I0670904

ISBN: 978-1-7330665-5-6

LEIGH ANDERS

TIDES OF CHANGE

A LOWCOUNTRY STORY

❧

Tides of Change is dedicated to anyone who longs for a family, but first has to remove obstacles that block their way. And to those who search for lost connections to the past, and find themselves in the process.

Special thanks to ZZ who shows me every day what real love is and how sad it would be without family.

Thanks to my amazing family. I treasure your love, and value the support you always give me. A big thanks to all who shared their knowledge and expertise with me while putting this book together.

CHAPTER ONE

Charlotte Christine Rainier, or Charley, as her friends and family called her, swiped the roll of packing tape across the top of the last moving box, then pushed it across the floor to join the others at the edge of the living room. She stretched, loosening her back, then walked to the fireplace hearth and sat down for a break. She looked around the room, checking to see if she might have missed any objects in her packing. All she saw were a few scuff marks on the walls and a couple dust bunnies where the sofa had been. She'd leave those for the realtor.

The furnishings and paintings that normally filled the room were gone, leaving behind an echoey, empty shell. Charley's gaze moved outside, through the town house's full-length windows, and toward the distant New York City skyline. It was a typical, late-March, New York morning. Dense fog draped the tops of the buildings much like a gray bandana, and blocked several floors from view. Small silvery streaks from a weak sun was the only light in the monochromatic sky as it tried to pierce through the dark clouds. Gray, plus even more gray. Even the colorful hydrangeas in pots that normally brightened the balcony were dead due to the lack of attention in recent months—a metaphor for her marriage. The dreary weather hanging over the city matched Charley's pensive mood.

Charley's life was changing, or more accurately, had changed already. Her divorce from Daniel was finalized six months ago. The time for analyzing and questioning what went wrong was over. She was well aware of how she got here—sitting alone in an empty house—but she hadn't yet figured out how to move on from this point. Bluntly put, she had been abandoned—again. She was on her own, except for Aunt Beth and Uncle Lance.

"Difficulties in life create new paths to opportunities," Charley's divorce attorney had said in an effort to bolster her spirit as she signed the final divorce papers. He was offering a 'lemonade from lemons' moment. He didn't give further advice on how to create that new path.

"Where do I go from here?" Charley asked the empty room. "What do I do now?"

Whatever you want, answered her inner voice, the name she called the chatter in her head. The chattering voice added, derisively, *Decide! You have only yourself to please—no one else. Be bold!*

"Be bold?" Charley asked out loud, annoyed that her inner voice was reminding her of the obvious: that she should view this break as the chance to make radical changes in her life. She was aware of that too, but right now she just wanted to get away from all the clutter and noise surrounding her life and not think about any of it. "I'm barely up to 'timid' this morning, much less 'bold.'"

Charley was frustrated that she felt frozen in place, and unable to decisively make a plan. She was stalling, dithering, and avoiding a decision about what to do next, or if *'next'* should be in a totally different direction. Her jumbled thoughts jumped from one possibility to another and all the heavy thinking was making her more confused. Yes, she was procrastinating, but caution overrode boldness at the moment. She had learned that lesson the hard way.

Charley sometimes ignored her instincts, or head chatter, and that usually led her straight toward disaster. A prime example was her months-long experiment with Daniel, when against her better judgement she agreed to stay with him to try and save their marriage. She ignored the warnings that Daniel couldn't be trusted to fulfill his part in the arrangement. Her decision prolonged the inevitable and the experiment ended as suspected, in bitter disappointment.

The divorce had not come as a surprise. The collapse had been gradual and began long before it ended with her signature on the official papers. She and Daniel had parted ways emotionally long before they reached that point. The wheels first fell off around their first anniversary—or, at least, that was when she found out that Daniel was cheating on her. There was a good possibility that it was not the first time he had strayed.

Charley accepted her part in the marriage's failure. Her job as a photographer and writer for a travel and adventure magazine took her away from home frequently. Daniel was often left alone in New York, but this shouldn't have come as a surprise to him. He knew what her job was when they married. The reality of an absent wife didn't fully register with him until a few months into the marriage.

Daniel, a Wall Street investment banker was a New Yorker to his core. No other place in the world measured up to New York City and no other profession was as good as his. Charley, on the other hand, liked to travel to interesting places and photograph sites ranging from the mundane to the exquisite. If the trip resulted in a great photo shoot, she was happy.

Despite pressure from Daniel, Charley couldn't give up the job she loved and become his shadow. She made concessions, though. She gave up her position as a staff photographer and writer and went freelance for the same magazine. She was basically doing the same job, but could pick and choose her assignments. Yet even as a freelancer, she was away from home more than Daniel wanted. In hindsight, Daniel's unhappiness with her job might have been just a cover for his unhappiness in their marriage.

A few months after Daniel vowed that he wanted to save the marriage, their story became the cliched, worn-out story of so many couples who try to repair something that isn't repairable. Daniel fell back into his old patterns of late nights at the office, late business meetings, and not returning Charley's calls. He soon admitted that he was back with the woman—a coworker in his office—he had been seeing before they agreed to try to piece their marriage back together. They finally—and mutually—agreed that divorce was the best solution for them both. Charley had given all she could to the marriage, but still it failed. Their union was over—kaput!

The divorce presented Charley with the perfect time to make changes in her life and a clean break from the past three years. Yet here she sat, brooding about moving on from an empty house that was filled with more bad memories than good ones. True, she had only herself to please, but taking a leap into the unknown by altering her life in a major way suddenly seemed scary. Daniel's infidelity still smarted and made her leery of her judgement. Could she be bold, change course, and strike out on a completely different path? Or should she stick with the safe choice—and continue in the same rut—sans Daniel? Recognizing that she was in a rut was a step forward by itself, wasn't it?

Most people would have figured out by age twenty-eight

what they wanted from life, both professionally and personal. She once thought she was one of those people, and one who always had the answer. Without her usual routine and structure, she was feeling oddly disconnected from her life at this moment.

No wonder her thoughts about her future were muddled; her past was muddled, too. Her life had cracked open like an egg when she was eight years old, and sometimes it felt like pieces were still missing. Even *she* sometimes wondered exactly who she was. Was she Charley Mathews, the frightened child who had been abandoned by her mother after her father's sudden death? Was she Charley Rainier, the polished and confident professional photographer and content writer? Was she Ce Ce Kane, the pseudonym she used in art gallery exhibits, and whose unique perspective was gaining recognition in the world of visual art? Was she Charley Phillips, the wife of Wall Street banker, Daniel Phillips?

"I can scratch Phillips off the list," she acknowledged. That narrowed her list of identities by one.

For the past six months, she had held onto the Phillips name and the Upper West Side town house—for convenience's sake—while she finished work assignments in Italy, the Mediterranean, and Germany. Keeping the name Phillips, and the town house was easier than explaining to her co-workers that her marriage had fallen apart again—completely, this time.

Daniel had been pressuring her to move out so they could sell the town house. Charley had a short break from work so she had agreed that now was a good time. Her entire life and three years of marriage were now shoved into twenty boxes—all closed and taped—ready to be taken to a storage facility near her Aunt Beth's New Jersey home. Yesterday, she had donated several boxes of items she no longer wanted or needed to a women's shelter Giving away parts of her old life, while a small step, had inched her closer to the final break.

The few pieces of furniture Daniel hadn't previously re-moved had been picked up two hours ago and taken to the auction house. More strings cut. The movers would soon return to pick up her remaining boxes, and that would sever all remaining ties to her life of the past three years. Mrs. Daniel Phillips would be left behind in the echoes of the empty rooms, and a new-old Charley Rainier would exit the town house.

Which brought her to her next step?

Charley loved photography, and after years of working in that profession, her future would be connected to it in some way. But there were other ways to use her skills without constant travel. She was tired of living out of a suitcase.

Charley smiled ruefully at that thought. Daniel would say, "*Now* you decide to stop traveling?"

She had several options; stay where she was or move to a different magazine; concentrate on visual art—exhibits and gallery shows; hire an agent and become 'a camera for hire', or open a studio of her own. But, the vast array of possibilities was actually complicating her decisions. Her fall back option was to just run away and hide.

Charley hadn't meant to join a one-person pity party when she sat down on the hearth to rest. But the empty house and the sad reflections of her marriage reminded her of another previous tragedy that had forced her to give up her home. Memories of the past and why she moved from Atlanta to New Jersey suddenly rose to the forefront of her mind. That period of her young life could best be described as "a period from hell", but she was eight, so at that time she didn't have any concept of hell. Now, twenty years later, her ordeal felt surreal, but "hell" still applied.

Charley was a sad and frightened child when she enrolled in Twin Pines Elementary School on the outskirts of Linden, New Jersey. She was plopped down in unfamiliar territory without friends or even her parents to protect her. Two boys in her class set out to make her life miserable. Even now, she could still hear their voices and see their jeering faces as they taunted her.

On her very first day, the two bullies immediately recognized the new girl's shyness and uncertainty. She was a new target, and they were experts in the game of tormenting someone whom they saw as vulnerable. She endured the bullying for about three weeks before it reached a breaking point. That day was fresh in her memory even now.

"I'm not an orphan," Charley cried as she backed into the corner at the end of the long corridor just outside her classroom. She wanted to run down the hallway and out the front door, but two boys from her class blocked her way.

"Ha! Ha! You're an orphan! You're an orphan," taunted one boy as he stuck his face close to hers. "You don't have parents." Charley shrank further into the corner. "And you talk funny," he added. Charley flinched and closed her eyes. She prepared herself for a physical strike from the boy named Tyler, but he just shifted his backpack and laughed, pleased that he had the power to cause her fear.

"I have a mother," Charley protested. "I had a father, but he died," she finished weakly.

"Yeah, you're like Tiny Tim," yelled the other boy, ignoring her comment. "You're a poor street urchin! You'll starve."

Charley wished Mrs. Fernandes hadn't read *A Christmas Carol* to the class because it had taught the boys a new word—urchin—and they didn't waste any time in using it to taunt her.

"No, I'm not!" she yelled back as her eyes filled with tears.

"What are you boys doing?" Principal Hawley asked from behind them as his hands closed over the shoulders of both boys. He didn't wait for an answer. "March! Now! To the office." He turned the boys in the direction of his office and firmly prodded them down the hallway. Charley didn't hesitate. She ran around them and scampered down the hallway. "Charley!" Principal Hawley called after her.

She didn't want to talk to Principal Hawley. She was an outsider, and if she told on the boys, it would only make the bullying worse. Today was the last day of school before Christmas break. She just wanted to get away from the boys, from the school, and from Principal Hawley. She ran through the school's front doors and out to Aunt Beth's car that waited at the curb.

Charley's face was smudged with tears as she climbed into the back seat and fastened her seat belt. What had she done to cause the boys to hate her? She hadn't wanted to come to their school in the first place, and it was clear that they didn't want her here, either. She'd much rather be in Georgia with her familiar surroundings: her mother, her best friend, and her school.

"Okay, sweetie, out with it. What's going on?" Aunt Beth asked when she saw Charley's face. She put the car in gear and pulled away from the curb.

Charley didn't want to tell Aunt Beth about the bullying, either. Aunt Beth would be in Principal Hawley's office immediately, and the incident would be all over school. No one would accept her as their friend and she desperately wanted to fit in. If she remained silent, maybe the boys would get tired of their bullying and leave her alone.

However, after some coaxing, Charley hesitantly spilled the details of the perpetual bullying campaign the two boys had begun on her very first day. By the time they pulled into the garage at home, Aunt Beth was seething with anger.

"Charley, why didn't you tell me this sooner?" Aunt Beth asked. "I wish you had. I can't bear to think you've been treated this way and didn't tell me. I promise you by the time you go back to school in January, things will change. You can count on it."

As Charley enjoyed her after-school snack in the kitchen, Aunt Beth and Uncle Lance huddled in their office. Charley could hear the low mummer of voices, frequently punctuated by voices raised in anger. She guessed that they were talking on the phone.

Why was this happening to her? Not that long ago, she and her parents had been a happy family, living in their home in the suburbs of Atlanta, Georgia. Her life had been that of a normal eight-year-old enjoying a new school year as she entered the third grade. She had tons of friends and a best friend, Melissa Colson, who lived next door and was also in her class this year.

Charley's happy life came crashing down around her when they were notified early one evening that her father had been killed in a terrible auto accident. A drunk driver had hit his car head on as he was on his way home from his job as the president of a major bank in Atlanta. Everything in her life became a nightmare after that. And the nightmare continued to rage on even after she moved to New Jersey.

Charley had been devastated by the loss of her fun-loving dad. He made everything a game, and he constantly made her laugh. She was in shock for days after the funeral. She couldn't process his death or accept that he wasn't coming back. Charley's mother was even worse off. She was inconsolable, debilitated by her grief, and incapable of accepting her new reality as a widow. She began to drink heavily. She was more interested in finding a full bottle of whiskey than seeing to Charley's needs. She forgot Charley existed. Charley fell back onto her regular routine to get by. She got herself ready for school each morning

and ate whatever she found in the kitchen. She cared for her
mother as best she could, coaxing her to eat at least a few bites
at mealtimes.

At first, there were lots of choices for food to eat. Neighbors
and her father's associates had brought food to the grieving
family. But after a few weeks, all Charley could find in the house
was boxed cereal, toast, crackers, and peanut butter. She took
money from her mother's purse to purchase school lunches
and thus had one hot meal each day during the week. After a
few false starts, she figured out how to operate the washer and
dryer, so she kept her clothes clean. She managed her bathing
and shampooing well enough so her teachers didn't suspect her
secret life.

Charley, embarrassed by her mother's behavior, hid their
situation from the neighbors. She concocted a story about her
mother being sick so that she could ride to and from school
with Melissa. Mrs. Colson agreed to give her a lift, although she
questioned Charley as to why her mother hadn't been the one to
ask. Charley lied and said her mother wanted Charley to ask.

Debra took to her bed.

She remained there for almost a month until one day, Charley couldn't wake her. Her mother would mumble and open
her eyes, but immediately go back to sleep. This odd behavior
frightened Charley. She didn't understand what was happening,
but she recognized that her mother needed help.

A desperate Charley found her mother's address book.
She bypassed her mother's parents' phone number. They had
moved from Atlanta to Arizona a few years earlier because of
her grandfather's breathing problems and hoped the dry air of
Arizona would help. The address book didn't list any contact
numbers for her father's parents or any of his relatives. Charley's
eyes paused on her mother's sister's phone number. Aunt Beth
was Charley's favorite person in the whole world, outside of her

mother. Aunt Beth and her husband lived in New Jersey.

"Mama's sick," Charley said when Aunt Beth answered the phone. "I'm scared. She wakes up for a few minutes, then goes back to sleep." Charley tried to get her mother to talk with Aunt Beth, but she couldn't manage more than a few incoherent grunts into the phone.

"I'll be there as soon as I can catch a flight," Aunt Beth promised.

She arrived that evening. Charley had not prepared her aunt for all that was wrong in the Mathews house. Aunt Beth looked around, horrified at what she saw: a nearly comatose sister, an unkempt house, and a confused and scared niece. The cupboards were practically bare.

Whereas hardship had crippled Debra, the situation only revved Aunt Beth up. She took charge, straightened the house, and despite Debra's protestations, pulled her sister from her bed. She ordered Debra to clean up and to eat the meals she prepared.

Aunt Beth spent the rest of the week searching for a rehabilitation facility for Debra; her sister had become an alcoholic or was at least depending on alcohol to avoid the sad reality of her life. She was neglecting herself as well as Charley.

"Debra," Aunt Beth said, "I'm not asking whether you want to go get treatment. You *are* going, and if you care one iota for Charley, you will not stall. Now, pack your bag and get in the car. Or do you want Charley taken away from you by the authorities?"

Aunt Beth's firmness and the mention of Charley's precarious position finally penetrated Debra's alcoholic haze. She agreed to Aunt Beth's plans. She also agreed that Charley should return to New Jersey with Aunt Beth and live there until she was better able to care for Charley like a mother should.

"Just until I'm well," Debra assured Charley. "Mommy's

sick."

Charley left her familiar surroundings and moved to New Jersey to live with Aunt Beth and Uncle Lance.

Now, Aunt Beth exited the office, entered the kitchen, and interrupted Charley's thoughts, saying, "Get your coat, Charley."

"Where are we going?" Charley swallowed a mouthful of milk. It stuck in her throat. Aunt Beth had a determined look, the one she had whenever she meant business. Was Aunt Beth going to the boys' homes to confront them or maybe to see Principal Hawley?

"We have an appointment. With our attorney. Uncle Lance is warming the car up now."

Charley sighed, relieved that they were going someplace other than to confront the bullies.

Aunt Beth and Uncle Lance took her to a meeting with their family attorney. Within a few days, the attorney had her mother's notarized signature on the necessary documents. A court date was set, and Charley's last name was changed from Mathews to Rainier. Charley's aunt and uncle hadn't officially adopted her, nor did they officially become her guardians, but they had given her the protection of their last name for as long as she wanted to use it. Charley would be treated as their child. She carried the name of two people who would be surrogate parents until Charley's mother recovered and was ready for her to come back and live with her again.

When Charley returned to school after the Christmas break, she was escorted to class by her Aunt Beth and Uncle Lance. Her classmates' eyes widened as the famous NFL wide receiver Lance Rainier escorted Charley into the classroom. The students knew who he was. They had watched him every Sunday during football season, until he had retired earlier that year.

Aunt Beth and Uncle Lance introduced themselves to the teacher, and then, Uncle Lance turned to address the class.

"This is Charley Rainier, our daughter," he told Charley's class-mates, placing extra emphasis on 'our daughter.' "I'm sure you'll make her welcome, won't you?"

A chorus of "Yes, Mr. Rainier" arose from the class.

The bullying ended that day, and Charley was no longer treated as an outcast.

Charley's mother eventually recovered from her depression and alcohol addiction, but she was never the same as she had been before Charley's father's death. She never asked that Charley return to live with her. Aunt Beth took Charley to see her mother during the summer and on holidays. Debra still struggled to take care of herself, so taking care of a child was more than she was capable of at the time.

Debra was thirty-four years old when she lost the love of her life. After her stint in rehab, she gave up alcohol, but then became a serial dater. She had affairs with one man after another, but they never lasted long. When she didn't find a love like she'd lost when her husband died, she quickly moved on to the next man. Charley continued to live with Aunt Beth and Uncle Lance. She graduated from high school in New Jersey, went to college at NYU, and graduated with a degree in fine arts.

The last twenty years had passed quickly, and here she was, once again at a juncture, and about to begin another new phase of her life. At least, she was better equipped this time.

The doorbell rang, snapping Charley out of her memories from twenty years ago. Who could that be? She didn't expect the movers for another hour. Maybe the traffic was light this morning, and they were early.

A man—not the movers, but a courier—stood outside the door when Charley opened it. "Mrs. Rainier-Phillips?" he asked.

"Yes. What can I do for you?" Charley looked at the courier curiously.

"I have a letter for you. Please sign here," the courier said as he presented Charley with a mobile device to sign.

Charley signed for the letter and closed the door. She frowned as she read the return address—James Lewis, Attorney at Law, Charleston, South Carolina. She tore open the seal and began to read. She made her way back to the fireplace and sagged down onto the hearth.

What was this all about?

Charley looked again at the letter in her hand. The contents were baffling to say the least. She scanned the letter again, hoping that the reason it had been sent to her would become clear. Still not understanding, she read it again.

The information began to sink in on her third read-through: "Dear Mrs. Rainier-Phillips, we wish to inform you that upon the death of Annabelle Travis, you have been bequeathed one section of beachfront property on Turtle Island, South Carolina, consisting of one house and three-quarters of an acre of land. Please contact the number below for more information."

Charley blinked. This couldn't be right. Obviously, Mr. Lewis had confused her with someone else. "Who is Annabelle Travis, where is Turtle Island, and why would a stranger leave a house and property to me?" Charley asked out loud.

She folded the letter and stuck it in her purse. Maybe Aunt Beth would know who Annabelle Travis was.

"I don't know an Annabelle Travis," Aunt Beth said after she read the letter and handed it back to Charley.

Charley had unpacked and was settled in the guest room at Aunt Beth's house. She had joined Aunt Beth at the bar in the kitchen to have a glass of iced tea.

"Your dad's family was from South Carolina," Aunt Beth continued, "so I imagine it's through the Mathews side of the family. Other than that, I don't know anyone named Travis. Just call the number and see what Mr. Lewis can tell you."

"Since my father was from South Carolina, how did my parents meet?" Charley asked. She usually avoided discussing the painful topic of her father's death, but this also meant that she avoided the subject of his life as well. As her memories of him had faded over the years, the busy life of a teenager, followed by the even busier life of an adult, had pushed aside any curiosity she might have about her father's early life—until now.

"George transferred to a bank in Atlanta from Charleston," Aunt Beth replied. "He met your mother at a bank-sponsored charity event. I think they fell in love the night they met. They were inseparable from that point on. Your mother always bragged that she and George were the perfect couple and had the perfect marriage. She was right about that. They were two halves of one person."

"I guess that sort of thing doesn't come along very often," Charley said.

"No, it doesn't. And that can be both a good thing and a bad thing. Your father didn't ask it of Debra, but she lost herself in him. Once he was no longer around, she couldn't cope. A large part of my sister died with him. But, Charley, to have a happy marriage, you don't have to completely give up your own identity."

"You mean like Daniel wanted me to do?"

"Exactly, like Daniel. Ever since I met your Uncle Lance at the University of Georgia, I never once asked him to give up his love of football or his locker-room buddies. And he's never once asked me to give up my textile-design business or any of my friends." Aunt Beth had worked for a fashion-design house in New York City, but started her own textile-design company from home when Charley came to live with them. It gave her the flexibility she needed, since she suddenly had a child to care for. Over the years, she had built it into a successful business.

"Aunt Beth, I'm sorry I disturbed your life and caused you to give up your career in New York." Charley had thanked Aunt Beth before, but she wanted to tell her again. "I'm grateful for everything that you and Uncle Lance did, but I regret what you gave up to do it."

"Having you around gave us more joy than I have words to describe. Lance and I always wanted children, but since we couldn't have any of our own, you became our own. Having you come to live with us prompted me to start my own business. That was the best decision I could have made, career-wise." Aunt Beth reached out and squeezed Charley's forearm. "It would have been painful to lose you," she continued, "but I was always willing to let your mother take you back if she straightened out her life. She wasn't able to do that, especially at first. It wasn't that she didn't love you, but her grief wouldn't let her see anything beyond her personal pain. She didn't realize that you were hurting, too. But to her credit, she did recognize her inability to care for you. She did the right thing by letting you live with us." Aunt Beth suddenly chuckled. "Plus, it gave Lance a reason to strut around your school and scare the bejesus out of those bullies."

Charley smiled at the memory. Uncle Lance appeared at school periodically after that initial visit and volunteered for school functions. Each visit he made was a message sent to the bullies that he was keeping an eye on them.

"Are you going to call the attorney in South Carolina?" Aunt Beth asked.

Charley hesitated before she answered. "I don't know why I'm stalling, Aunt Beth. The Mathews family has always been a mystery to me. I guess I'm just hesitant to open all that up again. What my mom did to them must have been very hurtful."

Charley never understood why her mother had cut off all contact with the Mathews family after her father's death. They had just lost a son and were as heartbroken as their daughter-in-law. But Debra Mathews had not been reasonable during that time. Her confused mind seemed to want to punish them in some way for her broken life. Or perhaps Debra's avoidance of her in-laws was because she was ashamed of her conduct and who she became after her husband's death.

"Debra wasn't just horrible to the Mathews family, she struck out at the world and everyone in it. Even *our* parents didn't want to be around her," Aunt Beth said sadly. "She eventually got over her anger, but by then, she had driven away everyone who cared for her—and, by extension, for you. A person can only take so much screaming and vitriol before they stay away for good. If I hadn't had you to think of, I probably would have cut ties with her myself. I hate to admit that, but it's true."

Charley touched Aunt Beth's hand. "I know she hurt you, but I'm glad you stuck by her—and me."

"Sticking by you was never an issue."

Charley finished her tea, then went to the office to call the lawyer, Mr. Lewis. She expected him to inform her that it was a mistake, that the letter should have gone to someone else.

"Mrs. Phillips, thank you so much for calling," Mr. Lewis said when he came on the line.

Charley didn't correct him on her name. She figured it would be a quick call, so the name wasn't important. "I don't want to waste your time, Mr. Lewis, but I think you have the wrong person," Charley stated. "I don't know anyone who lives in Charleston or even in South Carolina."

"We're confident we have the right person." Mr. Lewis laughed and added, "You made it a little difficult to find you. Aliases always complicate legal matters."

Charley didn't think of her various names as aliases, but again, she didn't correct him.

Mr. Lewis paused, and when Charley didn't say anything, he went on, "You were born in Atlanta, weren't you?"

"Yes, sir. I was."

"Good. Annabelle Travis left her property to her nearest living relative. She was confident that's you." He gave Charley a few more details and ended with, "Why don't you come down and take a look around—see the property? I also have documents for you to sign."

Charley hung up the phone with a promise to let Mr. Lewis know what she planned to do by the next day. Uncle Lance was with Aunt Beth when Charley returned to the kitchen. Charley shared what Mr. Lewis had told her.

"You should go down there and look over the property," Uncle Lance said. "What do you have to lose? You need to take a break from traveling and everything else going on right now—at least for a short while—so this would be the perfect chance to get away."

"But I'm scheduled to go to Costa Rico next week," Charley said.

"No problem. You can fly out of Charleston," Uncle Lance said. "If you leave for Charleston this week, it'll give you enough time to visit the property. You might even make a decision about it right away, before you leave for Costa Rico. I think you should go."

Charley felt a stirring of excitement over the prospect of a road trip. That sounded like fun. She traveled a lot in her job, but those trips involved airports, strange hotels, and hurried meals at whatever restaurant was nearest—quick in, do the shoot, quick out. She had never taken a leisurely trip where she absorbed the local culture and got to know the people and places she photographed.

"I'm going to drive," she stated excitedly as she made her decision. "I've always wanted to drive along the ocean highway." While in Charleston, she could absorb the feel of the city where her father had lived. Maybe she could reflect on and reconnect with the happy memories of their time together, many of which had slipped away from her over the last twenty years. If nothing else, the trip would be a visit to the South—the region of her birth.

CHAPTER TWO

C harley drove straight through from New Jersey to Charleston, stopping only to eat and fill her car's tank with gas. Once she had decided to make this trip, she was anxious to see the property her relative had left her and find out more about Annabelle Travis. She still had only the information that Mr. Lewis had given her and his assurance that Annabelle was indeed related to Charley.

She arrived in Charleston in the evening and checked into a hotel on Meeting Street, within walking distance of Mr. Lewis's law office. She was tired from the long drive, but she grabbed a quick meal in the hotel dining room and then took a walk around the area. A short walk would give her a preview and a small sense of the city where her father and grandparents had lived.

An awesome thought came to Charley as she strolled down Meeting Street. The sidewalk beneath her feet could be the same path her father once trod. Perhaps his spirit was walking with her on her evening stroll. The idea gave her goose bumps.

Charley stopped in front of St. Michael's Cathedral at the

corner of Broad and Meeting Street. The tall structure was beautiful. According to the plaque out front, the church had stood there for centuries—since 1761. Charley gazed upward toward the top of the cathedral, noting its magnificent stained-glass window and unique architectural design. Her fingers itched to snap some photos, but she had left her camera in her room. There would be time for that before she left town—if she left town.

Whoa! Charley's wandering mind came to a halt at that thought. When did a visit to check out the beach property turn into 'if she left town'? Had she already made her decision without realizing it? No, the decision to stay on Turtle Island would be made in a rational and informed manner. She brushed away all thoughts of any plans beyond a visit to the island and an inspection of her inheritance.

Inheritance from someone she didn't even know? Now, that was a development she never thought would apply to her. Of course, her 'inheritance' in this instance could turn out to be nothing more than a ramshackle hovel that needed to be condemned and torn down. But the land should be worth something. So, she *had* inherited something of value. Just how much value was to be seen.

Charley finished her walk and returned to her hotel room. She showered, then collapsed on the bed. She fell asleep as soon as she pulled the covers over her.

She was up early the next morning, anxious and nervous about her meeting with the attorney. She walked to his office just down the street from her hotel and arrived moments after they opened at nine a.m.

Mr. Lewis welcomed her, and after the customary greetings, he got down to business and recapped what he had told her on the phone: "Annabelle Travis left you a beach house and a nice piece of land—larger than most beach lots. It's been in her family for a very long time and was purchased back before there was much development on the barrier islands."

"I still don't know who she is," Charley said. "Do you know how she's related to me?"

"She's your father's aunt. Travis is her married name."

"I see. She didn't have any children?" Charley asked.

"She had a son, but she lost him in the Vietnam War. Your family has had a lot of death and tragedy. Surviving members are scarce," Mr. Lewis replied. As a shadow darkened Charley's eyes, he added, "I'm sorry. That was inexcusably rude of me to remind you of the loss of your father."

"It was a long time ago." Charley nodded and accepted his apology. "So, I'm the closest living relative? How do you know I'm the one you're looking for?" she asked.

"Annabelle is the one who located you. She was sure. There are a few distant cousins on the Travis side of the family, but this property was Annabelle's before she married into the Travis family."

"She was certain I'm the person she was looking for? There are others with the same last name," Charley said, still unable to let go of the idea that they had the wrong person. It was also weird to think that strangers had been nosing around in her life without her knowledge.

"Annabelle didn't share the details of how she found you, and she didn't broadcast the fact that she was leaving her property to you. People get hurt and angry if they feel they are being cut out of someone's will, and relatives often come out of the woodwork when there's money or property involved. Annabelle wanted to avoid any such potential drama. But it doesn't matter. She left the beach property to you. She was sure you're her closest relative on the Mathews side, Mrs. Phillips, and she wanted the property to stay in the Mathews family."

"I'm actually no longer using the name Phillips—since my

divorce. I should have mentioned that when we talked on the phone."

"No problem, but I'll have to change the name on the documents before you can sign. But that shouldn't keep you from moving into the property as soon as you like."

Charley suddenly had an idea. She had meant to do this for some time now, but between her job's travel schedule and her recent personal problems, she kept putting it off. Now, with Mr. Lewis's comment that there were very few members left on the Mathews side of her family prompted her to broach the subject.

"I wonder," she said hesitantly, "if you could do an official name change for me—since you have to redo the paperwork anyway." Mr. Lewis looked at her, a question in his eyes. "My name was changed to Rainier when I was a child. I'd like to add Mathews back to my name. Can you do that? Since you need to amend the documents for the property, maybe you…?"

"Yes, we can do that." Mr. Lewis dug around in his desk until he found the file he was looking for. He pulled out a petition for name change form and pushed it toward her. "I can file it with the county clerk for you, but there are additional requirements that only you can do, like fingerprints and an appearance before a judge."

"I can do that," Charley agreed. She filled out the form, including her new preferred name, "Charlotte Christine Rainier-Mathews," and handed it back to Mr. Lewis, along with her driver's license, social security card, and birth certificate, which she had brought along in case they were needed to claim her surprise inheritance.

Mr. Lewis took the identification cards and petition for name change form and looked them over slowly.

"I know it's a long name," Charley apologized after several seconds had passed. "The Rainiers raised me, so I feel I ought to keep the Rainier name, but I owe it to my father to also use my birth name."

"We are who life makes us," Mr. Lewis philosophized. "I think your father would be pleased."

He then called in his secretary to make copies of everything and notarize Charley's signature. He promised to keep her updated on the status of her petition to change her name and to let her know when the documents transferring the beach property to her were formally recorded. He ended by handing her the keys to the beach house.

Charley left Mr. Lewis's office and started walking back toward the hotel where her car was parked. She cut through a side street she had noticed earlier and wanted to explore. She walked quickly, feeling energized after making the decision to change her name back to her birth name. Her decision to come to Charleston suddenly didn't seem as crazy as it had when she first received Mr. Lewis's letter. She was moving forward with her life. Even if the beach house turned out to be a dump, she was glad she had made the trip.

Charley smelled food even before the delicatessen came into view. She started to walk past Benji's Sandwich Shop, but the smell wafting from the deli made her stomach rumble and reminded her that she hadn't eaten much for breakfast. She had been too excited about her meeting with Mr. Lewis to consume more than a cup of coffee. A sandwich to eat on her drive to the beach suddenly sounded good.

Charley stepped up to the door and yanked on the handle. The force of her pull and the weight of the heavy glass door propelled it outward—and much wider than Charley had expected. She heard an "Ouch!" from behind her. She glanced back to find a tall, dark-haired man standing just behind her. He held one hand over his right eye, and a red welt was rising on the skin above his eyebrow.

"Oh!" Charley exclaimed. "I'm so sorry. Forgive me. You

were too close. The door… it just flew open… wide." Charley's voice trailed off as she tried to explain that the door had practically opened itself. The hinges and the door's weight should have stopped it from swinging back so far. But they hadn't. She had hit the man in the face. "I'm so sorry," Charley repeated. She looked closer to see if there was any blood from the cut. She didn't see any, but offered all the same, "Do you need a tissue?"

"You're not from around here, are you?" the man asked simply, ignoring her apology. He stared down at her with one hand still cupped over his right eye. He frowned slightly as he rubbed the red mark over his eye.

"What? Not from here?" Confused, Charley looked down at her navy-blue cropped jacket, white shirt, skinny jeans, and ankle boots. Her hair was pulled back in a loose chignon, and she was wearing oversized dark sunglasses. Did her outfit scream "New York" and broadcast the fact that she wasn't a local? From what she had read and seen since her arrival, Charleston was not some backwater town, but rather a modern, sophisticated city. She didn't think her clothes were in any way different than what South Carolinian women were wearing.

She thought she looked appropriate for her meeting with an attorney—"stylishly casual". And the business suit that this man was wearing—his tie casually loosened at his neck—was of the latest style. It was rude of him to criticize what she was wearing even if he thought she was dressed inappropriately.

"No, I'm not from here. But…" Charley adjusted the front of her jacket, ready to defend her fashion choices.

"The door," the man replied, pointing to the door that she still held open. "It's been broken for years now. Benji refuses to get it fixed. As far as he's concerned, it still closes and locks, and that's good enough for him—and, apparently, the city inspectors. Everyone around here knows you have to open it *carefully*." He emphasized that last word, as if he were speaking to someone who was slow to comprehend. "So, you must not be from here. Otherwise, you'd know that." He looked satisfied with his explanation, as though she should see the connection.

"Oh!" Charley said. He meant that she wasn't from the immediate area around the deli, not that she was from another state. "The door? No, I didn't know. I'm sorry. Can I buy your lunch to make up for hitting you?"

"No, that's not necessary," the man replied. He then sighed, loudly. "I'll live. But I'll probably have a permanent scar. Maybe I'll sue."

Charley glanced up at him with another apology on her lips. His earlier frown had been replaced with a smile, and his blue eyes crinkled at the corners. His injury forgotten, he was now apparently enjoying her discomfort.

"I'm kidding. I'm fine," the man laughed. "After you." He pointed toward the open door.

"Sue me? Ha!" Charley retorted. "A comedian—and not a very funny one, at that!" She tugged slightly on the door as she stepped inside and then released it to close on its own. The man caught the door just in time to keep it from slamming in his face. Charley didn't look back to see his reaction.

"Hey, Alex," a man behind the counter called in welcome. "What can I get you?"

"My usual," Alex replied, "Reuben on rye. But help the lady first. And Benji, fix that damn door before someone gets badly injured."

"Sure, Alex," Benji replied. "It's next on my list of things to do."

Judging by the disgusted snort Charley heard from the man named Alex, he had heard that reply from Benji before. Alex walked toward a table and began talking to a couple seated there while he waited for Charley to complete her order.

Charley placed a to-go order—a Rueben on rye sounded

good to her, too—paid for her sandwich, and left the shop. She opened the door carefully this time. Alex was still talking to the couple at the table, but he glanced her way as she stepped out onto the sidewalk. She closed the door behind her with exaggerated care and met his eyes with a challenging look. Her tilted chin dared him to make a gesture or say anything. A half-smile lit his face, and he gave her a slight approving nod. He got her point, even though her eyes were hidden behind her dark sunglasses. Charley felt his gaze stay on her until she walked beyond the window of the deli.

Charley's thoughts lingered on the man she had just met—or, in this case, just injured with the door—as she walked toward her car. If Sandwich Shop Alex was an example of the men in the Lowcountry, they were a handsome lot, indeed. He had the classic good looks of an old-time movie star: tall, square-jawed, with dark hair and smoky-blue eyes. But she wasn't here to check out the local male population—even someone as handsome as Sandwich Shop Alex. Charley's photographer's eye had just been doing its usual job: analyzing something that was pleasant to look at. Sandwich Shop Alex definitely fit that description.

"Even you don't believe photography has anything to do with why you're still thinking about him," Charley muttered to herself. "All it proves is I'm a living, breathing female." That she had noticed an attractive man—or any man at all—was reassuring after everything Daniel had put her through. But she firmly reminded herself that Daniel had been good-looking, too, although in a less rugged way than Sandwich Shop Alex. And Daniel's attractiveness hadn't gone any deeper than his polished surface. First impressions don't always hold up to close scrutiny.

Charley came to a small alcove located just off the sidewalk. A wrought-iron bench sat in the shade under an oak tree, next to a fence covered in bougainvillea. The red blooms were just

starting to open. A private home was on the other side of the
fence, but the bench was obviously there for use by pedestrians.
Was this a thoughtful gesture by the friendly Charleston home-
owner, or was it placed here by the city? Whoever was responsi-
ble, it was an inviting place to rest.

Charley's feet propelled her toward the bench. It seemed like
a more relaxing place to eat her sandwich than in her car while
driving. She sat down, opened her sandwich, and tuned into
her surroundings. She enjoyed people-watching, and by paus-
ing here, she could absorb the atmosphere of this part of the
city. The area was a mixture of historic homes hidden behind
trees and fences, as well as small businesses that opened on to
the sidewalk. Multifloored office buildings could be seen in the
distance.

Traffic moved slowly along the street in front of Charley.
Pedestrians, some in business suits and others who were obviously shoppers or tourists, strolled leisurely along the sidewalk.
Despite the number of people walking by and the traffic on the
street, it was much quieter than a morning in New York City. A
morning there would be filled with horns blasting, and everyone rushing and pushing to get to their destination as quickly
as possible. Normally, she'd be pushing and shoving along with
them. She'd never take time to sit and rest on a shady bench in
the middle of the city.

But as much as she would enjoy spending the rest of the
morning people-watching, she couldn't linger in this pleasant
spot much longer. She had a beach house to visit. Charley finished her sandwich, then made her way to her car.

As Charley climbed into the car's driver's seat and buckled
her seat belt, she thought more about what she had done this
morning. She was officially becoming a Mathews again; she'd
discovered a previously unknown aunt, and she was in a city
for the first time where her ancestors had resided. Many were

probably buried in some of the cemeteries she had driven past when she arrived. These were important things to Charley. The sudden and tragic loss of her father had disconnected her from her own past, and squashed her life into a fragment of what was normal for most people. Until now, her father had been seen only through the eyes of eight-year old Charley. Maybe she'd get an adult's view of him by spending time in the region and absorbing the culture and atmosphere of the place where he was born.

As Charley started her car and put it into gear, she was more eager than ever to learn more about her great-aunt Annabelle, and to see the island and beach house she had left her.

CHAPTER THREE

Charley's silver-gray SUV, its back seat and cargo space loaded with essentials for the beach house, sped along the route toward Turtle Island. According to Mr. Lewis, the island was about a thirty-minute drive from the city of Charleston—provided traffic was moving and none of the bridges were closed.

Charley's photographic brain was in high gear as she left the city limits and entered the highway leading toward the islands. Her head whipped back and forth like a bobble head doll, first right then left, as she tried to take in everything at once on both sides of the highway. Today, rather than silencing the annoying voice on her car's GPS, she welcomed the voice's directions to keep her on track while she took in the scenery.

The waters of the West Ashley River shimmered like glass in the midday sun as she took the exit to the expressway bridge that led over the channel. From the high point on the bridge, Charley had a panoramic view of a hazy blue sky that stretched far across open waters, then thinned to a dark-blue ribbon where the ocean met the horizon. Below the bridge, lots of activity was going on in the channel. Seagulls darted about, looking for chum as they followed a large container ship and a couple of barges that hurried toward the inland port of Charleston. Charley spotted a boat, farther out in the channel, that was loaded with tourists and headed toward Fort Sumter—the famous outpost and site of two major battles between the Union and Confederate Armies during the Civil War.

Charley had familiarized herself with some of Charleston's historic sites before leaving New Jersey. At the apex of the bridge, she was able to see the top of one of those sites—the restored Morris Island Lighthouse. It now listed slightly to one side, but had stood guard in Charleston Harbor since 1876. The historic landmark had been decommissioned as a working lighthouse, but had been restored, and was now a major tourist attraction.

The landscape surrounding Charley was fertile ground for a photographer like herself. She automatically framed and visualized finished photos of the beautiful scenery she drove past. The magazine she worked for sent her to mostly foreign lands, but Charley planned to suggest they look south and closer to home.

Charley's fingers drummed impatiently on the car's center console as she sped along. Just like the container ship that was hurrying to its port, she was in a hurry to reach her port too and the end of a long drive. She was road weary from the fourteen-hour trip from New Jersey yesterday, and was ready to reach her property on Turtle Island.

She left the Charleston Harbor behind and crossed the bridge over the Stono River that led to Johns Island. Live oak trees covered in Spanish moss and palmetto trees lined the highway on both sides of the road. A road sign advertised Johns Island as home to the famous sixty-five-foot tall Angel Oak tree, reported to be four-to-five hundred years old. Charley added it to her running list of sites she planned to photograph.

According to Mr. Lewis, Johns Island, the largest island in the state, would be the longest portion of her drive before she reached Turtle Island. Still, it didn't take her long to come to the end of the main road. Charley made a left turn and after a couple miles, she approached a small bridge. A sign next to the bridge read 'Turtle Island.' She crossed the bridge, then over a small bump and her tires touched the soil of Turtle Island. She was almost there—her new home. *Temporary home*, she corrected herself. A thought, one she'd been toying with this morning, came to the forefront. If livable, the beach house would be her home for at least the summer. Annabelle's desire that the property remain in the Mathews family had nixed any idea of selling it. Her great-aunt had gone to extraordinary lengths to find her, and Charley would not go against Aunt Annabelle's wishes. Spending time here was necessary in order to decide how an inherited beach house fit into her life.

Charley followed a narrow two-lane road that wound along the ocean. She rolled down the car's window and let the sea breeze blow in. It ruffled her hair and filled the car with the sweet, fresh scent of the ocean. Large sand dunes now outnumbered the live oak and palmetto trees that had lined most of her route to the island. Sea oats and beach grasses covered the dunes and waved in the constant breeze. Small yellow flowers, hardy and determined, dotted the beach and the surrounding landscape. They grew profusely in the hot, shifting sand.

As Charley traveled further east along the ocean road, houses began to appear on her left. The houses were weathered, battered wooden structures that faced the beach, with sandy yards brightened by splotches of blooming red oleanders and orange-yellow lantana bushes. Sturdy and resolute, they managed to withstand a relentless, sand-laden breeze.

Charley's research before leaving New Jersey had indicated that Turtle Island was a small barrier island, about ten miles long, and five miles wide with a year-round population of approximately nine hundred people. The island was not as developed as some of the bigger, better-known islands. According to an online article she'd found in a local paper, the residents waged a constant battle to keep development out, and to maintain their slow and peaceful way of life.

The major businesses on the island consisted of a grocery store with a filling station, a couple restaurants, a few small coffee shops and cafés, and some mom-and-pop stores that sold fishing gear and hardware items. There was an excursion business that offered deep-sea fishing and island tours. There were no major retail stores, but shopping was not that far away, located on the nearby islands or in the city of Charleston.

The island got its name because it was a favorite spot for nesting female sea turtles. As the easternmost barrier island, it was easier for the turtles to reach than the islands located further inland and closer to the mainland. The turtles' instincts led them out of the sea to dig deep pits on the sandy beaches, lay their eggs, and then return to the sea. Charley's assessment regarding the turtles' nesting habits: they were trusting creatures to leave their young behind and in the hands of humans.

Charley soon spotted 204 Sunrise Way. She turned into the driveway. The crunch of her tires on the crushed seashell drive was a welcome sound. She parked a short distance from the house, unbuckled her seat belt, and leaned back in her seat. She closed her eyes for a moment to let the sounds of her surroundings replace those of the tires and the road. The pounding of the surf on the beach and the calls of the seagulls flowed through the car's open window. Charley took a deep breath and felt her tensed shoulders relax. She got out of the car, then stopped to survey the two-story clapboard beach house. A shiny tin roof sparkled in the bright sunshine.

The house was perched on pilings that raised it out of the

way of storm surges. It looked old, but solid. Beneath the main house was an empty space—perhaps for parking—with a door to a storage space near the back of the structure.

Mr. Lewis had told her that after Hurricane Hugo devastated the area in 1989, Annabelle had raised the original house on pilings, repaired the damage, added the staircases and the storage space, and made a few other modern upgrades. Beyond that, the basic structure of the cottage remained the same as it had been for decades. The house had been vacant for the last year, but a caretaker checked on it frequently to ensure that everything was in order. The utilities had been turned on as soon as Charley informed Mr. Lewis that she was on her way to Charleston.

Charley pulled out her camera and began taking pictures. She wanted to document this day through photographs—a visual record of her first visit to the beach house that now belonged to her. Much of the exterior's blue painted clapboards had weathered to a soft gray, while specks of the original blue stood out in places, having resisted the sand, wind, and spray from the ocean not far away. The speckled boards reminded Charley of a robin's egg and just added to the house's charm. The portion of the house that instantly drew Charley's eye and made her fall in love with it was the porch that wrapped around at least the three sides of the house that she could see from the driveway. A live oak tree, shrouded in Spanish moss, towered behind the structure and shaded one side of the porch. Two sets of stairs on the front of the house—one on either end of the front porch— were separated by a tall trellis, which was currently covered in red blooming bougainvillea.

A weathered sign hung between the steps, near the edge of the porch, reading, '*Leig Anail.*' Charley knew the gist of the phrase's meaning from her travels to Ireland and Scotland. It was Gaelic and loosely translated as "have a rest" or, by some interpretations, "to breathe."

"The sign couldn't be more appropriate, Aunt Annabelle," Charley whispered. "At this point, I need both—to rest and to breathe." She swung her camera over her shoulder and began pulling her bags from the car. She was anxious to see the interior.

Charley climbed the stairs and paused on the landing at the edge of the porch. She turned and faced the ocean. The water was placid and peaceful at the moment, but dark clouds billowed in the distance. It was too early for hurricane season— that much she knew about beach life—so the clouds probably signaled nothing more than an afternoon squall. She glanced over at her nearest neighbor's house. It was similar in style to the Travis house, but had a wide single staircase instead of two and a porch that ran across the front of the house. It appeared to be empty now, so perhaps it was a rental property and too early for vacationers.

Charley unlocked the door. It stuck, but with an extra shove, it opened into a hallway. As Charley stepped inside, a fine layer of sand crunched under her shoes. The doors and windows apparently didn't keep all the sand and wind outside, but it was on the beach, after all. A thorough cleaning would be the first thing on her agenda once she unpacked.

"Oh my! This is nice!" Charley thought in surprise as she stepped into the living room to the left of the hallway. A galley kitchen filled the rear section of the living room and was separated from it by a long bar-like counter. The kitchen had all the necessary appliances—in retro white, but they fit the style of the house. The living room was furnished with the usual: sofa and coffee table, two over-stuffed chairs, a TV, end tables with matching lamps. The furnishings were old but in good condition.

Charley started to step back into the hallway to inspect the

rear portion of the house when she noticed a framed photo on
the wall behind the sofa. Charley moved closer for a better look.
It was one of her photos—a beach scene she had shot in Pan-
ama a few years ago. Three ragtag children played on a sandy
beach not far from a row of dilapidated houses that were barely
standing. They appeared ready to fall at any moment. Laun-
dry was spread over the rickety balconies and fluttered in the
breeze. In the distance, modern, expensive high-rise buildings
were outlined against the sky. Charley had captured the juxta-
position of grinding poverty located within the shadows of the
wealthy upper class. Her pseudonym, Ce Ce Kane, was signed
in the photo's bottom righthand corner.

She had exhibited the photo in a New York gallery about
two years ago—the last showing of her work—just before her
marriage with Daniel fell apart… the first time. She hadn't
shown anything since, because Daniel didn't want her to spend
the time it took to put together the photos for an exhibit. Charley suspected his attitude might have been due to jealousy over
the attention she received—attention that didn't revolve around
him. Had Annabelle known who Ce Ce Kane was? Had she
been at the exhibit and bought the photo that night? *I doubt I'll
ever know*, Charley concluded.

Charley made a quick inspection of the rest of the house.
A bedroom and bathroom were located on the first floor. The
room was fairly large—larger than the bedroom in her first
apartment in New York City. It opened onto a deck that ran the
width of the backside of the house and was partially shaded by
the oak tree. She stepped outside to look around. Her neighbor's
house had a similar deck.

She found two small bedrooms upstairs and another bathroom. The front bedroom had been used as an office, and a desk
sat in front of the window that looked out onto the beach and
the ocean. Charley could see herself working here, editing pho-

tos, writing on her laptop, or posting or emailing her stories. *Or not.* Mr. Lewis said the island had acceptable cell service, but very slow internet. If the internet wasn't sufficient for her needs, she'd ask Mr. Lewis if she could use his office until she found a different work-around. Then again, who would want to work when they had such a gorgeous view before them? The rolling waves and sandy beach calling them to come outside and play would be hard to resist.

Charley finished unpacking and putting away the household items, cleaning products, and food she had brought from New Jersey. The kitchen pantry was empty, but she'd brought boxed crackers, chips, some canned goods, drinks, and a few other staples. She wouldn't starve immediately, but once she had the place cleaned and straightened, she'd make a grocery run to supplement the pantry.

Two hours later, Charley was sitting on the front porch, watching the ocean. A tuna salad sandwich, chips, and a glass of soda sat on the table beside her chair. She was rethinking her plan to make a trip to the grocery store today. She had scrubbed the bathrooms and the kitchen, swept the floors, put clean sheets on the bed, and opened the windows to air out the house. Once that was finished, she was unable to go any farther than the rocking chair on the porch. Shopping could wait.

Charley's road trip from New Jersey and all the excitement of arriving at the house had caught up with her. If she leaned back in the chair and let the ocean breeze blow through her hair, she could easily fall asleep here on the porch. She grimaced as she recalled that four days from tomorrow, she would board a plane bound for Costa Rica to spend almost a week photographing the rain forest. For the first time in a long time, Charley was not excited to be flying off to a new place for a photography shoot.

CHAPTER FOUR

Y ou want me to do what?" Alex looked incredulously at
his father.

Bob Morgan was seated behind his desk in the law
offices of Winston, Morgan, and Gilbert. It was a cool morning
so the window behind his father's head was open and the sound
of traffic on Broad Street came through in a low hum.

When he was first summoned to his father's office, Alex had
expected a conversation about his clients or his workload as
a senior member of the firm or even possibly a sermon about
some decision he had or hadn't made. But Alex had never expected… this.

"You want me to spy on some unsuspecting woman? A
stranger? Why would I do that? Why do I *need* to do that?"

"It's not spying… exactly. I'd never ask you to do anything
illegal. You just need to get to know her, find out who she is," his
father replied.

"That's the definition of spying. And what's this all about?"
Alex leaned forward, rested his elbows on his knees, and
scowled at his father. The explanation had better be good,

though he doubted it would be. His bosses sometimes had crazy ideas, but this might be the craziest he'd heard to date.

"Mrs. Maitland has asked us to find out who this Charley Phillips or Charley Rainier person actually is. According to Mrs. Maitland, she's used several names, so it's hard to get a clear picture of exactly who she is." Mr. Morgan shifted in his chair. "It's very important to Mrs. Maitland, though I'm not sure why." Mr. Morgan nervously fingered some papers on his desk. He was evidently as uncomfortable with what he was asking Alex to do as Alex was in hearing it. Just more evidence that this was a bad idea.

"This is Mrs. Maitland's idea? You know she doesn't always use logic when she gets something in her head," Alex cautioned. Mrs. Maitland's schemes were the craziest of the three of them—her, Mr. Winston and his father—and that was saying something. "Her main objective is getting her way—always!"

"Well, she's one of our biggest, most influential clients. She went directly to Mr. Winston. Apparently, he didn't ask for details, or if he did, he didn't share them with me. When Mrs. Maitland talks, he listens and doesn't ask questions. She told him that it's extremely urgent that we find out the truth behind this Charley Phillips. She suggested you be the one to do it."

"Why?" Alex needed more to go on than just a crazy request from a woman whom he referred to as "The Bulldozer." The name was sometimes used affectionately, but it always accurately described Mrs. Maitland's business tactics.

The Maitland family was one of Charleston's oldest families and one of its wealthiest. They had been in the shipping business since pirates hid in the coves off the coast of South Carolina. And like her predecessors, the pirates, she wasn't above using blackmail to get her way or above using threats to take her considerable wealth to another firm if she didn't get what she wanted.

"Mrs. Maitland thinks 'Rainier' might be her maiden name and 'Phillips' her husband's name," Mr. Morgan added, "but apparently, neither of those names is the one she's looking for."

"Two names aren't a *lot*, and if this woman uses different names, maybe she doesn't want anyone to know who she is. That's not a crime. And since when did we become private investigators?" Alex asked. "Or spies?"

"Since Mrs. Maitland fired the private investigator she hired for the job."

"A PI? She hired a PI to investigate this woman? This is crazy." Alex shook his head as he leaned closer to his father, hoping he heard wrong. "You must be kidding. A PI?"

"A PI, yes. And he must have found something that makes Mrs. Maitland believe this woman is the one she's looking for, regardless of what name she currently uses. But before the PI found positive proof, he was involved in a break-in on one of his other jobs—caught on camera—which makes one question his ethics and his abilities. He'll probably lose his license. Mrs. Maitland doesn't want to hire another PI and take a chance that he might do something illegal, too—and in her name."

"You know what they say about getting fleas from lying down with dogs," Alex replied.

"Mrs. Maitland got rid of him before his fleas contaminated her search for this woman. But now, she wants our help to finish the job."

"Why me?" Alex asked. "I'm not an investigator."

"You're the natural choice. You're free and not in a serious relationship right now. It wouldn't be strange for you to get acquainted with her." Mr. Morgan paused as Alex grimaced. "It's been over a year since you and Rebecca broke up. Alex, it's time you started to get to know other women."

Alex frowned at his father. Rebecca hadn't merely broken up with him. She had broken up with him when they were practically at the altar. Yes, it had been over a year, but that didn't mean it still didn't smart. Besides, he hadn't met anyone since that he wanted to date on a regular basis.

"It's time to rip the Band-Aid off and get on with your life," his father continued. "I know you were hurt, and I don't want to sound cruel, but unless you get out there and start dating again, you'll be old, alone, and still clinging to what might have been."

"Wow, you hit all the clichés in that one sentence. And for someone who doesn't want to be cruel, you're doing a great imitation," Alex accused. "I've dated other women since Rebecca."

"Please! You've escorted a few women to organized events, but you've rarely *dated*. You've taken Mrs. Maitland out more than eligible women."

As exasperated as he was with his father at the moment, Alex had to smile at his comment. Mrs. Maitland, his client, was sixty, or close to it, and yes, he had escorted her to some fundraising events around town. It was true that immediately after he and Rebecca broke up, he was vocal about his anger and didn't hesitate to voice his cynicism about love and romance. If his memory was correct, he had sworn off of getting involved with anyone ever again and had given up on the idea of ever having a family. With time, he had backed off from such vehement claims. He didn't think he had become a grouchy hermit at the age of thirty-two. Still, just in case his father was right, he'd try to go out more often for pleasure… when he had the chance. He spent most of his time working right now.

Still, that didn't mean he wanted any part of Mrs. Maitland's scheme.

"Why me?" Alex asked again. "What makes you think I'll agree to do your spying?"

"Like I said, you're a natural choice. Plus, a good-looking guy like you won't have any trouble striking up a friendship with this woman. Who knows, maybe you'll sweep her off her feet and learn what you need to know right away?"

"She'll fall for my looks?" Alex grunted. "You make this woman sound shallow. My character doesn't matter? That would just be another reason to avoid her. Besides, what will her husband say about a strange guy hitting on his wife?" Alex asked. "Other than call me a homewrecker and challenge me to a duel at the Angel Oak at dawn?"

"They were divorced some time ago." Mr. Morgan ignored Alex's sarcasm and adjusted some folders on his desk. "She might be ready for… uh…you know, some male companionship by now."

Alex's eyes widened, then he frowned at his father. "What? Your implication is, at best, crass and unkind to this unknown woman. And to me. Sounds like what you're looking for is a gigolo."

"I apologize," his father replied. "That came out wrong."

"And by the way," Alex continued, "are you calling me 'good-looking' because everyone says I look like you?"

"Actually, you get your dark hair and gray eyes from your mother. My only contribution is your height. But you're taller than I am now. You get taller every time I see you."

"Don't try to distract me by switching topics!" Alex replied. "Most people have stopped growing by my age. Maybe you're just shrinking. And how long has it been since you looked into Mom's eyes? They're more blue than gray."

"Counselor, you're asking me to give out intimate details about my private moments with your mother," his father replied. "Blue-gray, then. Whatever the color, her eyes are lovely. I look into them often."

Alex flushed slightly as a sudden visual of his parents' private moments flashed before his eyes. His father's twisting his question to make him uncomfortable reminded Alex of what a good a litigator he was. He had the skill to turn innocent comments into lines of attack against his targets and was an expert at confusing witnesses and making them uncomfortable during questioning. Alex admired his dad's abilities as a lawyer, but Alex wasn't without skills of his own—in a courtroom setting. Lately, his father had accused him of being too serious. When his father tried to engage him in a debate over a legal case, Alex didn't push back the way his father wanted him to. It had been different when he was in law school. Then, he was always willing to go toe-to-toe with his father. One would think the two men were mimicking the great debaters and orators of history and were competing to see who could keep up the argument the longest. It was a game they both enjoyed—back then.

To be honest, Alex felt a bit disenchanted with his profession at the moment. Helping rich people get even richer had lost some of its appeal. He'd much rather help a fledging environmental group fight the very corporate clients he was sometimes representing. But he couldn't live on pro bono work. Which brought him back to the scheme his father—one of his employers—was proposing.

"Here's the dossier on the woman." His father pushed a blue folder toward Alex.

Alex pushed it back. "'Dossier'? This is becoming a scene right out of a gangster movie. 'Go out there, Joey, and get the goods on this dame,'" Alex said, mimicking Al Pacino. "I can't believe that you're involved in this and that you want to implicate me, as well. Next, you'll be asking me to bring back a lock of her hair or a finger."

"That wouldn't be a bad idea—the hair, I mean. A source for DNA." His father laughed. "But I don't think that's part of our task... yet."

"What exactly is our task?"

"As I understand, all you need to do is find out as much as you can about this woman's past and report what you find to

Mrs. Maitland. That shouldn't be too difficult if you become friends with her."

"Hmph! And you say this isn't spying?" Alex retorted.

"Read the folder." His father pushed it toward him again.

Alex refused to pick it up. This whole scenario was creepy, and he was searching for ways to duck any involvement in it. "Where do I find this mysterious woman? Just so you know, I'm not interested in making a trip to Podunk, USA."

"You'll like this part. It's another reason why you're perfect for the job," his father replied. "According to the PI's report, he located this Rainier or Phillips or whatever her real name is in the New York and New Jersey area. But she's here now—on Turtle Island. According to Winston, by way of Mrs. Maitland, this woman inherited the old Travis place."

"Here? Annabelle left the beach house to her?" Alex's interest perked up. The old Travis place was right next to the beach cottage he had bought two summers ago. The reason he had been selected for this "spy" job was becoming clearer. He visited the island as often as possible.

"If you do this… just think! You'll be free of your regular duties here and can spend the whole summer out there. I know you aren't happy with your work in acquisitions and mergers right now, so this would give you a break and time to think about your future with the firm."

"I do my job," Alex insisted.

"You do your job and do it well, but I know environmental law is your first love. I also know that you've been advising environmental groups pro bono in your free time." His father paused, then continued, "But back to our current situation. Mr. Winston is so anxious to please Mrs. Maitland that he has agreed to let you spend all your time at the beach and just monitor your cases from there. Your interns can help, but you may need to come into the office occasionally to meet with clients.

But a summer free of your duties here in the office would give you time to step back and think—decide what you really want to do *and* keep Mrs. Maitland happy at the same time." New interest sparked in Alex's eyes. Then, his father added the clincher that made it hard for Alex to say no: "You don't want us to send Eric Winston out there, do you?"

Alex flinched at the mention of Eric Winston. Eric never saw a "dame" that he didn't want to chase. He considered himself a ladies' man and had meddled in Alex and Rebecca's relationship, though he wasn't the cause of their breakup. He had constantly pressed Rebecca to ditch Alex and go out with him instead. Rebecca had ditched Alex, but at least it hadn't been for Eric.

"Are you trying to bribe me?" Alex asked. Spending time at the beach was an attractive prospect, but he was still uneasy. His father was asking him to spy on a stranger.

"Is it working?"

"Maybe. If I do this, will you let me pitch a proposal to Mr. Winston that would allow me to take cases for and represent some of the conservation groups using the firm's name? I don't want to leave this firm, so I'd still keep my regular caseload, of course. Can you get Mr. Winston to at least listen?"

"I believe I can, and I promise to try. He's very anxious to please Mrs. Maitland." His father pushed the folder toward Alex again.

Alex still didn't pick it up. "This just seems wrong on so many levels. I won't accept any payment for doing this," he added emphatically. "If Mrs. Maitland is billed for my time, donate the money to charity." The queasy feeling in the pit of his stomach about the whole crazy plot hadn't lessened. Invading someone's privacy and deceiving them for a hidden purpose went against everything he believed in. But he didn't want Eric Winston turned lose on an unsuspecting woman, either. And the chance to add environmental cases to his day job was hard to resist.

"I'm not asking you to break any ethical standards," his father replied. "But take the folder just in case you need to verify information you uncover against information the PI found."

Alex's stomach clenched as he looked at the folder. It probably contained details about many areas of this woman's life. Whoever she was, she deserved her privacy. She shouldn't have her life picked apart by him or by anyone else, for any reason. He couldn't believe he was agreeing to do this. But, "In for a penny, in for a pound," as the saying went. "How do I recognize this woman?" he asked. "Is she old? Young? Covered in warts?"

His father pulled a photo from the folder. "No warts" was all he said as he pushed the photo toward Alex.

Alex stared down at a professional headshot portrait of a young woman whom he guessed was around his age, maybe a little younger. The photographer's lens had captured a halo of golden-brown hair, highlighted and intensified by the studio lights. The woman's green eyes sparkled, yet Alex recognized a vulnerability, or maybe it was distrust and sadness in their depths. He had seen the same look in his own eyes after his breakup with Rebecca.

There was something vaguely familiar about the woman. Her mouth and the way she held her head sparked a memory buried somewhere deep in his brain. He strained to recall if or where he had met her. He probably hadn't met her, though, because those green eyes would be hard to forget.

As Alex's eyes roved over the face of the woman in the photo, he almost told his father the deal was off. He didn't want to deceive someone whom he suspected had already suffered heartbreak and disappointment.

Alex returned to his father's proposal. If not him, then who? His reluctance was overridden by concern for the unsuspecting woman, Charley Phillips. Alex knew Mrs. Maitland well. She wouldn't give up her search, regardless of whether he helped her or not. She'd just find someone else and run over this woman in the process.

Alex studied the photo and felt a flicker of interest. *Get outside your comfort zone, Alex, and start experiencing life again,* he thought. He had no idea if he and this woman would even hit it off. They could be enemies the moment they met, or they could have nothing at all in common. But at least he would be meeting someone interesting and his attention would be on someone and something other than himself and his workload. Even if the spy game was a failure, he would have spent time with a beautiful woman. But were his personal reasons good enough for him to spy on this stranger? Was he letting his own self-interest talk him into participating in a scheme no one other than Mrs. Maitland would dream up?

As Alex struggled with the ethics of what he was agreeing to, he decided that Mrs. Maitland, his father, and Mr. Winston would only get the information that he decided to share with them. He had control over that much, at least. Alex reluctantly picked up the folder and slipped the photo back inside.

"I won't look at this report and be influenced or prejudiced by it. I still can't believe I've let you talk me into this shifty plot." He rose from his chair. "One more thing. If I become uncomfortable with this plan, I won't hesitate to pull the plug and quit."

As Alex walked out of his father's office and closed the door, his uneasiness returned. He almost turned around to tell his father that he'd changed his mind, but he spotted Eric Winston entering his own office just down the hallway. The sight of Eric reminded Alex of one of the most powerful arguments his father had used to get him on board. His participation in the plan was a blocking move to keep Eric away from the woman.

Be honest, Alex thought as he walked toward his office. *A beautiful woman and a summer at the beach! You're not actually being as altruistic as you want to pretend.* It looked like he was now going to spy on his neighbor. He just hoped he didn't come to regret it.

For the rest of the day, Alex wrapped up what he could of his current caseload. For the cases he couldn't finish, he made notes on what needed to be done, who needed to be called, and all other pertinent information. His father could expand upon his notes before sharing them with the intern who assisted Alex. That done, he gathered up the paper files and carried them to his father's office. His father wasn't there, so he dumped them in the middle of his desk. He wrote a quick note and stuck it to the top folder. The note read, 'Gone to the beach.'

Alex ran a few errands, picked up some groceries, and then closed up his house in Goose Creek. He loaded Rex, his dog, into the back seat of his pickup and drove to Turtle Island. A burnished-gold sun was sinking in the west when Alex pulled into the driveway of his beach house. A silver-gray SUV was parked in the driveway of the adjoining property. His interest and curiosity were piqued, but for reasons other than Mrs. Maitland's scheme. Just who was this woman—Charley Phillips—and how was she connected to his friend Annabelle? She must have meant a lot to Annabelle, since she left the beach house property to her, yet he had never heard Annabelle mention her.

"What do you think, Rex?" he asked the Sheltie resting in the rear seat. "You suppose she likes dogs? You need to stay away until we find out, okay?" Rex tilted his head, looked at him, and barked. "I'll take that as a 'yes.' Come on, boy. Let's go inside."

Alex carried the bag of groceries up the steps to the house as Rex bounded ahead of him. Rex loved the beach. When Alex took him for walks, he raced around the sand dunes with gusto, chasing after and barking at any seagull that came into his line of sight. He never caught any and didn't really want to. Catching them wasn't the point.

Alex felt the tension leave his shoulders, and his muscles uncoiled as he entered the house. He always felt more relaxed and more carefree here on the island. But for one reason or another—work, family gatherings, and so on—it had been a few weekends since he was last here. Alex went from window to window, opening them to let the sea breeze flow in and air out the house.

When he and Rebecca had been together, he hadn't visited the island as often as he wanted to. Rebecca hated the beach. This was a major point of contention between them. She liked Charleston's social scene, hobnobbing with the rich and power-ful, and networking for her interior design business. The feeling of sand in her shoes drove her mad. Well, that was water under the bridge, or—to use a better beach analogy—that problem had floated out to sea on the evening tide.

Alex took the burger he'd picked up in Charleston, along with a beer from the fridge, out to the front porch. As he ate, he watched his neighbor's house. There didn't appear to be any ac-tivity outside or inside the house. What nefarious doings could his mysterious neighbor be plotting on this beautiful evening? Burying money from a bank heist on the beach? Plotting to sell secrets to the enemy? Maybe she was a secret agent and chased bad guys for the government. His rambling thoughts amused him, but that's about all they were—entertaining and amusing. He'd never make it as a crime novelist. Mrs. Phillips's photo didn't look like his image of a Mata Hari—or of any spy, for that matter. The word *spy* brought the queasy feeling back to his stomach. He was the spy, not his neighbor.

Alex finished his dinner and took Rex for a walk. As he

passed the Travis place on his return home, there was still no movement around it. He thought for a moment that maybe he should check on her just to make sure she was alright. He quickly squashed that idea. He was not that anxious to set *his* nefarious plot in motion.

Charley stretched, yawned, and scrunched her eyes against the blinding light that pierced her eyelids. Her hands flailed as she tried to push the light away. But the light refused to budge. She moved her head to the right and back again, but the light persisted. She opened one eye. A bright beam of light hit her squarely in the face. Charley instantly came fully awake, sat up, and looked around. A bright morning sun was shining through the window. The sun's rays struck the appliances in the kitchen and bounced straight back across the room and into her eyes where she lay on the sofa.

Oh! Aunt Annabelle's beach house. She rubbed her eyes and stretched again. Everything that had happened yesterday came into focus. She remembered now. She had lain down on the sofa, hoping the sound of the ocean waves would relax her and help her sleep once she went to bed. Obviously, the sound had relaxed her. She had spent the entire night sleeping on the living room sofa. A glass of red wine, still nearly full, sat on the coffee table in front of her. Charley stretched again and looked at the clock. Eight o'clock. She had slept eleven straight hours. She must have been more exhausted than she realized.

Charley got up, showered, dressed, and then made a pot of coffee. She poured herself a cup when it was ready, grabbed a protein bar, and took them outside to the morning coolness on the back deck. As she passed through her bedroom, Charley remembered her plan to drag the area rug out onto the back deck to air it out and remove the musty smell, the result of the closed-up house.

She leaned back in the wicker chair and took a sip of coffee. It was muddy and not very good—not nearly as good as the coffee from the corner coffee shop she regularly frequented in New York. But it was loaded with caffeine and was hot, so it would do the job of jolting her out of her sleep-induced stupor.

Charley had finished her second cup of coffee before she felt sufficiently awake to tackle the rather large rug. She rolled it up and began pulling it across the room. It was heavier than she had anticipated. Sweat beaded on her forehead as she twisted and yanked it toward the door to the deck. As she tugged, the rug came partially unrolled and one side caught on the side of the doorframe. She yanked, but it didn't budge.

"You want some help with that?" a voice asked from behind her. Charley let out a yelp, dropped the end of the rug, and quickly spun around. Her head bumped against the side of the door. The owner of the voice was a tall man who smiled widely at her from the top of the stairs that led up to the deck from the yard. A reddish-brown and white dog sat at his feet, staring at her.

"You! Sandwich Shop Alex! What are you doing here?" Charley asked, her eyes round with surprise. She was staring into the face of the man she had met yesterday—or, rather, the man she had injured with the door yesterday.

"I live here," Alex replied, equally surprised. "And I see we've already met. Your hair is different, and you're not wearing those dark sunglasses, but there's no mistake—you're the woman who tried to poke my eye out yesterday. And before you try to injure me again, I'm just here to welcome you to the island." He held up his hands, as if to ward her off.

"You scared me half to death," Charley exclaimed. She

pressed her hands to her chest. "I'm sorry about hitting you." Her eyes went to his forehead. The mark above his eyebrow had faded. Charley rubbed the spot on the side of her head where she had bumped it.

"And I'm sorry I scared you. Let me look at your head." He didn't wait for her reply, but approached and pulled her hand away from the spot she was rubbing. He placed his hand under her chin, tilted her head to the side, and parted her hair to inspect her injury. He gently touched the spot. "It doesn't look too bad. A little red, but no blood. No stitches required." There was a smile in his voice as he removed his hand from under her chin and stepped back. "I think we'll both survive our wounds."

"It's the heart attack you caused by sneaking up on me that might leave lasting damage. I might sue," Charley said, reminding him of his comment from yesterday.

"You don't have a case. The witness won't corroborate your story." He smiled and nodded toward the dog who sat looking from one to the other. "In shared fault cases, it's always best for parties to just drop the cases and avoid the hassle. Most are frivolous."

"Shared fault? A heart attack versus a bump on the forehead? I'll check with my attorney, if you don't mind," Charley stated, then realized how grumpy she sounded. She amended her comment. "I guess you're right. A lawsuit might be excessive for someone guilty only of sneaking up on me."

"I didn't sneak up on you," Alex insisted. His smile made Charley question his denial. "I'm Alex, by the way—your neighbor." He nodded to the house next door. He stuck out his hand. "And I'm rarely referred to as 'Sandwich Shop Alex.'"

"Oh!" Charley blushed. "I'm Charley." She clasped his extended hand. She had blurted out the nickname she had given him when he suddenly appeared out of nowhere. "I heard Benji call you Alex. I have a habit of assigning names to interesting people I see, but don't actually know."

"So, you think I'm interesting?" Alex asked with a broad smile. "Maybe 'Interesting Alex' would be a better name than 'Sandwich Shop Alex.' That one just conjures up the smell of pastrami and garlic."

She had walked into that one. She stared at him, searching for an appropriate reply. He still held her hand. He now appeared to be close to laughing at her, but she couldn't think of a retort that might wipe the teasing smile off his face. Something cold touched her free hand. Charley looked down at the Sheltie who had moved in between her and Alex. She pulled her hand free and bent to rub the dog's head, happy for the distraction. "Who are you? You sure are a pretty thing."

"That's Rex. He considers himself handsome, not pretty," Alex explained.

"Well, you are indeed handsome." Charley scratched Rex behind his ears. He plopped down by her feet and looked up at her adoringly.

"You have a friend for life," Alex noted. "Here, let me help you with that rug. Where do you want it?" He went around Charley and Rex without waiting for a reply. With one tug, he had it out on the deck.

Charley directed him to hang it over the deck railing. "I want to air it out. It smells musty."

"The place has been closed up for over a year, ever since Annabelle got sick." Alex spread the rug over the railing. Grains of sand fell off of it and onto the deck. "You might want to vacuum it once it's aired. Annabelle kept a vacuum in the storage room beneath the deck. I can bring it up, if you want."

"No, but thanks. I'll get it later. You seem to know a lot about Annabelle."

"I knew Annabelle for several years before she passed. I used to help her with small repairs around here—whatever she couldn't do herself." Alex crossed his arms and casually leaned against the deck railing. "I'm personal friends with the kitchen faucet. If you ever have problems with it, just ask."

The morning sun had now risen over the top of the beach house and filtered through the canopy of the live oak tree. Its dappled rays created a patchwork of light and dark shadows across the deck. It exposed sun lightened strands where it touched Alex's dark hair. His blue eyes squinted against the morning light as he waited for her to answer. "Thanks for the offer. I'll keep that in mind. So far, the faucet's working fine," Charley replied. Rex stood up and nuzzled her hand again. Charley looked down, patted his head, and scratched him behind his ears. She looked back at Alex. "But maybe you can help me with something else. I need to make a grocery run. Does the grocery store on the island carry the essentials, or do I have to go to a store on one of the other islands?"

"It depends on what you call 'essentials.' If you're a gourmet cook, then no. You'll need to go to a grocery store on one of the bigger islands. But if you want the basic staples—bread, milk, coffee, eggs, butter, stuff like that—you can find them at the island grocery store."

"I've never been accused of being a gourmet cook," Charley laughed. "I'd describe myself as an 'eat on the fly' kind of cook."

"In that case, why don't I take you? I need to get a few things, too. I can show you around the island along the way," Alex offered.

Charley hesitated. She didn't know this man, but he seemed nice, and if Annabelle thought he was alright, who was she to disagree? Of course, she didn't know Annabelle, either, she reminded herself. Charley's desire to see the island quickly overrode any concern she had about going with Alex. They were neighbors, and this was technically their second meeting. So he wasn't exactly a stranger.

"If you're sure it won't inconvenience you."

"No trouble at all. I'll pick you up out front in, say... ten minutes?" Alex moved toward the stairs leading down to the yard.

"Ten minutes is perfect."

"Come, Rex. You have to stay home for this trip." The Sheltie rose from his resting place on the deck and obediently followed Alex.

CHAPTER FIVE

lex's first stop on the guided island tour was a small inlet not far from their beach houses. They exited the pickup truck and approached the inlet. Egrets—the long-legged coastal wetland birds—flew from the trees, their roosting places disturbed by the visitors. Alex stopped when they reached a wet, spongy area.

"This is the jewel of Turtle Island: the salt marsh. You might call it the canary in the environmental coal mine," Alex explained. He waved his hand to encompass the entire wetland preserve. The tide had recently pushed more water into thick patches of reeds, tall grasses, and bushes that grew out of the waterlogged ground.

"How so?" Charley asked, then wrinkled her nose at the pungent scent in the air. "What's that smell?"

"That sulfur-like smell is from pluff mud. It's caused by the decomposition of animals and grasses at the bottom of the marsh. Some liken it to the smell of rotten eggs, but it plays a unique role in keeping the marsh healthy," Alex explained. "The mud forms a rich, healthy base for sea life, such as oysters. It also supports the plant life you see all around us. The tides bring in nutrients from the ocean and deposit them in the marsh. Then, the water flows out to sea again."

"Oh, I see. It's sorta like nature's cleansing system," Charley said.

"Something like that," Alex said, nodding. "Or you could call it nature's co-op. Each element depends on the other. In return for the nutrients from the ocean, the marshes provide homes for fish, birds, and other wildlife, as well as plant life. The vegetation that grows from the rich soil then becomes the first line of defense in stopping erosion of the beach and shoreline. And the plants assist with flood control when hurricanes or tropical storms move in."

"You called it an environmental canary. That usually means a warning sign. Doesn't everyone want to take care of the marsh?" Charley asked. It seemed very simple to her.

"Profits get in the way of common sense. The island is under constant threat from development," Alex replied. "Runoff from construction sites have destroyed marshes on several of the other islands. Thus far, we've been successful in stopping large-scale development here on Turtle Island, but that doesn't mean the developers have stopped trying to get a foothold. It would take just one builder to come in with a bulldozer, and all of this would die." Alex frowned as he stared at the marsh. There was no mistaking his passion for the subject. He was serious and not joking around as he had earlier.

"You seem to know a lot about the ecology of the marshes," Charley stated.

"I've fought to save them since I learned how important they are to life on the islands—since I realized the marshes all along the coastline are at risk, not only from developers, but also from rising sea levels. I've won some court battles, and I've lost some. But losing hasn't stopped me from doing whatever I can to save all this." Alex swept his hand in a wide arc.

"Oh, so you're an environmental attorney?" Charley asked.

"No, corporate, but I represent some environmental groups who can't afford an attorney. I believe this marsh is worth the fight. You could call it my second job, but I've been accused of making it my first priority."

"A passionate man with two mistresses," Charley stated with a laugh.

"I prefer to think I have two top priorities and no time for mistresses." Alex smiled in return.

"Well, I can tell you're passionate about all this," Charley said, gesturing to the marshland around them. Passion for a cause—was that what was missing in her life of late? Was she passionate about what she was doing with her life right now? Did she want to spend the rest of her life running from airport to airport, never staying in one place for very long? This was a question that kept circling in the back of her mind lately.

"It's an uphill fight," Alex continued. "As with most environmental issues, it's hard to persuade people that just because you can't always see what's happening, it doesn't mean bad things *aren't* happening. Sometimes, by the time you can see it, it's too late."

Alex stared at the marsh for a moment longer, then turned to Charley. "Enough of that. Let me show you the rest of the island and your neighbors."

"Let's go," Charley replied. She followed Alex back to his pickup truck. She was ready to see the rest of the island and learn about the other people who lived here. Maybe she would get to know some personally before the summer was over and she had to leave.

They left the marshland, and Alex took the road that circled the beach front, then, he cut across the middle of the island. Along the way, he pointed out the houses that had been rebuilt after recent storms and those that had miraculously managed to survive the same damaging hurricane winds. Alex knew the names of all the houses' occupants, even if he was not personally acquainted with many of them. Obviously, he spent a lot of time on Turtle Island.

It didn't take them long to see most of the island. It was small in size, but appeared to have all the things necessary to make it a community. Charley was disappointed when the tour was over and they parked in front of Whitaker's Family Market. She enjoyed listening to Alex talk as he told her about life on the island—even down to the plant life. According to Alex, the hardy yellow flowers that grew on the dunes—the ones she had spotted yesterday when she arrived—were seaside daises, or commonly called beach daisies. They mixed with evening primrose and added color to the sandy backdrop of the beach.

Whitaker's Family Market was a one-story building located in the middle of the island and away from the beach. Elevated on large, thick pilings, it was protected from rising water, because powerful storm surges caused by hurricanes could easily reach the interior of the island. The residents of Turtle Island occupied a precarious position, but they were all apparently willing to accept and prepare for the danger in exchange for the pleasure of living here.

Charley loaded her shopping cart with items she considered essential due to her limited cooking abilities. She purchased only things that would keep until she got back from her trip to Costa Rica at the end of the coming week. Alex picked up a few items—mainly treats for Rex. She questioned his need to come to the store at all, but she was happy he had accompanied her. His tour of the island had been both informative for her as a newcomer, as well as entertaining.

When they returned from the grocery store and parked in front of Charley's beach house, Rex could be heard barking furiously from Alex's house next door. Alex quickly gathered up most of Charley's groceries and then turned to her. "While I carry your bags up, would you mind letting Rex out before he tears down the front door? The door's unlocked."

"Sure. He does sound anxious to get out."

"He loves attention, so I think he misses his new friend," Alex replied with a grin.

Charley climbed the stairs to the porch and had barely opened the front door to Alex's house when Rex bounded out. He danced around her on the landing. "Are you happy to see me, or would anyone who opened the door do for you?" Charley bent down and rubbed his head. "No one has been this excited to see me in many years."

Rex followed Charley back to Alex's truck. She picked up the remaining bag of groceries and carried it up the steps and into the house. When she pushed the front door open, she saw Alex standing in front of the photo from her New York art show.

"Are you interested in photography?" Charley asked. She set the bag down on the kitchen counter, then came to stand beside Alex.

"Interested, but I'm more of a point-and-shoot photographer. I don't have the eye this photographer has."

"Do you know if Annabelle was? A photographer, I mean."

"Nah, I don't think so. She just liked beautiful pictures that tell stories."

"Do you know where she got this photo?" Charley held her breath while she waited for Alex's answer. She already knew where it had originally been displayed. She just didn't know how it came to be here.

"I do. I took Annabelle to an art exhibit in New York shortly before she got sick. Not just any exhibit would do, though. It had to be this one."

Charley felt chills run up her arm. Annabelle and Alex had been at her show.

"That was nice of you," Charley said in an even voice, but her heart jumped at the news that her great-aunt had made a special trip to New York just to be at her art show.

"Well, she was going regardless. I moved up a scheduled business appointment I had in New York, so it worked out for both of us. I couldn't let an eighty-eight-year-old woman go into that jungle by herself."

"Did you meet the photographer?" Charley knew the answer to that question, too. The gallery owner, Regina, a friend of Charley's, had asked her to stay away to maintain the mystery of the elusive photographer. Regina had created this mystique for Charley at her first showing. For artists like Charley, new to exhibiting their work, Regina felt the mystery would generate more interest and sell more photos. Regina never displayed a picture of the photographer at Charley's shows.

Charley went along with the arrangement, but for her own personal reasons. She wanted to maintain the separation between her life as Charley Rainier and her life as a visual artist and photographer. When she first started showing her photographs, she didn't want her day job as a staff photographer for a travel magazine—the job that provided her income—to be affected by praise or criticism of her work as an exhibiting photographer. Her acceptance of this anonymity might also have been due to her lack of confidence at her first gallery showing. Either way, she went along with Regina's strategy, and the mystery had built from there.

As it turned out, she didn't need to worry about merging her two lives, because both careers were successful. But people seemed to like the mystery, so Charley and Regina never divulged that Charley Rainier and Ce Ce Kane were one and the same.

"No, we didn't meet the photographer," Alex replied to Charley's question. "A prior engagement—she was out of the country or something. Annabelle was very disappointed." Alex turned toward Charley. "I'm glad to see that she left the photo with the house."

"Me, too." Charley felt slightly uncomfortable about not admitting to Alex that she was the photographer, but the time just didn't feel right. He didn't know anything about her life, so he probably wouldn't believe her if she suddenly claimed to be the photographer. One day, she would have to bring the charade of Ce Ce Kane to a halt. But when and how to do so was the problem.

"I bought a photo at the exhibit, too—two elks in Alaska, butting heads with their antlers locked. It's hanging in my office." Alex turned away from the photo, walked to the kitchen counter, and began taking the groceries out of the bags. Then, he stopped. "Is it okay if I unbag these for you? I'll let you put them away."

"Sure, and thanks," Charley replied. Hmmm. Alex was a very thoughtful and helpful man, even with household chores—something she had never counted on and never received from Daniel. Charley began sorting through her grocery purchases as Alex removed them from the bags, separating refrigerator items from those to be stored in the pantry.

"The elk photo spoke to you, didn't it? Did it remind you of a personal story—two headstrong males fighting… probably over a female?" Charley remembered the photo very well. She and her guide had taken a floatplane to one of the few islands where elk could be found in Alaska: Raspberry Island in the Kodiak Archipelago located in the Gulf of Alaska. She had lain in the bushes for three hours, snapping photos of wilderness scenes and the wildlife in the immediate area, waiting and hoping that elk would appear.

Her guide kept assuring her that elk would come. She couldn't believe her luck when a group of ten wandered into the clearing. Much like some humans she had known, two males started fighting—an exercise to impress the females in the herd. Each male was trying to dominate and overpower the other. Another human trait. The two rutting bucks, framed against the snowcapped mountains, with fire in their eyes and their muscles tense as they locked antlers, made for the perfect shot. It was one of her favorite photos. She was glad it was in the hands of someone who appreciated it.

"No, nothing that romantic," Alex replied with a chuckle. "Actually, it reminded me of my brother. As teenagers, Robert and I would often lock horns—or, in this case, antlers. Not over females, but over everything else. He always had to get in the last word or the last punch. He's younger, so I was usually the first to back off. I'm not sure what we were trying to prove. Of course, we drove our parents crazy. We eventually grew out of it… for the most part."

"Do you have any siblings other than your brother?" Charley had always wondered what it would be like to have a brother or sister. Even in Alex's story of sibling rivalry, his voice held obvious affection for his brother. What was it like, sharing such a deep connection with someone that nothing—no matter how much you fought or what words you said—could break it? The blood that ran through your veins wouldn't change, no matter what happened between you.

"No. I just have one brother." Alex smiled. "At one time, I would have gladly traded Robert for a sister, but my parents wouldn't let me. Do you have siblings?"

"No. Just me. I can't imagine what it would be like to have someone to share things with or to fight with, even." Charley picked up a bag of sugar, walked into the alcove where the pantry was located, and placed it on a shelf. She lingered there for a few seconds. She wanted to avoid discussing any part of her life as a child or have Alex question her about it.

"As teenagers, fighting was something Robert and I did very well. But sharing? Not so much." Alex laughed as Charley returned to the kitchen. He folded the empty paper bags and stacked them on the counter. Then, he dusted his hand, turned, and started to walk toward the door to go home.

"Uh… listen. There's one place I didn't show you this morning." Alex turned back to Charley. "It's the Tides of the Marsh restaurant on the other side of the salt marsh. You haven't had shrimp until you've eaten Manny's fried shrimp—or any other way you like it. Want to go? Maybe around seven?"

"You don't have to mess up your evening. You've already done so much for me today: the tour of the island and the trip to the market. You've been very kind and helpful," Charley replied.

"No problem. I'd like the company. And trust me, the food is great!"

Charley hesitated only a moment longer. She *did* want to go with him. Spending the evening alone wasn't very appealing to her, either. "Okay. Seven it is."

After Alex and Rex left, Charley grabbed a quick bite for lunch and then went back to the cleaning she had intended to do when Alex appeared on the deck. She found a broom in the kitchen pantry and swiped it across the rug hanging over the deck railing several times. Grains of sand tumbled from the rug onto the deck

"Cleaning one thing begets cleaning another," Charley grumbled as she began sweeping the sand off the deck. She continued on, making her way around the porch. Once she had finished sweeping all sides of the porch, she moved down the stairs and began sweeping the concrete floor of the open space under the house. The soft breeze from the ocean suddenly picked up in intensity and deposited more sand around her as she swept. Charley stopped sweeping and looked around. The space looked somewhat cleaner than before, but with the perpetual breeze, she didn't expect that state to last very long.

Charley gave up her fight against the wind and sand and instead decided to get ready for her dinner date.

"It's not a date," she scolded herself as she dressed in denim, knee length skimmers, a loose flowing shirt, and sandals. "Just neighbors having dinner together."

She checked herself over one last time in the hallway mirror, then walked outside to sit on the porch's lower steps to wait for Alex. He was right on time. Punctuality was another quality that differentiated him from Daniel. He came out of his house right at seven o'clock. He had changed from the beach shorts he wore earlier into denim jeans and a knitted pullover shirt. He climbed into his truck, started the engine, and backed out of his driveway. Charley walked to the edge of the yard and climbed into the passenger side when Alex stopped the pickup in front of her.

They drove to the restaurant, companionably chatting about things they saw along the way. Charley had many questions about the islands and the Charleston area. What was it like to live in a place with so much history at your fingertips and in a state that protected it as fiercely as the state of South Carolina did? Of course, there was a lot of history around the New York and New Jersey area, too, but with her busy life, she hadn't always noticed it. There were too many other things to do. The history of the Northeast had gotten lost in her hectic life of constant travel to foreign lands and hustle to advance her career. "What's it like to live here—on the island—all the time?" Charley asked.

"I don't live here all the time," Alex replied. "I have a house in the Charleston suburbs. But I stay here a lot on the weekends—as often as I can."

"It's not the weekend." Charley stated the obvious. "So how is it that you're here now?"

Alex was slow to answer. "Well, I, uh, I'm taking a few days off here and there this summer. I'm, uh, trying out the carefree life of a surfer dude. I plan to let my hair grow long and get a surfboard. You think it'll fit me?"

Charley looked askance at him, noting his well-trimmed hair and nails. "You don't look the part—yet. But seriously."

"You can do this when your father is your boss," Alex explained with a laugh.

"I see. I wouldn't know. I have to work." The fact that she was also thinking about taking the summer off passed through her mind.

"I have to work, too. I'm not an entitled son of a rich man," Alex replied testily. "I earn everything I get."

"I'm sorry." Charley reached out and touched his arm where it rested on the truck's center console. "I didn't mean that the way it came out."

"I get your point, though." Alex's mouth twisted in an ironic smile. "You wouldn't be the first to think that my father paves the way for me. Those people don't know my father or know the pressure I'm under at times. And, sometimes, it's *because* I'm his son."

"I'm sorry," Charley repeated.

"No problem. I get prickly—too prickly, maybe—when people think my father's personal accomplishments transferred to me at birth." The frown left Alex's face. "We're here." He nodded toward the restaurant as he pulled into the parking lot.

Alex parked in a space beside a ramshackle, rambling building set up on tall pilings near the water's edge. A sign read, 'The Tides of the Marsh,' an obvious play on the line, "Beware the ides of March," from Shakespeare's play, *Julius Caesar*.

"Clever name," Charley remarked as she and Alex exited the pickup truck and walked toward the walkway that led to the front door.

"Most locals have shortened the name to just 'The Tides.' Manny originally thought about calling it 'The Phantom of the Marshes,'" Alex commented with a laugh, "but he ditched that name because he was afraid it might frighten patrons away. Manny is a walking contradiction. Part 'theater rat' as he calls himself and part Lowcountry chef."

Alex's hand was warm on Charley's back as he guided her up to the ramp to the front door of the restaurant. "Manny is a transplanted New Yorker. Alex continued. "According to him, he once dreamed of becoming a star on Broadway. He hung around off-Broadway productions for a few years, but he never landed any roles beyond background extra work, so he moved south and took up his second obsession, cooking."

"That's quite a career change."

"He still acts a little. He belongs to a community theater group in Charleston." Alex reached out to open the door to the restaurant. "I'd prefer to open this door myself, if you don't mind."

"Still not funny!" Charley retorted as her eyes again went to the area above Alex's eyebrow where the door had hit him. "But please." She motioned to the door and stood back to let him open it for her.

Charley preceded Alex into the crowded dining room. Business at the restaurant was apparently very good. Waiters bustled about, serving the patrons that filled most of the tables in the room. Two additional rooms had been added to the original restaurant at some point. The walls, constructed of newer lumber, rambled off in random directions, forming nooks and private spaces, much different from the original large dining room. The haphazard construction gave it a happy, causal, and beachy feel.

"Hey, Alex!" Several people at the bar turned, waved, and shouted a greeting. Alex acknowledged their greetings with a nod.

"Would you like your usual table?" the hostess asked as she stopped in front of Alex. "It's available."

"That would be perfect."

The hostess led them to a table near a window on the ocean side. Alex greeted other diners as they passed. He held the chair for Charley as she sat down. She looked out the window, taking in the peacefulness of the view of the open water. Twilight was descending over the ocean, and a rising moon was a tiny glimmer on the distant horizon. The incoming waves lapped at the pilings under their feet. It was a gorgeous location for a restaurant, and the view of the approaching evening over the water gave the oceanside table a romantic feel.

"You're a popular guy, I've noticed. Are you known at all the eating establishments in the Charleston area?" Charley asked after the waitress had brought their menus. "You're known by your first name at Benji's and also here."

"Maybe I'm just known for eating out a lot," Alex replied as he studied his menu.

"You have a favorite reserved table," Charley pointed out. "In a very romantic spot. There must be a story here—and it involves a woman. Won't she be upset that you're sharing her spot with another woman?"

"Humph," Alex scoffed. "It's not what you think, but she was an extraordinary woman."

"I knew it!" Charley affirmed. "I can spot these things. Handsome single guy, romantic table. I'm very good at picking up on small details. My ESP is usually spot-on."

"Not to burst your clairvoyant bubble and your amazing ability to add up small details, but I used to bring Annabelle here," Alex replied. "This was her table when she came here with her husband. No one dared deny it to her even after he died. I guess I inherited it from her."

"Oh." Charley was about as far off the mark as one could get. She took a sip of her wine. She hadn't anticipated that her great-aunt was the one Alex brought to the restaurant.

"You're not totally wrong, though. I did bring a girlfriend here a few times, but she prefers the fine dining establishments in Charleston. And yes, I do eat here a lot, and it's because of Manny's food—same for all the other diners in here tonight." Alex motioned toward the crowded restaurant. "Speaking of Manny..." He nodded as a short, stocky man in an apron approached their table.

"Hi, Alex. So, this is Charley, our latest islander. Welcome, Ms. Phillips."

Charley looked at him, a question in her eyes. She really did need to set that court date to change her name—and soon.

Manny answered her unasked question. "The Whitakers were in earlier. It's a small island."

Ah, the credit card she had used at the market. That was something else she'd fix once Mr. Lewis got her name changed. A failed marriage touched many aspects of one's life.

"And, of course, we're nosy, too. Everyone on the island is interested in the woman who's staying at Annabelle's beach house," Manny added for further clarification. He chatted for a few more minutes, then left their table with, "Enjoy your dinner," and moved on to welcome other diners.

Charley let Alex order for her. He recommended the fried shrimp that came with all the traditional trimmings, promising that she wouldn't be disappointed.

"So, you're from New York? The city?" Alex asked as they waited for their food. Before Charley could answer, he added, "I noticed your license plates. You aren't the only one who notices details." He smiled as he refilled her wine glass.

"Yes, New York City, New Jersey—that general area." Charley gave the briefest of answers, as she usually did in order to avoid questions of how she became a New Yorker.

"You don't sound like a New Yorker," Alex persisted. He looked across the table at Charley. The light from the candle placed in a mason jar in the middle of the table glinted silver in his blue eyes.

"Actually, I was born in Atlanta," Charley relented. Alex's interest was friendly chatter, so he wasn't expecting details. "But I've lived in New York and New Jersey for the majority of my life. I'm a mixture of all three—Georgia, New York, and New Jersey—a woman without a home, uh, state." She would share that much—her circuitous route from Atlanta to New York, but not how it came about.

Alex was practically a stranger, and discussing her early life with *anyone* made her uncomfortable. She couldn't explain further without dragging down what so far had been a pleasant evening. Charley didn't open herself up to most people, even friends. She probably had developed the habit early on in an effort to shield herself and hide her mother's conduct from questions and scrutiny. She wasn't exactly hiding her past, but she didn't want anyone to judge her by her mother's conduct or to pity her, either. This was another reason why she had so readily agreed to use a pseudonym for her art exhibits. If she gained fame as an artist, she didn't want reporters or art critics digging around in her life for dirt.

"Well, you'll be a South Carolinian in no time," Alex assured her without further questions. "When the Lowcountry claims you, you never want to go anyplace else."

The waitress delivered their meals. Charley relaxed as they ate, happy that Alex didn't pursue the subject of her life before she moved to Turtle Island.

"What was Annabelle like?" Charley asked. "You called her 'extraordinary.' What made her so?"

"You didn't know her?" Alex asked.

"I didn't even know she existed until I got the letter from Mr. Lewis informing me that she had left me the beach house. I don't know anything about her."

"Annabelle was a sweet lady. She was what most people would call a sophisticated, classy, Southern lady. She was a passionate supporter of the arts and the history of the area, as well as environmental causes. She left most of her estate to a variety of charitable organizations around the Charleston area."

"Her family lived here all their lives?" Charley asked. Annabelle wasn't from the plantation era, but Charley couldn't help but picture a young Annabelle in hoop skirts, floating down a spiral staircase to meet her beau at the bottom. The image fit the words Alex used to describe her.

"According to Annabelle, her family and the Travis family were part of the original colonists that came here in the 1600s. They were well-off by the standards of the time, but her family wasn't nearly as wealthy as the Travis family. I think both families made their fortunes through rice and cotton exports… and maybe a bit of war profiteering on the side.

"Annabelle was in her eighties, but age didn't stop her from keeping up with current events." Alex chuckled as he continued his story. "She could hold her own in discussions about politics, old and new music, movies, and the customs of today versus when she was young. Annabelle was a strong believer in climate change, and she kept up on that, too. It pained her to see her beloved city flood from rising sea levels and the beaches constantly eroding and shrinking."

"Sounds like you had something in common," Charley observed.

"I enjoyed her company." Alex leaned back and took a sip of

his wine. "She reminded me of my grandmother. I guess that's why we became good friends."

"Annabelle also supported the arts, you said?" Charley prompted. She was curious to know how she fit into Annabelle's life. "Was that why she wanted to attend the art exhibit in New York?"

"I don't know her precise reasons or why she insisted on going to that specific exhibit," Alex replied. "She didn't say, but she was adamant about it. She was always looking for new talent to support and liked to help new artists launch their careers. Maybe she had seen the photographs somewhere and admired the photographer's work."

"She does sound extraordinary," Charley agreed.

While they ate, Alex filled Charley in on the local historic sites she should visit while she was in the area. He described the people who lived in different parts of the state and what it had been like to live through Hurricane Hugo, the monster storm that had devastated the Charleston area in 1989. He had been a toddler at the time, but some areas still hadn't fully recovered. There had been other damaging storms since, but that one had touched so many lives.

They finished their meal and prepared to leave.

"The shrimp was delicious," Charley said as they approached Manny on their way to the door.

"Thank you, Charley. Have Alex bring you back again soon." Manny clasped her hand in both of his as he warmly thanked her. He then extended his hand to Alex. "Good to see you, Alex," he said, then added with a slight nod toward Charley, "with someone."

On the drive home, Charley wondered about Manny's pointed comment to Alex. Was there another story there, hidden in Manny's "with someone"? The girlfriend? Of course, a man like Alex probably had a girlfriend—maybe more than one girlfriend.

"I have some business that will take up most of tomorrow, but if it's not too late when I get back, maybe we could take a walk on the beach. I can show you the riptide area that you'll need to avoid if you decide to go into the water," Alex suggested as he walked Charley to her door. "And that's not a pick-up line. The riptide can be dangerous to an unsuspecting swimmer."

"Thanks for the warning. I'll remember that. A walk? Maybe...if you get back in time. Let's play it by ear," Charley replied noncommittedly. She needed to do some prepping for her trip to Costa Rica.

"Okay. Sounds good. Goodnight," Alex replied.

Charley thought for a moment that he was going to lean down and embrace her but then changed his mind. Or she could have misread the situation, and the thought of a parting hug had not even entered his head. The girlfriend he'd mentioned at the restaurant wouldn't be happy when she learned he had taken another woman to The Tides for dinner and shared his favorite table with her. She'd be incensed if he also embraced that woman.

But as usual, though, she was letting her imagination override reality. Southerners treated everyone like kissing cousins—or, in this case, hugging cousins—from what she had heard. And Charley wasn't looking to get involved with anyone. Alex was just being friendly by spending the day showing a newcomer around the island. Another Southern trait. That's what neighbors did.

She waved goodbye to Alex and watched as he quickly went down the steps to the yard and crossed to where his truck was parked. Charley stepped inside her house and closed the door. The evening—actually the whole day—had been pleasant. Alex was an interesting man. His was easy to talk to and well-versed on a wide range of topics. He listened attentively when she shared her thoughts or brought up a new topic—another quality that set him apart from Daniel.

For the second time in two days, you're thinking about a man you just met. And it's the same man, her inner voice chided. That was true. Analyzing Alex's goodbye in this much depth meant she was letting herself become distracted by a handsome man, and from the reasons she was here on Turtle Island: a break from the confusion that was her life and a beach house left to her by an aunt she didn't know. She didn't need to trade one uncertainty for another. Romance was not what she needed to focus on. Definitely not what she was looking for.

But all weighty topics, such as the beach house and her new life-plan, had barely been on her mind during the time she had spent with Alex today.

CHAPTER SIX

The morning following his day spent with Charley, Alex left the beach house with Rex in the back seat of his pickup. He drove toward Johns Island to meet with two members of SOI—Save Our Islands—a local environmental group. He didn'ʈ see any activity around Charley's house as he passed. Maybe she liked to sleep in on Saturdays, but it was almost ten o'clock. In Alex's view, this was a little late to still be asleep, especially since it was a beautiful April morning. Perhaps she was taking a walk on the beach. That's where he would be if he didn't have this appointment.

The day he'd spent with Charley had been fun. He hadn't gleaned one piece of information from her that he could pass on to Mrs. Maitland, but that hadn't been his intent. Fishing for information wasn't why he invited Charley to spend the afternoon and evening with him. She was simply fun to be around. She seemed reticent about sharing details of her personal life, and he understood that. They barely knew each other, so that didn't mean she was hiding deep dark secrets like those the gang from his office insinuated she had.

Alex drove over the bridge that connected Turtle Island to Johns Island and toward the spot where he had promised to meet Conner Guidry of SOI. He had previously represented SOI in a few court cases filed against land developers in the area. The cases mostly involved runoff from constructions sites. It was a recurring battle against a few specific construction company owners. They never looked beyond their bottom line to see the damage they were doing—even though it was also damage to their own future lives and businesses.

Conner had texted him yesterday just before he picked Charley up to take her to The Tides for dinner. Conner said that they needed to meet right away, but agreed to wait until this morning. Agreeing that the matter could wait surprised Alex. Conner and his wife, Mary, were passionate environmental warriors, often impatient with the slowness of investigations and the judicial process. Alex had to remind them frequently that the courts moved at their own pace but would eventually get it right. Conner, the more impatient of the two, wanted instantaneous results. Of course, wanting immediate action wasn't a trait unique to Conner. Alex wanted that, too. But he was also practical and familiar with the justice system, which some would say moved slower than a snail.

Alex pulled into the parking lot near the boat dock located at the end of Johns Island. Conner and Mary were pacing in front of their parked car, impatient to get on with what they wanted to show Alex.

"What's up?" Alex asked as he parked and got out of his pickup truck.

"There's illegal dumping taking place on Kings Island." Conner's voice was filled with urgency. "We found it yesterday."

"What kind of dumping?" Alex asked.

"Drums filled with some type of chemical," Mary replied. "There's hazard markings on the drums."

"My boat's over here." Conner didn't wait for Alex to agree to go with them. He and Mary turned and walked toward the dock where his boat was moored.

Alex quickly donned his wading boots, then he and Rex followed Conner to the boat dock. There was no use in trying to persuade Conner to slow down. If he spotted danger to any of the islands, he became fixated on the problem and was relentless until action was taken. Alex wanted to see the dump site for himself, so he climbed into the boat as Conner started the engine.

Soon, they were speeding toward a small, uninhabited strip of land not much bigger than a sandbar that was located southeast of Johns Island. Conner's boat cut through the water, leaving a trail of white rippling waves behind them as he hurried toward his destination. As usual, he was zeroed in on what he had discovered and single-minded in his eagerness to show Alex the barrels of chemicals. It wasn't long before Kings Island came into view.

Like Turtle Island, Kings Island was a nesting-ground for female loggerhead sea turtles. The loggerhead was the most common species of sea turtle in Carolina coastal waters, and Kings Island was another place they returned to year after year. It fell to humans like Conner and Mary and other environmental groups to protect their nesting grounds from predators—most notably, human predators.

The sea turtles' nesting period would begin in about a month, lasting from May until August. The turtles' instincts led them to the sandy beaches of the Atlantic Coast, but these instincts didn't keep them away from places that were dangerous to the survival of their hatchlings. On the developed islands, an army of volunteers worked to protect the nesting sites from foot traffic, storm damage, and erosion. The turtles would normally be safely away from humans on tiny Kings Island, but if Conner was right—and Alex didn't doubt that he was—the turtles were not safe even here on this small, uninhabited strip of land. The salt water would quickly eat away at the metal of the containers filled with hazardous chemicals. These chemicals would then leak into the marshy ground and poison the local food sources and damage the sea turtles' nests.

Once they had moored the boat, Alex commanded Rex to remain onboard. He didn't want to risk exposing Rex to the chemicals if they had already leaked into the water. Rex whimpered, but obediently lay down in the bottom of the boat and watched as Conner and Mary led Alex through the shallow wetlands toward the shore.

"They're over there," Conner said, "hidden in the trees." He picked up a recently worn path that led to a thicket of scrubby trees mixed with grasses and bushes. He parted the bushes and pointed to the pile of containers. Alex came to a stop beside Conner and stared at several drums that had been dumped on the ground. White labels identified the contents as dangerous if inhaled and a poisonous substance.

"Oh, no!" Mary exclaimed. "There's four more containers than there were yesterday. There were six yesterday, and now, there's ten. We watched the site for a good portion of the day, but they still dumped more."

"They're bringing them in at night," Alex said with barely suppressed anger. "The drums contain solvents. I think I might know where they're coming from." He raised his phone and took a picture. "Let's go. There's a place on the mainland I want to check out."

When they were back on Johns Island, Alex led the way in his pickup as Conner and Mary followed in their car. Alex drove across the bridge and further inland to North Charleston. He stopped a short distance from what used to be a custom auto paint and repair shop and an RV storage site. It had gone bankrupt about a year ago.

Alex regularly kept up with land and business purchases in the area. His job required him to know who was looking to sell their business, who was under financial stress, and who was facing bankruptcy. He also kept up with companies that were increasing their footprint in the business community by purchasing or merging with other businesses or through new construction. Dawson Construction had recently purchased the fifteen acres that had belonged to the auto paint shop. They had filed plans to build townhomes on the property. As an attorney for SOI, Alex had dealt with Dawson before over infractions at other building sites. Dumping hazardous chemicals, however, was a new low, even for Dawson.

Alex left Rex in the truck and motioned for Conner and Mary to follow him. They worked their way around to the wooden fence at the back of the paint shop. Alex loosened a board and peered through the opening. He counted approximately twelve containers stacked against the back of the building. Their labels were identical to the ones they had found on Kings Island.

In order to purchase the property, Dawson would have had to certify that he would properly dispose of the chemicals. Dumping them on Kings Island did not qualify as "proper disposal." But disposal of hazardous material was expensive, and Dawson was always looking for ways to cut corners. That was his modus operandi. Alex zoomed in with his phone and took more pictures. Then, he motioned for Conner and Mary to backtrack, and they returned to where their vehicles were parked.

"I'm going to notify the sheriff about what's going on, then file a motion with the courts for an injunction to halt the dumping. The sheriff will investigate. Once he's done an investigation, he can bring charges against Dawson," Alex said as he paused by his pickup.

"I can come back tonight and catch them in the act," Conner offered.

"No," Alex said sharply. "The sheriff will handle it from here. With your reputation, Conner, Dawson could easily accuse you of planting the chemicals on Kings Island just to cause trouble for him." Conner needed to stay far away from Kings Island and this repair shop site for the time being. In the past, Conner had occasionally used tactics that, while warranted—at least in his mind—had come close to crossing legal lines. His overzealousness had complicated a couple of cases for Alex. "Conner, I'll handle this in court. You stay away," Alex repeated his order. "Mary, you make sure he does."

After receiving assurances from Conner and Mary that they would let Alex handle the matter, Alex drove to his law office to draw up the documents he would need on Monday when he filed the injunction against Dawson Construction. He also called the local sheriff and reported the illegal dumping, its likely source, and whom he suspected of doing it. He then sent the sheriff copies of the pictures he'd taken.

Even with the court's involvement, the worst Dawson would probably face was a fine and an order to remove the drums of solvent from Kings Island. He'd be ordered to properly dispose of the remaining chemicals at the shop site, too. But he'd still be free to squeeze in as many zero-lot townhomes as he could build on the fifteen acres. Dawson's punishment should be stronger, but business development held a strong hand. As in most cities, the local government was always looking to expand its tax base. They didn't take Dawson's lawbreaking lightly, but they also didn't want to stop him from building in their city. The lawsuit would be a step, albeit a small one, toward keeping Kings Island free of dangerous chemicals. It would send a message to other would-be polluters that someone was always looking over their shoulders if they broke the law. But Alex knew some people would keep trying.

After Alex finished the paperwork for the injunction, he read over the messages in his email inbox from his intern concerning ongoing mergers. He reviewed the relevant files, then emailed detailed instructions to the intern. He moved on to requests from a couple of prospective new clients that had called wanting information on business opportunities in the area. Alex researched some local companies that would fit the interests of these clients, highlighting the ones who might be willing to sell or merge, and emailed responses to the companies who had inquired.

So much for having the summer off, Dad, he thought as he closed up his laptop. He woke Rex from his nap on the floor near his feet, and they left the office together.

Alex had spent longer in his office than he intended. He had missed lunch and worked past his usual dinner hour. It was dark by the time he reached the parking garage. He loaded Rex into his truck, then climbed into the front seat. He sat there for a few minutes, trying to decide what he should do. It was already late, and by the time he drove to Turtle Island, it would be even later. Charley would think he was crazy if he popped in on her at such a late hour. He was supposed to join his family for lunch tomorrow for his mother's birthday, and he had to be at the courthouse first thing on Monday morning to file the Dawson case. Staying on the mainland until Monday made the most sense. Besides, Rex needed to eat, and judging from the rumble in his stomach, Alex needed food, too.

There wouldn't be any walks on the beach tonight, Alex concluded as he started his truck and drove toward his home in nearby Goose Creek. He didn't have Charley's phone number to let her know that he wasn't coming back to the beach house tonight, but they didn't have a firm commitment to meet. Char-

ley had said to "play it by ear." She'd figure it out when he didn't
show up. But did a "no-show" qualify as "playing it by ear"?

Alex parked in his driveway, got out of his pickup, and let
Rex out of the back seat. He looked up at the sky and felt a
touch of regret. Tonight, would be a perfect night for a walk on
the beach. The night was clear, and the moon was high in a star-
filled sky. Along the beach, the moon would be even brighter
and the stars, even more plentiful. He could almost hear the
waves crashing on the shore from here in his driveway—the
perfect romantic place for a couple to get to know each other.

"Romantic place?" he muttered to himself. "That's not your
mission, remember? You don't even know this woman, and
judging by Mrs. Maitland's clandestine operation, she may not
be someone you *want* to know." In frustration, Alex kicked at a
clump of debris the wind had blown onto the sidewalk leading
to his front door. He couldn't visualize Charley in that way but
he was straying from his employers' orders. Romantic walks on
the beach had nothing to do with it.

His entire being balked at what his father and his two con-
spirators had tasked him to do —obtain information surrepti-
tiously, under false pretenses. He couldn't do it, especially now
that he had actually met Charley. Alex was back to his original
plan: his handlers would get only what Charley let slip and what
Alex chose to give them.

Alex admitted that his interest was piqued by Charley. Was
it interest in Charley, or was he just trying to prove to his father
that he wasn't the reclusive grouch he insinuated Alex had
become? Whatever it was, disrupting his evening with her was
just one more reason, to see James Dawson, owner of Dawson
Construction, punished for his illegal dumping. Dawson was
who had led Alex to his current foul mood, but it was the "Gang
of Three" from his office, and their secret operation, that made
him suspect this would not end well for him.

By the time Alex had fed Rex and made himself a sandwich, he had his frustrations under control and reason returned. His runaway fantasies about romantic walks on the beach were just that—fantasies. A huge factor was the fact that Charley might not be a willing participant in his fantasy. Another factor was him. Was he ready to trust someone again?

Alex's experience with Rebecca had proven that he wasn't very good at interpreting signals from women. He had missed all the signs that Rebecca was involved with someone else. Maybe Rebecca's devotion as his fiancée was nothing more than a blind assumption on his part. He hadn't wanted to see the truth. He still wasn't sure why he hadn't recognized that things were not right between them. He had gotten over Rebecca's leaving him for someone else, but his faith in his judgment where women were concerned was still shaky.

Mrs. Maitland's inference that there were dark details about Charley's life made her someone with whom he should not test the waters or count on to help him regain confidence in his judgment. A flashing red-light cautioned him to avoid involvement with her.

Alex had trouble squaring the woman he had spent the day with, with the woman Mrs. Maitland's cloak-and-dagger quest implied she was. But what did he know? After all, historically, he wasn't the best judge of women.

CHAPTER SEVEN

Alex drove back to Turtle Island on Monday morning after he filed the court documents requesting an injunction against Dawson Construction. By now, Dawson's attorney should have received orders to cease removing anything from the former paint shop in North Charleston. The sheriff had begun an investigation of the solvents stored at the paint shop on Sunday, and he had already made a trip to Kings Island to inspect the illegal dumping site.

As Alex neared Charley's house, he noticed her car was not in the driveway. Maybe she had business on the mainland, was visiting one of the other islands, or had more shopping to do. Alex had planned to stop by with an apology for not showing up on Saturday night. They hadn't made firm plans to meet, but an explanation was still the right thing to do.

Sitting on the front seat of his truck was a box of raspberry scones that he'd purchased at a pastry shop before leaving Charleston. He had hoped to present them to her, along with an apology, and after he explained why he was detained in Charleston, maybe they could take that delayed walk on the beach tonight.

"Damn!" he muttered in disgust. Even after all of his
self-analysis on Saturday night, he apparently hadn't let go of his
fantasy involving Charley. He was back to daydreaming about
walking a moonlit beach with a woman he didn't know. Alex
had found Charley to be a very interesting woman—smart,
funny, and beautiful. He had been distracted and completely
forgotten about his assignment during their day together. If he
let his mind wander into conspiracies, maybe that was Charley's
plan. Nah, he didn't believe that, *But, interesting, smart, funny,
and beautiful doesn't make her someone I should trust*, he reminded himself.

But the object of his speculation still hadn't returned to her
house when Alex looked for her again later in the afternoon.
And her car was still missing from her driveway when he took
his dinner to the front porch to eat in the early evening. Where
could she be? Had she already had enough of island life and left
the beach house for good?

Over the next few days, Alex looked out the window first
thing each morning, but the SUV still had not returned to the
driveway. Should he be worried that something had happened
to her? An accident, perhaps? Alex decided to give the situation
a few more days. There was a fine line between being a nosy
neighbor and a concerned neighbor. If she didn't return by the
weekend, he would call Mr. Lewis and ask if he could share any
information on where Charley had gone. Mr. Lewis might know
how to reach her family to check on her.

Alex tried to stay busy and keep his mind off of his elusive
neighbor. He followed up with the sheriff a few times regarding
the Dawson case. On Wednesday, he made a trip into Charleston to clear up a last-minute problem with an out-of-state
client's merger with a local business. Charley had not returned
to her house when he got home that night.

As Alex took Rex for a walk on the beach the next morning, his phone rang. The caller ID indicated that it was his father calling.

"Any new information on your neighbor?" his father asked getting right to the reason for his call.

"No, no progress yet. I don't even know where she is right now," Alex replied to his father's question about his assigned mission. "Her car is gone."

"Gone? You mean she's left the island."

"Yes, gone! She wasn't here when I arrived back on the island on Monday. It's now Thursday, and she hasn't been home. I've not seen her."

"That's very strange," his father commented. "She didn't tell you she was leaving? I wonder why?"

"You think it's curious that my neighbor, who I only spent a few hours with, didn't share her plans with me? I don't." Alex replied shortly. His father's comments were increasing Alex's own anxiety over Charley's whereabouts.

"Hmmm, it's just strange that she didn't mention her plans for the weekend," his father replied. "So, nothing at all going on around her place?"

"I've not seen any activity at her place since I last saw her on Friday night, but remember, I wasn't here for the weekend." Alex was getting annoyed with the interrogation.

"Do you think maybe she's fled the country. Mrs. Maitland isn't going to be happy if we've lost her already." His father kept asking questions that Alex could only answer in speculation.

"No, I don't think she's fled the country. I don't get the feeling that she's running from the authorities. And I'm really not concerned, at the moment, about Mrs. Maitland's happiness."

"I know, but her happiness seems to be Mr. Winston's biggest concern. And you don't really know this person," his father pointed out.

"Yes, Dad," Alex replied impatiently. "You're right. I barely know her." Alex sat down on the sand and watched Rex chase seagulls along the water's edge.

"Do you suppose she met someone and went away with them for a few days?" his father persisted even though Alex's knowledge of Charley's whereabouts was zero.

"No, I don't know! How would I know that?" Alex was irritated that his father had even asked such a question, and he was irritated at himself for having had the same thought several times. He was even more irritated that this particular thought bothered him.

"Mrs. Maitland is getting anxious to wrap this up, whatever it is, and find out who your neighbor is." Alex's father was back to Mrs. Maitland's vague plan.

"Yes, you've told me. Nothing new there. Mrs. Maitland is always anxious if it's something she wants. I checked the deed records when I was at the courthouse, and as of Monday, the name on the property was still Annabelle's. With our target gone, there's not much spying I can do." His father hated when he used the word *spying*, which was why he used it now to get under his father's skin. He felt cranky, and his father's interrogation wasn't improving his mood.

Alex's frustrations of late ran the gamut from not knowing why Mrs. Maitland was so interested in Charley to frustration that Charley had left without telling him that she was leaving. But why would she? They hardly knew each other—as his father had pointed out—and he didn't have a right to know her plans. She definitely didn't have to inform him that she was going away with someone for the week.

"I'll let you know if and when she comes back or if I find out where she's gone." Alex didn't wait for his father to end the call before he hung up himself.

Rex returned from chasing seagulls and sat down at Alex's

feet.

"Where has she gone, Rex? Do you know?"

Rex tilted his head and looked up at Alex. He barked once in answer, then spotted another seagull on the beach and took off running toward it. It flew away as he approached. He barked at the bird, then came running back to Alex.

Alex continued his one-sided conversation with Rex. "Do you miss her?"

Rex barked.

"Yes, I figured you did. She gives you hugs and treats."

Rex nuzzled Alex's hand, looking for sympathy.

When Alex went to bed that night, there was still no sign of Charley.

When he awoke the next morning and took his coffee out to the front porch, Charley's car was back and parked in her driveway. Alex blinked to make sure he wasn't dreaming. Nope! The car was still there. Charley was back! Now what? He was both relieved and anxious to see her again. He sorted through different scenarios of how he should approach her. Should he pretend he hadn't even noticed she was gone? That one wasn't credible. Should he storm over there and ask where she had been? He immediately discarded that option too. Charley, whom he barely knew, would think he was crazy, and she'd be right. Should he wait for her to contact him first?

Disgusted with his hesitation, he set his coffee cup down quickly, and his coffee sloshed over his hand. Fiery green eyes didn't burn as far as he knew. *Maybe not, but I have a better idea,* he grinned.

"Rex, go see if Charley is okay," Alex said as he opened the door and called Rex away from his food bowl. Rex didn't hesitate or need additional coaxing. He bounded down the stairs and raced across the adjoining yards. He ran up to Charley's door, sat down, and started barking.

Alex slowly followed Rex across the yard. He stopped at the foot of the stairs just as the door opened and Charley stepped out onto the porch. She bent to pat Rex's head. Her hair was a mass of curls, and she was dressed in a long sleep T-shirt. Alex felt a moment of guilt as he realized that Rex had awakened her from sleep.

"I'm sorry," Alex called from the foot of the stairs. "Did Rex wake you up?"

"What do you think?" Charley replied, motioning to her hair and attire. She squatted down and hugged Rex. "But that's okay, boy. I missed you, too."

Charley stood up and ran her hand through her tousled hair in a feeble attempt to tame her curls. Alex started to tell her to stop and leave them alone. Her sleepy green eyes and wildly tousled hair were sexy as hell. He now knew what a gut punch felt like. His mind zoomed past *interest,* blew past *attraction,* and went straight to *temptation.* He fought the urge to climb the stairs, pull her into his arms, and kiss her soundly.

All Alex managed to do was to stare up at her as he stood motionless and tried to kick-start his brain. A weight lifted off of him. He was relieved that she was safe and very happy she had returned to the beach house.

"What?" Charley asked when she noticed Alex's steady gaze.

"Nothing," Alex replied. He looked away guiltily and focused his attention on a car that drove along the dusty road in front of their houses.

"Oh, geez, I'm tired." Charley stretched her arms over her head and let out a loud yawn.

"I… uh… I have the coffee pot on, and I'm a master chef when it comes to pancakes," Alex said. "It's the least I can do, since my dog woke you up."

"That sounds great! You had me at coffee," Charley laughed. "Let me go change, and I'll be right over."

CHAPTER EIGHT

Charley stepped into Alex's house just as he was pouring pancake batter into a pan. She looked around the room. His place was laid out in much the same way as hers. Both houses had probably been constructed by the same builder and around the same time.

A cup of coffee was sitting on the bar that separated the kitchen from the living room. Charley walked to the bar, added cream to her coffee, and then closed her eyes as she took her first sip. "Ah, bliss! Good coffee. I might be alive, after all."

When Alex didn't respond, Charley opened her eyes and caught Alex staring again. "What?" she asked. His eyes fixed on her face, then moved and settled back on her hair. "My hair has a mind of its own. I should have combed it," she apologized as she pushed it behind her ears. "But the thought of coffee was the most urgent thing on my mind after brushing my teeth."

"No," replied Alex. "I like it like that."

The smell of hot batter turned his attention back to the pan on the stove. He flipped the pancakes, and soon had them plated up then sat them on the dining table, along with butter, syrup, and a bowl of fresh strawberries. He motioned for Charley to take a seat. Picking up her coffee cup, she moved to the table, and sat down. Alex refreshed her coffee and his, then sat down across from her.

"I saw my mother in Miami," Charley blurted out. She was wrestling with how to broach the subject of where she had been for the past week. Alex probably wondered why she had disappeared and to where. She had planned to tell him and ask him to watch her house while she was gone, but he hadn't returned to the beach over the weekend. She had an early flight on Monday morning. She started to add that she went on to Costa Rica from Miami, but Alex interrupted.

"Was it an emergency? Is your mother alright?"

"With my mother, it's always an emergency," Charley replied with a rueful smile. "She's fine. I met her husband—the third one since my father's death. She may have found a keeper this time, but who knows?" Charley chewed her lip nervously. Why was she spilling the sad tale of her mother's life to Alex? Maybe sleep deprivation over the last week had left her brain too foggy to filter her thoughts. But once engaged on the subject, her brain couldn't stop. "She wanted to apologize for abandoning me all those years ago."

As soon as the words left her mouth, Charley was ashamed. What she said was true, but there were extenuating circumstances—or at least her mother thought so. And now, either sleep deprivation or the presence of a good listener had Charley sharing personal information that she usually hid. She couldn't seem to stop the words from pouring out of her mouth.

"Abandoned you? Why did—"

"I'm sorry, Alex," Charley interrupted. "I didn't mean to say that. I guess the jet lag loosened my tongue a bit—or more accurately, disengaged it from my brain."

"It's quite alright. Sometimes it's better to say things out loud and just get them out. Did you accept your mother's apology?" Alex asked. He appeared ready to ask another question, but changed his mind.

"I did, but I forgave her years ago. I just hadn't told her before now. She hadn't directly apologized to me, either. We have a complicated relationship, and it wasn't changed much by our meeting, but it's a start. At least she's trying now."

On Sunday, when Charley had called to see how her mother was doing, she mentioned that she had a layover in Miami before flying on to Costa Rica. Surprisingly, Debra had asked if they could meet. She was waiting at the Miami airport with her new husband, Kenneth Stuart, when Charley deplaned.

The two women had hugged, Debra introduced Kenneth, and then, they found a seat in the waiting area.

"Charley," her mother quickly began, "I know this won't change the past, but I wanted to see you and apologize for the way I've behaved over the years… since we lost your father." Debra looked away, unable to meet Charley's eyes. "I don't know what happened. I just went crazy. And I'm sorry." Her voice trailed off before she turned back to Charley with tears in her eyes. "I'm so terribly sorry and ashamed for what I did to you."

Charley sat motionless. This was a new twist. Whenever she had visited her mother over the years, Debra had always pretended nothing was wrong. She refused to accept any responsibility or even acknowledge the separation between herself and her child.

Debra reached over and picked up Charley's hand. "Can you ever forgive me? I wanted to be different, I really did. But I couldn't figure out how to make myself do it. I don't know why," she whispered.

"She really means it, Charley," Kenneth added. "Apologizing to you is all she's talked about recently, even before you called."

Charley looked at her mother's face. Her eyes held a new look, an earnestness that hadn't been there before. The blankness Charley had seen in her mother's face for so long was now gone, replaced by sincerity and real sorrow. There was deep longing in her eyes. Debra was finally accepting blame and acknowledging her failure as a mother.

Charley had forgiven her mother many years ago, once she was old enough to recognize that her mother was not a strong person. Without Charley's father to love, she had shut down emotionally. Debra was unable to handle the tragedy that had blown her life apart. Armed with that acceptance, Charley had let go of her deep hurt and anger. Her mother's failure as a parent had toughened Charley and taught her resilience. It was a hard lesson but was what later helped her weather the heartbreak and disappointment in her failed marriage.

Of course, Charley was human, and she would always carry hurt and a wish that things had been different. But Aunt Beth and Uncle Lance had created a happy life for her and in many ways that had lessened the impact of Debra's abandonment.

"I forgive you, Mom." Charley returned the squeeze of her mother's hand.

Debra's apology and acknowledgement of what she had done was a start. They would never be best friends like most mothers and daughters, but they could have a relationship—hopefully one without rehashing the hurtful past.

Charley kissed her mother and Kenneth goodbye as her flight to Costa Rica was called. As she walked toward the security area, she looked back to where her mother stood. Kenneth had his arm around Debra as she waved goodbye to Charley. She looked happy. Kenneth was a retired architect, and based on their meeting today, he appeared to be a nice guy, unlike the addicted gamblers and grifters her mother had associated with in the past. As Charley waved back to them before taking her place in the security line, she wished only good things for her mother.

"A verbal apology always helps," Alex said, bringing Charley's attention back to the present. "Did you spend the week with her?" Alex refilled her coffee cup again and pushed the pitcher of cream toward her. "And you mentioned jet lag? From Miami? It's only about an hour-and-a-half flight and in the same time zone." Was that an accusation in Alex's voice that she was hiding something?

Oh! He didn't know about her assignment in Costa Rica. She hadn't told him that she was a photographer or discussed her career at all during their time together. There had been too many other things to talk about.

"This is great coffee, by the way." Charley added cream to her cup and stirred her coffee. "I guess I didn't mention that I work for a travel and adventure magazine. I had an assignment in Costa Rica. I'm a photographer and writer. After I left Miami, I had a photo shoot in the Costa Rican rain forest."

"I see." Alex nodded, with comprehension lighting his eyes. He leaned back in his chair. "No, I didn't know that. Actually, we didn't introduce ourselves properly when we met on your deck. The rug incident got in the way." He smiled and stuck out his hand. "Hi, I'm Alex Morgan, attorney-at-law, formerly known as Sandwich Shop Alex."

"Hi, I'm Charley Rainier." She laughed as she shook his hand. 'Mathews' was not yet an official part of her name, so until it was, she was still just 'Rainier.' At least she had unloaded Daniel's name from her mind as well as her life. "I'm a photographer and content writer—freelance at the moment."

Charley spent the next few minutes describing her trip and the photos she had taken in Costa Rica. The rain forest had offered a wealth of amazing subjects to photograph. She had come across a group of American tourists, and they agreed to let her photograph them on their first zip line adventure. One woman hadn't been enjoying the experience as much as others in her group. Charley captured the woman's fear as she strapped on her harness. She struggled to force herself push off, even as her husband coached her. Charley saw the woman later at the hotel. She posed for another photo as she excitedly told Charley how pleased she was that she had faced her fear and tackled something new and scary—and lived to tell about it, she added.

"How do you pick the photos to use in a spread?" Alex asked.

"I forward the best shots to my editor. Then, she decides which photos will actually be used in the magazine spread. After that, I write the accompanying article for the photos she chooses."

Charley quickly tired of talking about herself and her trip. She wanted to know more about Alex. "You told me that you were an attorney the other day," she said, changing the subject, "but how does an attorney find time to loll around on the beach as much as you apparently do? You denied it before, but confess! Your father *is* a very wealthy man, and you inherited a fortune. You're his spoiled heir and only play at working."

"Humph!" Alex snorted. "More ESP? As I also explained before, you haven't met my father. If you had, you'd know that he's not wealthy and that there aren't any laggards in his family. Does my battered pickup look like the vehicle of someone who's spoiled or rich?"

"That could be a ruse to throw people off the trail of what you're really up to," Charley replied with a smile.

At her comment, Alex rose, picked up the plates, turned his back, and walked toward the kitchen. Charley saw a flush rise on his neck from her teasing. Had she said something wrong? Was his family situation or his relationship with his father something he didn't want to talk about?

Alex frowned as he stacked the plates by the sink. "I'm just trying to decide what I want to do when I grow up." His frown was gone and he was smiling again when he returned to the table to get their coffee cups.

"Don't you like practicing law?" Charley asked, trying to recover the easy conversation from earlier. She had obviously stepped in something or hit a sore spot.

"I do, and I don't actually hate my current job, but I like taking on environmental cases and fighting for the little guy." Alex scraped the remaining food off the plates and into the trash can, then loaded them into the dishwasher. "What about you? Do you enjoy your job?"

"I enjoy photography, but I'm tired of traveling so much. I'd like to put together a book of photos and stay in one place for a while." Charley had actually published one book already, and her publishing company was pressuring her to do a second one. "I might take the summer off, too. There are lots of scenic areas around here that I'd like to shoot. But I'll have to talk to my bosses at the magazine first. I'm not a wealthy spoiled brat, either. I need a job to go back to this fall."

"So you plan to stay here, then? For the summer?" Alex asked. "Rex would love it if you did," he added.

Upon hearing his name, Rex came to stand beside Charley. He sat down and looked up at her.

"Maybe. I think so. At least for the summer," Charley replied. "I'll miss you too, Rex, when I leave," she said to Rex as she patted him on the head. "The summer should give me enough time to make arrangements for the beach house. Maybe I'll rent it out or something, but I'm not sure right now. By the way, is that how you met Annabelle—as a lawyer?"

"It was," Alex replied. He came back to the table and sat down again. "She was my first client out of law school. I think my father assigned her to me because I was new to the practice. She was a sweet lady, unlike some of the tougher and more vicious clients we have. We became friends. Annabelle was the person who let me know that this beach house was going on the market. Property on the island sells quickly, so I was able to buy it before a bidding war started."

"How did she end up with Mr. Lewis, then? Did you run her off?" Charley smiled, but a frown creased Alex's forehead. She quickly added, "I was kidding."

"Mr. Lewis is a family attorney. Our firm isn't. I set her up with Mr. Lewis for her estate planning, but I kept her as a client for her limited business needs."

"Was her estate large?" Charley asked, curious about the woman who had left her the beach house.

"She had a few holdings, but she wasn't super-wealthy by Charleston standards. She had a home in Charleston that she donated to the historical society, along with some of her remaining assets to help preserve the house long-term. The rest went to environmental groups—except, of course, the beach house that she left to you.

"I would've liked to have kept her as a client," Alex continued. "I suggested to Mr. Winston that the firm take some family law cases. I like helping regular people, getting to know them, and helping sort out their problems. To me, it's more challenging than representing impersonal and often cutthroat businesses—although I think I'm pretty good at that, too."

"Self-confident, too, I see," Charley teased with a smile. "What happened?"

"Mr. Winston shot down that idea, just like he did my pitch that we take environmental cases. Cases like those don't bring in big bucks. I assume that's why he's not interested." Alex leaned forward and rested his elbows on the table. This was a topic Alex apparently had strong feelings about. He was trapped into doing the bidding of his bosses.

As we all are, thought Charley. But she had a lot of freedom in her job when she went out on a shoot, and she liked her bosses. "Sounds like you may have to strike out on you own," Charley suggested.

"Maybe, but a firm like Winston, Morgan, and Gilbert carries a lot more weight in legal cases than a start-up firm would. I'm still hoping I can change Mr. Winston's mind."

"I hear determination in your voice, so I think you'll be successful," Charley stated. She reached across the table and touched his hand. "I don't know much about the practice of law, but I do know that attorneys who represent regular people and nonbusiness causes are needed. We all need a superhero at one time or another!"

"Ha! No Superman capes in my closet!" Alex laughed away Charley's compliment. "But you're right, and I'll keep pressing my case. Maybe I'll wear Mr. Winston down eventually. By the way, if you decide to stay here and do a book this summer, I can be your escort around the area, since I'm semi-free for the summer. I know some fantastic places, and they'll photograph beautifully. They'd be perfect shots for a book."

"That's nice of you. I just might take you up on your offer."

"Well, it might not be as generous as you think. You could give me some pointers on photography while we're at it."

"I think that would be a fair exchange," Charley replied. "What type of camera equipment do you have?"

Alex brought out a DSLR camera with a variety of lenses and other attachments and placed them on the table in front of Charley.

"When we first met, you said you were a point-and-shoot photographer," Charley commented, as she picked up the camera and examined it. "This is a pretty nice camera for an amateur."

"I'm an amateur at using it," Alex laughed, "but when it

comes to buying equipment, I'm a pro. And the salesperson was very helpful."

Charley sorted through the equipment while commenting on the camera's specific features. Then, she stifled a yawn. "I'm sorry. I didn't get home until after three this morning."

"No, don't apologize. I should apologize for letting Rex wake you up. As a further apology, why don't you let me fix dinner for you tonight? I have two very nice steaks just waiting for the grill."

"Can I have a rain check?" Charley asked as she yawned again. "I'm really tired, and I doubt I'd be very good company." She stifled yet another yawn. "I might fall asleep and face-plant into my salad." She tried to laugh, but it came out as another yawn. Her Costa Rican trip had been grueling—plotting an itinerary, arranging for guides, getting up early and to bed late after reviewing each day's shoot. The only glamorous thing about the life of a travel photographer was getting to see some amazing places. Charley was suddenly overcome with tiredness and couldn't stop herself from yawning. She felt she might nod off at any moment.

"Sure," Alex replied. "Another time, then. And I still owe you that walk on the beach. I'll walk you home."

"You don't have to do that," Charley protested.

"I insist. Besides, I'm going that way. Rex needs his morning run. He gets cranky if I don't take him out so he can harass the seagulls."

Charley said goodbye to Alex at the foot of the steps leading up to her front porch. She waved one last time at the top of the stairs as Alex turned and continued toward the beach with Rex. Charley went straight to her bedroom, collapsed on the bed, pulled the covers over her, and immediately fell asleep.

Alex was on his way back to the house from his walk when his phone rang. He saw his father's name and number on the caller ID. He hesitated and studied his phone for a few seconds, trying to decide whether he wanted to answer or let the call go to voice mail. More instructions from the "Gang of Three" for his spy mission? He decided to answer the call.

"Any update?" his father asked immediately.

"Yes, she's back. She was on a business assignment," Alex, answered his father's question. He sighed. Evidently, Charley's whereabouts was still the most important thing going on at the law firm. Mrs. Maitland had that kind of power. Alex longed to tell his father to just take him off the case, but he hesitated, remembering his father's threat that Eric Winston would replace him. Alex held his words, admitting that he was stuck doing something he didn't want to be a part of.

"I never told anyone here that she was missing, so I'm glad she's back." Alex heard relief in his father's voice. "Mrs. Maitland asked me to call and invite you and Charley to a charity ball with a dinner and fundraising auction. She wants to meet Charley."

"A charity ball? Fundraising and an auction? She wants me to bring Charley so that she can meet her?" Alex repeated what his father had just said to make sure he had heard it correctly over the sound of the wind that had suddenly picked up. Apparently, Mrs. Maitland wasn't waiting for him—or anyone else—to get the information she wanted. She was taking charge and wanted to see their target in person. What was she up to now? Alex was sure she was up to something.

"I can ask Charley." Alex paused while his father explained that the ball was to raise money for cancer research. "But what if she doesn't want to go?"

"It's for a good cause. How could she refuse?" His father asked.

"I agree it's for a good cause, but don't suggest that I kidnap her and force her to come if she doesn't want to." Apparently, his handlers thought he could just snap his fingers and make Charley do their bidding.

"She'll meet a lot of interesting Charleston blue bloods, business leaders, and politicians. Your mother will be there, and there's me." His father laughed as he added himself to the list of interesting people attending the ball.

"I'll invite her. That's all I can promise," Alex said as he ended the call.

CHAPTER NINE

Charley arrived at the courthouse in Charleston at one p.m. on Monday afternoon. Mr. Lewis had called that morning to inform her that a spot had opened up on the family court docket, and if she could come into Charleston, her name-change petition would be heard that afternoon. All the required paperwork had been filed, and to finalize the name change, she just needed to show up and answer a few questions. Charley hurried up the courthouse steps to join Mr. Lewis, who waited for her just inside the double doors.

Charley's petition was the next item on the court's afternoon schedule. Once they were seated and the judge entered the courtroom, Charley was asked to provide a brief history of how she began using the name of Rainier. She quickly explained that her name was changed when she went to live in New Jersey as a child. Her aunt and uncle had made a home for her and given her the protection of their name. Now, she wanted to reclaim her birth name, too. The judge listened to her story, then quickly granted her petition. Almost immediately after stepping into the family courtroom as Charlotte Christine Rainier, she left it as Charlotte Christine Rainier-Mathews.

"Good luck to you, Ms. Rainier-Mathews," the judge congratulated her.

As the judge addressed her with her new-old name, Charley pictured her father looking down on her smiling and with approval in his eyes.

Before leaving the courthouse, Charley signed the legal papers in front of a notary that would transfer Annabelle's property into her name. Mr. Lewis filed the deed and the accompanying paperwork with the county clerk, and Charley's inheritance was complete. She was now Charley Rainier-Mathews, owner of a beach house on Turtle Island, South Carolina. Two major events in Charley's life had been accomplished in what seemed like a matter of minutes.

Charley said goodbye to Mr. Lewis and walked along King Street, peering in the windows of the boutiques along the way. Alex had invited her to a charity ball and fundraiser to be held on Saturday night the coming weekend. Charley planned to shop for a ball gown before leaving the city.

The evening wear displayed in the shop windows brought back the memory of the carload of evening gowns she had donated to the women's shelter when she moved out of the town house in New York just a few weeks ago. Daniel's firm held frequent black-tie events, and he never missed any of them. Charley had accompanied him when she was not away on an assignment. She sometimes wanted to skip one and just stay home for a relaxing evening with just the two of them, but Daniel believed his career hinged on who he met and schmoozed with at these parties. Spending an evening alone with Charley was no substitute for an evening with his pals or prospective clients.

But that was then, and with everything that had happened to her, *then* seemed like a lifetime ago.

Charley was excited about attending the ball with Alex. She

would meet new and exciting people from across a wide spectrum of Charleston's society. The guest list would not be limited to stuffy financial people like Daniel's associates, who usually spent the entire evening talking only about the latest rich client they had landed or hoped to land. But Alex and his father were lawyers, and Alex specialized in mergers and acquisitions, so rich clients may be what they discussed, too. And according to Alex, the ball would be held at the home of one of the wealthiest business owners in Charleston. It may well turn out to be similar to the New York parties she had attended with Daniel. Still, it would be her first formal encounter with the citizens of Charleston.

Charley passed a variety of clothing stores along King Street that sold everything from casual, to business, to evening wear. She paused in front of one, then stepped into the cool interior of Haley's Evening Apparel. A sales associate was at her elbow immediately. She guided Charley through a maze of designer evening dresses, discarding some and recommending others that would be appropriate to wear to a charity fundraising event.

After searching through the available styles, Charley chose a black one-shouldered gown with a long, flirty skirt and a slit that ended just above the knee. It was a classic design and appropriate for any formal occasion. The black color brought out the blonde streaks in Charley's hair, which had only become blonder since she had moved to the beach.

The dress fit Charley perfectly and didn't need any alterations. She purchased black pumps to wear with it. The sales associate assured Charley that she would blend in well with the members of Charleston's society that usually attended such events.

In the week that followed, Charley and Alex set out each day to photograph the historic and beautiful scenes of Charleston and the surrounding area. Alex drove to the Island Café each morning to pick up muffins or bagels for breakfast and sandwiches for lunch. He appeared at her door each morning with his camera and a cup of coffee, ready to guide her to the best photography sites in the area. Alex proved to be an eager student and attentively listened to her instruction on how to get the most out of his camera equipment. Charley showed him what to look for when choosing his subjects; how to find the best angle, and how to recognize when the light was right. She explained the part patience and long waits played in getting great shots, especially when photographing wildlife subjects.

Photography was Charley's profession, but it was about more than just how she earned a living. She was a visual artist who never took shortcuts. Her goal was to showcase a subject in the most favorable way possible. Each time she pointed her camera at something or someone, she sought to create a product she could be proud of. She hoped to pass along the same standards to Alex.

Alex had a new and different location to show her each day. They took a boat to Morris Island, the tiny island in Charleston harbor, and took photos of the lighthouse that Charley had spotted when she first arrived. A local organization, Save the Light, had restored the lighthouse and made it a favorite tourist attraction.

Alex took Charley to other islands and beaches—Folly Beach, Isle of Palms, Bulls Island, and Sullivan's Island—which were much more developed than Turtle Island. Charley photographed the Angel Oak on Johns Island—the large and very old live oak tree that was so well-known and visited so frequently that a park had been built around it.

They spent a full day on Wadmalaw Island, a less populated island with green landscapes, and marshlands, and was the location of an American tea farm called the Charleston Tea

Plantation. They enjoyed a glass of wine on the shaded patio of the Wadmalaw Firefly Distillery.

Alex's abilities with his camera improved throughout the week. He quickly learned from Charley's instruction—except for the lesson on patience. They had good-natured arguments whenever he insisted that what he saw through the viewfinder of his camera was good enough. Charley felt that Alex disagreed sometimes just to hear her response. She looked forward to the give-and-take of their friendly arguments, and their disputes became as much a part of each day as getting the best photo of the subjects they were shooting.

"I warned you that I was a point-and-shoot photographer," Alex whispered one day when they were crouched in the damp marsh grasses waiting for three fledgling egrets to take flight from the nest nearby. "Wallowing in the mud was not what I had in mind." The baby birds had made several feeble attempts to fly, but had yet to make it into the air.

Charley had crouched for hours in past shoots, waiting for the perfect action shot, so this exercise was nothing new to her. Anticipating the habits of wildlife could be tricky, but she believed it was only a matter of minutes before she and Alex would get a photograph that was worth the wait. In Charley's opinion, waiting for the subjects to do what you wanted them to do was as much a part of the job as snapping the picture.

"And I told you that if I teach you, you have to follow my lead. Now, shush," Charley whispered back. She held up her hand. "Get ready! You need to snap the photo just as they leave the nest. Then, follow them into flight." The snowy birds emerged from the nest and teetered on the edge. They flapped their young wings a couple of times, and then, the first one lifted off into the air. It was immediately followed by the other two. They wobbled a little at first, but soon, instinct took over, and they straightened their bodies, expanded their wings, and soared higher with each flap of their wings.

The clicking of Charley's and Alex's cameras and the call of the egrets were the only sounds in the early morning hush of the marsh. It was a beautiful experience, and they had captured it all on their cameras.

"That was amazing!" Alex whispered excitedly. He grabbed Charley by the shoulders and pulled her toward him in a tight hug. His lips brushed her forehead. Then, before Charley could react, his lips traveled down to settle on her lips. The contact caught Charley off guard. She leaned in as Alex deepened the kiss. As the kiss ended, reason slowly returned to Charley. She pulled away and stared at Alex. He appeared to be as surprised over what had happened as she was.

What was she doing? What was Alex doing?

Alex was the first to speak. "Sorry. I got carried away. That was a wonderful thing to experience… uh… the photo, I mean," he said, clarifying. "The kiss wasn't bad, either," he added with a mischievous smile. He reached out and pushed a stray strand of hair that had come loose from her ponytail behind her ear. His fingers remained gently resting against her cheek.

"I told you that patience would pay off," Charley whispered back, ignoring Alex's comment about the kiss. She pulled away from his fingers, reached up, and tightened the band around her ponytail. Their subjects, the egrets, were gone, so why was she still whispering? "Remember? Patience! Maybe you'll listen to me in the future," she added more loudly. She took a deep breath and to distract herself from Alex's steady gaze, she pointed upward toward the direction the egrets had flown. They were now just small dots in the blue sky as they circled in high arcs above the marsh. The birds were enjoying their newfound freedom.

"Yes, ma'am. I promise to listen," Alex replied as he looked to where she pointed. "That shot was definitely worth the wait."

His focus turned to reviewing the photographs he had just taken. "These are great!" He turned his camera toward Charley to show her the picture he'd snapped just as the egrets lifted into flight. "This is good, don't you think? Are we finished here?"

"Yes, we're finished," Charley replied as she inspected Alex's photo. "We won't get any better shots than that one." Charley kept her face turned away from Alex to hide her reaction. One kiss from a man she barely knew, and she was rattled! Apparently, Alex was not affected the same way. He joked and appeared unaffected. She would treat it the same way. They had simply become caught up in the excitement of a great photo shoot. She was making a bigger deal out of the incident than it deserved.

Then why was she still obsessing over it several minutes after it had happened?

Charley's inner voice gave her a mental shake and ordered. *Stop! One small kiss means nothing. You've been kissed before! Forget it!*

A summer romance with a handsome man like Alex was tempting, but not worth the pain that would surely follow once it ended. Someone usually got hurt and her job was to make sure it wasn't her. She carried a lot of baggage from her marriage to a cheating husband and their subsequent divorce. She never wanted to feel or experience anything similar again.

As Charley packed up her camera gear, she reminded herself of yet more reasons why a summer romance was a bad idea. She enjoyed her outings with Alex—a lot—but her life and future plans were still unsettled. If she returned to her life and her job in New York, they would naturally go their separate ways. That would be much harder to do if she let herself get involved with him, provided of course, he was a willing participant. He might still be in love with the girl he had mentioned previously. She was Alex's photography coach, he was her student, and their relationship needed to be strictly friendship. Alex seemed to feel the same way. They were back to easy conversation as they walked out of the marsh and climbed into Alex's pickup truck. They drove home in silence, tired but pleased with the day's successful shoot. Shots like the flight of the baby egrets were rare.

The next morning, Alex arrived at her door as usual. If he remembered the kiss she had termed "their moment in the marsh", he didn't show it. He was still the same friendly, knowledgeable tour guide he had been before. He announced that their destination for the day was to an entirely new location. "No sandwiches for lunch," he said. "I want you to experience the local cuisine of Pawleys Island. You're in for a treat."

"Another restaurant where they know you by name?" Charley asked with a grin.

"They do know my name. But… well, you'll see."

Alex drove north from Charleston, taking US Highway 17—the coastal highway and the same one Charley had traveled down the day she first arrived in South Carolina. Alex kept up a running commentary as they drove toward Pawleys Island. He pointed out landmarks along the way. As he drove, they passed a billboard advertising Brookgreen Gardens straight ahead.

"I'll take you there on a future excursion," Alex promised. "The gardens aren't too far north of where we're going today. It's a large property made up of themed gardens with native plants and sculptures, and it also functions as a wildlife preserve. It's a photographer's dream."

Just south of Myrtle Beach, Alex turned eastward and crossed the Southern Causeway that lead to Pawleys Island, a long narrow peninsula and small barrier island on the Atlantic Coast.

"This land was once a rice plantation," Alex explained as he reached the end of the causeway and turned onto a winding two-lane highway. "Some descendants of the people who used to work the land still live here." He pointed toward a scattering of wooden cottages that lined the road. "But many of these houses are vacation rentals now. The island's narrow peninsula-like location makes it a frequent target of hurricanes and tropical storms. Despite the damaging storms, many of the islanders keep building back."

"They must be strong people to continue to live here under those conditions," Charley commented. "It's admirable when people value their ancestral lands and refused to leave despite the hardships they faced."

"They are hardy people—as most of the inhabitants of the barrier islands are, or, at least the older folks are—and they fiercely cling to the land and their traditions. Some of them hunker down and refuse to evacuate during storms. But there aren't that many of them left now. Probably less than two hundred are year-round inhabitants. The young people grow up and move to the mainland to find jobs and an easier way of life."

"Even on the mainland, young people are drawn by the jobs, social life, and entertainment they can find in the cities," Charley noted.

Alex continued familiarizing Charley with the island's people. "Some of Pawleys's old-timers merge the Gullah Geechee culture brought from Africa centuries ago with today's modern life. Their language can be unique, too. They speak English, of course, but like to mix in their own special Creole words. I guess it's their way of keeping the language alive."

Alex stopped his truck in front of a wood-framed house set high on pilings. It was the same weathered gray color as the others they had passed along the way. Large pots of blooming flowers sat on either side of the steps leading up to the porch.

"Welcome to our home, Alex," a tall man called out as he stepped out onto the porch and came down the steps to meet

them. He was dressed in jeans and a T-shirt and moved slowly with a regal bearing and spoke in a cultured British accent.
"And who is this beautiful lady you have with you?"

"Hello, Bowen," Alex replied as he shook the man's hand.
"This is my friend Charley. Charley, this is Bowen Harrison.
Watch out for him. He's a silver-tongued devil if there ever was
one."

"Do not listen to him, Charley," Bowen replied as he bowed
low and kissed Charley's hand. "Ah, Alex, my friend, do not
worry. I will not steal your lovely lady, although she will be hard
to resist."

"Okay, Bowen," Alex chided, "cut the fake accent! Your
smarmy act as an African tribal chieftain isn't fooling anyone,
especially me." Alex turned to Charley. "Bowen and I went to
college together. I went on to law school, and he became a college professor. He teaches African Studies at Carlton College in
Columbia. Don't be fooled. He's as much a native South Carolinian as I am."

"If my act works with the ladies, why change it?" Bowen
dropped his fake accent, laughed loudly, and added, "I'll give
you tips, my friend."

Alex started to reply, but was interrupted by a plump woman who called from the edge of the porch, "Bowen, stop harass-
ing our guests. Ignore him, both of you. Come inside."

Charley and Alex followed Bowen up the steps and onto
the porch, where they were immediately hugged by the woman.
"Welcome, Charley. I'm Bowen's mother," Mrs. Harrison said as
she opened the front door to the house. "Come in. I'm so glad
you came. Lunch will be ready soon."

Charley and Alex stepped into a small, neat living room.
Charley gazed around at the décor in the room. The pride the
Bowen family took in the African heritage their ancestors had
brought to South Carolina was displayed in the paintings that

lined the walls and the artifacts on the shelves. Sweet grass baskets woven with intricate designs and pottery of various shapes filled every corner of the living room. Mrs. Harrison's speech was clearly American English, but as Alex had said, she occasionally interspersed words of the Gullah Geechee language into the conversation.

Charley was instantly drawn to the paintings on the wall. As a visual artist herself, she immediately noticed the clever use of color and the painter's unique style. She stopped in front of one of the paintings. an obvious scene from Pawleys Island.

"My daughter, Gena, did this painting," Mrs. Harrison said from beside Charley. It was a beach scene that showed a large loggerhead turtle crawling back toward the ocean. It left a visible double trail in the sand, first leading away from the ocean and then moving back toward it from a disturbance in the sand—the nesting pit where the turtle had just laid her eggs. The colors in the sky as the early morning sun was just beginning to rise over the ocean were vivid and beautiful. As a photographer, Charley appreciated the talent that went into each brushstroke. At the bottom of the painting was scrawled the word '*cootuh*' and the name G. Harrison.

"It's beautiful. Such rich colors," Charley marveled. "What does '*cootuh*' mean?"

"It is Gullah for 'turtle.' Appropriate, don't you think—since it's a painting of a turtle?" Mrs. Harrison laughed. "And I agree. It's the colors in the sky with the rising sun that catches the eye."

"Where is your daughter now?" asked Charley.

"She lives in Charleston with her husband and two of the most perfect grandchildren a grandmother could want." Mrs. Harrison beamed as she mentioned her grandchildren. "But she still paints every chance she gets. She sometimes shows her paintings at a small gallery in Charleston."

Charley nodded and moved on to the other paintings. They

were all done with the same technique and bright, vivid colors. Charley was quickly caught up in the scenes and the people in the paintings. The artist had created a rich illustration on canvas of life on Pawleys Island.

Mrs. Harrison left Bowen to entertain Charley and Alex while she finished preparing the food in the kitchen. Soon, she announced that lunch was ready. They filed into the kitchen and sat down at the table.

"*Nyam*," Mrs. Harrison instructed, "eat." She pointed to the food set out on the table. Bowls of rice with shrimp, fried okra, sweet potato pie, surrounded a small mound of firepit-roasted oysters. The food looked and smelled delicious. Charley and Alex were happy to oblige Mrs. Harrison's command to eat. As Charley ate, she was content to just listen to the conversation that went on around the table. She sat quietly, absorbing the warmth and hospitality of Mrs. Harrison as she told stories of life on the island. Charley only took part in the conversation when Mrs. Harrison or Bowen asked her a direct question.

As Bowen and Alex reminisced about their college days together, they often argued over the details of their stories. Charley suspected the stories were embellished and exaggerated. Perhaps none of the details were close to one-hundred-percent accurate.

Finally, Alex pushed back his chair. "Mrs. Harrison, thank you. I don't think I can eat another bite. I have to stop now, or I won't be able to move. And then, you'll be stuck with me for the night." Charley seconded Alex with compliments of her own.

"You're both welcome in my home any time," Mrs. Harrison replied. "We can never thank you enough, Alex, for what you did for us."

"Nah." Alex waved away Mrs. Harrison's thanks. "Right is right, ma'am."

Charley made a mental note to ask Alex later what Mrs.

Harrison meant by her comment. What could he have helped them with? A legal matter, Charley guessed.

Charley and Alex offered to help Mrs. Harrison clean up the kitchen, but she shooed them out to the living room. She soon joined them, and they visited for a short time until Charley and Alex had to leave. They thanked their hosts and happily accepted an invitation to visit again.

After leaving the Harrisons, Alex guided Charley around the island. He stopped the truck whenever Charley spotted something she wanted to photograph. He didn't take his camera out of the truck today, preferring to just watch Charley in action.

They drove to one of the beaches, where Charley found multiple subjects to shoot. Several small children played tag with the waves and tried to race them to the shore. The joy on their faces as they played made Charley laugh as she took their photos. She moved on to photograph the intense concentration on the faces of three other children as they diligently worked to build a sandcastle on the beach. Pride in their accomplishment quickly turned to dismay as they watched a wave come in, wash over the elaborate castle, and pull it toward the ocean. Charley used her long-range lens to photograph, but not disturb, three fishermen near the pier. Their faces showed how serious they considered their task, as they patiently waited for the fish to bite.

After Charley had finished taking her photos, she walked back toward the pickup truck. Alex leaned against the truck, his feet crossed at the ankles, and his hands partially stuck in the front pockets of his jeans. His hair ruffled in the soft ocean breeze. Dark sunglasses covered his eyes, but Charley felt his eyes were on her as she approached him. She stopped several feet away, lifted her camera, and snapped his picture. As she checked the results of the shot and looked at his face, she couldn't help but think back to the kiss in the marsh yesterday. Their excitement over taking a rare photo had led them to do something they wouldn't normally do, but the spontaneous "moment in the marsh" was still pleasant to think about.

"I don't know about you, but I'm exhausted," Charley said as she reached the pickup truck.

"It's probably from the large lunch we ate," Alex replied. "Ready to go? Did you take all the shots you wanted?"

"I did." Charley put her camera in the back seat, then climbed in beside Alex. "It's been a very productive day." She leaned her head back and closed her eyes as Alex started the pickup and drove out of the beach parking lot. They were almost back to Charleston before Charley remembered Mrs. Harrison's grateful comment to Alex.

"What did Mrs. Harrison mean by 'what you did for us'?" Charley asked.

"I helped her with a court case concerning her land. It's an age-old problem on many barrier islands. The land is in high demand, and some developers will try anything they can to take it away from the people whose families have lived here for centuries. The problem actually dates back to after the Civil War, when African Americans bought or were given property, and the deeds were not properly executed. Fast forward to today, and the ownership of that same parcel of land is divided among all the heirs that descended from the original owners. This complicates the situation even more. This is called heir property."

"What happened?" Charley asked. "Did someone try to swindle the Harrisons out of their land?"

"It's complicated, but basically, yes. The Harrison family has lived on this land for centuries, but Mrs. Harrison didn't have a recorded deed. A developer tried to take the land by claiming that without a deed, Mrs. Harrison couldn't legally own it. Bowen called me and asked for my help. I represented them in court. It took about four months and lots of research—mainly a title search and then a land survey. But the hardest part was tracking down all the living heirs across several states."

"That must have been a huge chore," Charley said, "trying to find that many people."

"Thankfully, Mrs. Harrison had records of her family's genealogy. That's another flaw in the heir property system: all the heirs have to agree to any arrangement involving the land. In Mrs. Harrison's case, they all did agree to keep it in the family. All the heirs now have a clear title to their portion of the forty acres of property," Alex sighed. "It doesn't always turn out that well. I was happy to help them get what was rightfully theirs."

Alex's efforts on behalf of the Harrison family didn't really surprise Charley, but hearing that he had been successful impressed her. "That's amazing, Alex. And I know you did all that at your own expense."

"There wasn't that much expense. My labor was free and…" He trailed off. "Well, I did have to hire an assistant to track down the heirs. But I'd do it again."

They drove the rest of the way home in silence. Charley relaxed and was almost dozing when Alex stopped the truck in her driveway. She heard Rex barking as she opened the pickup's door. "Someone's happy you're home," she said as she climbed out. Alex got out of the pickup and followed her to the foot of the steps.

"Rex? Nah, he just wants his run on the beach. I have some business in Charleston tomorrow, but I'll pick you up around six thirty for the charity ball. If that's alright, of course."

"Sure. Six thirty sounds fine. See you then." Charley waved and turned to climb the steps leading to the front porch.

Charley had plans for tomorrow, too. She had an appointment at a spa on Johns Island for a full range of services. The technicians had their work cut out for them, especially when it came to her nails and her hair. The days she'd spent crawling around in the sand and bushes with her camera had not been kind to her hands. The sun and salty air had been even less kind to her hair.

CHAPTER TEN

Charley took one last look at herself in the hallway mirror. Her hair sparkled with the highlights and lowlights
she'd added at the spa that morning. She wore it pulled
back in a loosely braided chignon, and long tendrils softly
framed her face. Her dress fit perfectly, and the slit in the skirt
gave it an elegant, sophisticated look. She was satisfied with her
appearance, and was ready to meet Alex's family and friends as
well as Charleston's high society.

Charley sat down on the living room sofa to await Alex's
arrival. She reviewed some of the photos from their visit to
Pawleys Island yesterday. She had a nice selection. Alex was
right when he'd promised she'd find many subjects to shoot.
Over all, she probably now had enough photos to complete the
book her publisher had been pushing her to do—a book about
the Lowcountry of South Carolina.

Charley laid her camera down on the table when Alex
pulled into the driveway in front of her beach house. She hadn't
seen him all day. He must have stayed on the mainland to dress
for the evening. Alex knocked softly on her door promptly at

six thirty. She had noticed his punctuality before, and it hadn't been a fluke. He was always on time.

"Oh my," she breathed as she opened the door and stared at him. His dark hair gleamed in the fading light of the setting sun, and his black tie and tuxedo jacket contrasted sharply with the pristine white shirt he wore. The bright smile and the admiration in his eyes caught and held her attention. She took a deep shaky breath.

"You look beautiful. But I'm not surprised by that," he finally said.

"So do you. Uh… I mean you look gorgeous. Uh… handsome." The sight of him made her question her earlier decision to by-pass a summer romance. Most men looked their best in a tuxedo, but Alex turned the look up a notch. His tall frame and broad shoulders filled out the formal wear better than anyone she had seen at any New York gala. Make that better than anyone she had seen anywhere! Charley suddenly remember her manners. "Do you want to come in?"

"I think we should be going. It's about a forty-five-minute drive to the site of the ball. Do you have a wrap?"

Charley picked up her wrap and clutch purse. Alex draped the wrap gently around her shoulders. Goosebumps raced up and down her arm as his fingers lingered on her bare shoulders. She smiled up at him, then laced her hand through the arm he offered.

"Oh! The rich spoiled son *does* have a fancy car!" she teased when they reached the black BMW parked in the driveway.

"Spoiled, maybe, but not rich. It's my mother's," Alex replied. "Like a male Cinderella, I'll be back in my battered pick-up truck by tomorrow."

On the way to Charleston, Alex gave Charley a brief overview of the Maitland family, including their extensive ties throughout the Lowcountry and their vast businesses. Mr. Maitland had passed away, and now, Marietta Maitland, his widow, was in charge of the empire. She was active in the Charleston community and frequently held charity balls for one reason or another. Last year, it had been to support various Charleston arts programs. This year, it was to raise funds for cancer research.

"Charley, I need to tell you something," Alex said hesitantly as he stopped at a red light just inside the Charleston city limits.

Uh oh, Charley thought. *This sounds ominous.* "What? What's wrong?" Charley braced herself, unsure of what to expect. Was the news bad and would it affect her, directly? She had spent a lot of time with him recently, but she still didn't know much about him personally. Alex was basically a stranger, so was he about to share a deep dark secret?

"Don't sound so worried." Alex reached over, caught her hand, and shook it gently. "Relax. It's nothing bad, really. Just information I think you should know before we get to the Maitland estate. My ex may be at the ball."

"You were married?" Charley asked. The idea that he might once have been married had never entered her mind. But it should have. He was in his thirties, with a successful career, and was extremely good-looking. A marriage in his past wouldn't be unusual. "Why haven't you mentioned it?" Charley's next thought was to commiserate with him. She had a failed marriage in her past, too.

"No, that's not it. I've never been married—but I was engaged. The day before our wedding, Rebecca, my bride-to-be, decided she wanted to marry someone else—a junior partner in my law firm."

"Oh! How horrible! When did this happen?" Charley looked at Alex and noticed a tightening of his jaw. It still bothered him, but that was natural, regardless of how long ago it had been. As she well knew, it was hard to get over the loss of trust in a partner you cared enough for to start a life with. Or, in Alex's case, a promise to start a life with.

"A little over a year ago," Alex replied. "Aside from being dumped and humiliated by my bride, I've often wondered how I could have been so stupid to miss the signs. How did I not recognize that she was sleeping with someone else even as we were planning our wedding?"

"I'm sorry, Alex. Being deceived by someone you loved will probably hurt for some time. But it's good that it happened before you were married. I had been married to Daniel for over a year when I realized he was cheating on me. After that, we wasted another year trying to make things work. Of course, that experiment was a failure. Once trust is broken, it's practically impossible to put it back together again."

"I was clueless," Alex added in disgust. "I'm still stumped as to why I didn't recognize she was in love with my coworker, someone I saw practically every day. How did they hide that?" Alex's mouth tightened. "I suppose I should be happy that she didn't wait to ditch me as we stood before 150 invited guests. Everyone tells me that one bad experience doesn't mean all relationships will fail. My head tells me that's right, but it's shaken my confidence in relationships."

"Trust me, I know. We're quite a pair, aren't we?" Charley said. "Do you ever think, though, that you're giving too much power to the very person who broke your heart in the first place? You're letting them ruin your life even more." Charley's past with Daniel had given her insight and taught her this lesson—twice. It was easy to acknowledge these wise words, but heeding them was the hard part. Charley glanced over and caught Alex looking at her. "Not everyone is untrustworthy, Alex."

"Yeah, I know. I believe that now." Alex looked back at the road.

"So, do you want me to act all lovey-dovey with you to-night? Make Rebecca jealous and regret what she threw away?" Charley asked. "I can lay it on thick, if you want."

"Only if you mean it," Alex replied. He smiled and raised an eyebrow at her. Then, he became serious again. "You'll have to let me know if and when you mean it. I'm over the dumping and humiliation—or, mostly over it. I realize now that I didn't offer Rebecca what she wanted, but I can't figure out why I didn't recognize that sooner? I'm still unreliable in deciphering signals."

"I seriously doubt that." Charley suddenly felt flirty. She gave him a flirtatious smile then added, "Maybe you haven't found the right woman, yet."

"Maybe," Alex replied shortly without looking at her, then fell silent. So much for flirting and fishing for a compliment. Obviously, she needed to practice her flirting skills, or maybe Alex was right and he hadn't recognized she was flirting. Or maybe he was remembering what might have been with Rebecca.

Alex remained quiet as he took the bypass road around the Charleston business district, then turned northwest toward Summerville. The Maitland estate, officially named Oak Lane Plantation, was located south of Summerville, about fifteen miles from Charleston. After a while, they turned into a long driveway marked by a sign that read 'Oak Lane Plantation.' The driveway was lined by a canopy of oak trees covered with Spanish moss. For tonight's gala, the tree trunks were wrapped in strings of white lights, giving arriving guests a lighted path to the house.

Alex stopped the car in front of a large, red-brick, planta-tion-style two-story house with a white portico centered on the front. A uniformed valet opened Charley's door and took the keys from Alex to park the car among other vehicles in a large clearing nearby.

Charley and Alex were met at the door by a butler who led them toward the back of the house. They could hear the murmur of voices and laughter as they neared the ballroom. The room, they entered was filled with guests, some mingling in small groups, while others were already dancing beneath a large sparkling chandelier. Tables covered in white tablecloths and set for dinner ringed the dance floor. At the back of the room a polished dark wooden staircase spiraled upward to rooms on the second floor. Waiters crisscrossed the room, passing out hors d'oeuvres and glasses of champagne. Charley paused just inside the door for a moment, struck by the grandeur of the large ballroom and the beautifully dressed guests.

Alex guided Charley into the room, then snagged two glasses of champagne from a passing waiter and handed one to Charley.

"This is how the Charleston wealthy *actually* live," Alex leaned close and whispered. "The Morgan household is nothing like this. That's our hostess." He nodded toward a woman surrounded by a group of guests on the other side of the room. "I'll introduce you later."

"Hey, big brother," a voice said from behind Charley, "don't hog the lady."

Charley turned to see a young man standing behind her. He was fairer and a little shorter than Alex, but he had the same smoky-blue eyes and wide, friendly smile.

"Hi," Charley said as she stuck out her hand. "You must be Alex's brother."

"Charley, this is my brother, Bobby Junior. He prefers to be called 'Robert.' He thinks it makes him sound grown-up."

Robert ignored Charley's hand and bent to kiss her lightly on the cheek. "Now I understand why my brother has been skipping work and spending so much time at the beach," he remarked as he stepped back. He slapped Alex on the back. "There's hope for you yet."

"Did you bring a date, or couldn't you find someone who wanted to be seen with you in public?" Alex retorted good-naturedly.

"I did bring a date: Corine Dawson," Robert replied as he looked around the room. "She's around here somewhere. And before you get hot under the collar, she's not the enemy. She's not her father."

"It's your love life." Alex shrugged. "I just don't want you to get involved with the wrong person."

Charley glanced between Alex and Robert. This appeared to be a conversation they'd had before. Was Alex imparting a general lesson as an older brother or a specific lesson he had learned through his experience with Rebecca? Maybe his warning was more about the last name of the person Robert was dating.

"Not all women are the same, Alex, and in Corine's case, not all are like their parents," Robert replied.

Alex had told her about the case he had filed against Dawson Construction and the subsequent investigation by the sheriff's department. Robert's date was apparently the daughter of the defendant in Alex's suit. Robert was right: not all children were like their parents. Charley could attest to that.

"I know. I'm just being your wiser older brother." Alex placed his hand on Robert's shoulder and shook it affectionally. "I don't want you to get involved in something where you're forced to take sides."

"I know. Don't worry about me. As your wiser younger brother, I say you should concentrate more on your own love life—or lack thereof," Robert replied with a laugh. "I know what I'm doing."

"I hope so." Alex frowned and started to say add something,

but his parents, Bob and Karen Morgan, joined them at that moment.

"Charley, I'm so happy to meet you," Karen said warmly. "Alex has told us so much about you and your photography lessons. I hope he's being a good student." Both she and Bob hugged Charley. "We have a table over there." Karen pointed to a large round table not far from the dance floor. "You and Alex have a reserved seat, so come join us for dinner and the auction so we can talk and get to know you better."

The band, a popular local cover band, positioned on a raised platform at the end of the room, switched from an up-tempo number to a slower tune. The female singer began singing a rendition of Lady Gaga's seductive song, "Always Remember Us This Way." Bob wrapped his arm around Karen's waist, and with a wave goodbye, they walked toward the dance floor.

Alex gently elbowed his brother away from Charley's side and offered her his hand. "Care to dance?" he asked.

Charley nodded and nervously accepted his hand. Alex took the glass of champagne from Charley's hand and placed it on a nearby table.

It had been a while since Charley had danced and visions of tripping or stepping on Alex's feet raced through her mind as he led her to the dance floor. It soon became evident that tripping wouldn't be a problem with Alex as he expertly led her into the slow dance.

Alex tightened his arm around her, pulling her closer, then dropped his head and rested his chin against her temple. He softly hummed along with the lyrics. Charley relaxed, laid her head on his shoulder, and breathed in the masculine scent of his cologne. The pulse in his throat beat softly against her forehead.

Charley completely lost herself in the feel of Alex's arms around her as their bodies moved in rhythm with the music that flowed through the room. She let go and floated, breaking free from past hurts and struggles. All decisions about her future were pushed aside. Her resolve not to think of Alex romantically, weakened even more as he held her and swept her away from the crowded ballroom. It was just the two of them, alone in a beautiful world of their own. She was on a sensual ride, and she welcomed the invitation to just let go, stop thinking, and follow Alex wherever he took her.

The song came to an end, but Alex didn't immediately release Charley. Still caught up in the magical moment she didn't step away either. Alex kissed her lightly on the temple. She was jolted from her fantasy when Alex suddenly stepped back. He turned toward a man standing just behind him. The man had tapped Alex on the shoulder.

"It's my turn with your beautiful partner." The man's hand was extended toward Charley.

Alex's mouth tightened, and he scowled, but he nodded and stepped to the side. "Charley, this is Eric Winston." Alex made the introduction in a voice that was less that friendly.

"Hey, gorgeous. Let's dance," Eric said as he pulled Charley close without giving her a chance to accept or reject his invitation. She pulled back, putting some distance between them. "I hear you're from New York," Eric continued as he began leading her in the dance. His hand dropped low on her back. She not-so-gently elbowed his hand up to the middle of her back.

"I love New York," Eric said without waiting for Charley to comment. "Maybe we can get together when you go back. I make frequent trips up there—sometimes for work, but usually for the nightlife. Beautiful women are plentiful up that way, and they trawl the nightspots—looking for me, I hope." He smiled at Charley and looked at her for comment. She was at a loss as to how she should respond to such an egotistical statement. Her silence didn't seem to bother him, because he quickly resumed his chatter.

As Charley looked up into Eric's arrogant face, she quickly sized him up. Now *this* was an entitled, spoiled rich boy. She'd met men like him in New York City. She could spot them easily, and as the old saying went, she could quickly "separate the grain from the chaff." Men like Eric were caught in their own narcissistic bubble and assumed that everyone saw them the same way they saw themselves. Eric Winston was obviously impressed with himself. As he moved Charley around the dance floor and chattered on, it never occurred to him that she might not be as enthralled by him as he thought. He was enthralled with himself, and that was all that mattered.

Charley looked away from Eric's smug face. She missed a step when she caught sight of Alex across the room, dancing with a tall redheaded woman. Instinctively, Charley knew the woman was Rebecca, Alex's ex. They appeared to be engaged in a serious conversation. Charley wondered who had asked whom to dance. She grudgingly admitted they made a beautiful couple. Rebecca, if that was indeed the woman in Alex's arms, was tall—probably at least five-foot-eight. For the first time in her life, Charley's five-foot, four-inch frame felt inadequate when compared to the woman in Alex's arms. Charley straightened her back and pulled herself up to her full height. She felt a prick of jealousy and then felt ridiculous. Who Alex chose to dance with wasn't her business. But she had felt a deep connection with him as they danced and thought Alex had felt it too. But that could have been her imagination.

Charley finished the dance with Eric, though she pulled away each time he tried to pull her closer. When the music finally stopped and the band laid down their instruments to take a break, Charley quickly excused herself, happy to escape Eric's roving hands. She made her way to the ladies' room to freshen up.

When Charley left the ladies' room, she slowly retraced her

steps down the corridor that led back to the ballroom. On the way, she paused to examine the paintings that lined the wall. In what she assumed was chronological order, based on the clothing each subject wore, were portraits of the Maitland family going back many generations—probably to the earliest days of Charleston.

"That's my husband's father," a voice said at her elbow.

Charley turned toward the voice. A woman, who appeared to be in her late fifties or early sixties, and who Alex had identified as the hostess of the charity ball, Mrs. Maitland, stood next to her.

She peered closely at Charley's face for a few minutes, then nodded toward the stern-looking man in the portrait that Charley had been examining. "He died tragically when a horse threw him headfirst into a stone fence. His neck was broken, and he died instantly."

Charley was startled by the woman's directness. This was the grande dame of the Maitland empire, a woman who bluntly said what was on her mind. According to Alex, her company controlled most of the shipping industry in Charleston and had expanded farther up the East Coast as well. Mrs. Maitland was known as a formidable, no-holds-barred businesswoman. She had the reputation of being even tougher than her husband after she took over the empire upon his death. *Tough, as well as blunt and direct*, thought Charley.

"Your family has a long and, from what I hear, distinguished history, Mrs. Maitland." Charley nodded to the paintings.

"We can trace the Maitland family line back centuries. They started a company that has only become larger and more important as the years have gone by. Some would call that luck. Others would call it ruthless business savvy and smart strategies." She chuckled, then sobered as she motioned for Charley to move further down the hallway. She stopped in front of another portrait. "The Maitland family has been both smart and lucky, but they've had their share of troubles, just like everyone else: death, sickness. Success in the business world doesn't cure all adversity." Mrs. Maitland turned and pointed to a younger version of her father-in-law—the last picture in the row. "That's my husband, Arthur. I lost him far too early. To cancer."

"I'm sorry for your loss," Charley replied. What Mrs. Maitland had said was true. Wealth and success didn't prevent tragedy. "That's the reason for the fundraiser tonight, correct? For cancer research?"

"Yes. Cancer touches many lives. Young or old, it doesn't care." Mrs. Maitland didn't elaborate further. She stared at the portrait for a moment longer, then turned back to Charley.

"I'm truly sorry," Charley repeated.

Mrs. Maitland acknowledged Charley's condolences with a nod. "I believe your name is Charley? A friend of Alex Morgan's?"

"I'm sorry," Charley replied. "I was distracted by the paintings and didn't introduce myself. Yes, I'm Charley Rainier-Phillips." The words were out of her mouth before she even realized that she had used her former married name. Old habits were hard to break. Mrs. Maitland looked at her quizzically, but didn't say anything. *Oh,* thought Charley, *she's probably heard that my name is just 'Rainier.'* "My last name is complicated," Charley stated by way of explanation. "It's a long story."

"I would be interested in hearing it sometime," Mrs. Maitland replied as she began to walk down the hallway toward the ballroom. "But right now, I have hostess duties to see to, and you need to get back to the party. Dinner will be served soon, and the auction will begin soon after. And I see that your date, Alex, is waiting for you."

Charley looked toward the end of the hallway. Alex was indeed waiting for her, casually leaning against the wall just outside the corridor.

"You two have met, I see." Alex frowned at Mrs. Maitland as he took Charley's hand in his.

"We have," Mrs. Maitland replied. "I was telling Charley about the Maitlands' long lineage. It was very nice to meet you, Charley. I hope we can visit again soon and you can tell me all about yourself. Enjoy your dinner." With that. Mrs. Maitland turned and briskly walked away.

Alex frowned as his eyes followed Mrs. Maitland for a few minutes. He then placed Charley's arm through his and escorted her to the table occupied by the Morgan family. Robert introduced his date, Corine Dawson, as Alex held Charley's chair for her, then took a seat beside her. He leaned toward her and whispered, "I apologize about Eric." The waiters interrupted before he could say more, as they began serving dinner.

The dinner was a three-course meal of Southern favorites including petite filet mignon, broiled lobster, and grilled asparagus, finished off with a dessert of chocolate raspberry cake. Charley was welcomed and included in the conversation of the other diners at the table. Corine and Karen wanted to know what it was like to live in a city like New York. Charley's reply was mostly in generalities about the people who lived there, the international dignitaries who visited, the trials of navigating the city's subway system, and the Broadway plays and other entertainment venues. She didn't share many personal details, such as her divorce from Daniel. She preferred not to discuss topics that might ruin what to her had thus far been a beautiful evening—except for the wrestling match with Eric Winston.

"Where in the city do you live?" Corine asked.

Charley stalled her answer as she waited for the catering staff to clear the table in front of her. How could she answer Corine's question without bringing up the very topic she wanted to avoid—her failed marriage?

"Want a refill?" Alex asked, further delaying Charley's reply, as he picked up the bottle of wine and refreshed each glass on the table.

Charley was still formulating an answer to Corine's question when the auctioneer took to the podium to announce that the auction was about to begin.

Charley turned her chair around so she could face the auctioneer. Alex follow suit and aligned his chair with Charley's. He laid his arm across the back of her chair and cupped his fingers around her shoulder and began lightly caressing her bare skin with his thumb.

Alex's arm and fingers caressing her shoulder was a possessive move. Was his display of affection for Charley's benefit; directed at Eric, who sat at the table behind them; or for Rebecca, who sat at the table to their right? Just in case it was directed at Rebecca, Charley leaned closer to Alex's side. After all, she *had* promised to act lovey-dovey with Alex to make his ex-fiancée jealous. She looked up at him and met his eyes. He smiled at her and squeezed her shoulder. *Hmmm. Who exactly,* thought Charley, *was benefiting from the warm glow that spread through her as she nestled even closer?*

Out of the corner of her eye, Charley caught Karen's gaze shifting back and forth from Alex to her. When Charley looked over, Karen smiled warmly, then looked away with a pleased expression on her face. Charley forced her attention away from the pleasant and soothing feel of Alex's fingers on her shoulder to concentrate on the auctioneer's voice as he described the first item to be auctioned off for charity.

The items up for auction ranged from all-expenses-paid trips and spa treatments to motorcycles, a car, and sculptures and artwork by local artists. All items had been donated by citizens and businesses of Charleston. Bids on the items came in quickly from the guests in support of cancer research.

Charley's mind wandered as a motorcycle went up for auction and quickly went to someone in the back of the room. Then the auctioneer made an announcement that brought her attention back fully on the auction. Caught off guard, she almost gasped out loud.

"Our next item," the auctioneer said, "is a sixteen-by-twenty signed, limited-edition, framed photograph by Ce Ce Kane, a famous New York photographer. It was donated by the Lower King Street Art Gallery of Charleston. Do I have an opening bid of three thousand dollars?"

Charley sat dumbfounded as the auctioneer held up one of her photographs, which she had taken in the Falkland Islands. A large group of gentoo penguins were lined up in single file, readying themselves to dive off the frozen blue cliffs into the cold waters of the South Atlantic. Charley vividly remembered the day she had taken that photo. The temperature had been brutally cold. She had to keep blowing on her frozen fingers so they wouldn't stiffen up and prevent her from operating the camera. There must have been at least twenty-five penguins lined up on the ridge, and more were marching into view from behind the plateau. They followed each other like soldiers. None hesitated at the edge, but just jumped off the cliff, one after another. She had managed to catch four in flight on their dive down into the icy water below. The shot was as perfect as the shot of the baby egrets in flight that she and Alex had photographed this past week.

"Three thousand," shouted someone.

"Five thousand," shouted another. Charley recognized the voice and turned to see Eric Winston holding up his auction paddle.

"Ten thousand," Alex bid.

Eric answered with fifteen thousand.

Everyone else in the audience stopped bidding, as they recognized that a bidding war was brewing between the two men that would price the photo out of their bidding range.

The bids went back and forth until Eric raised his bid to twenty-five thousand.

"Thirty thousand," Alex countered.

Eric laughed, then threw up his hands in surrender.

Charley was mortified and shocked that Alex had bid so much for the photograph. And she felt guilty. She couldn't give him a copy of that specific photo, but she could give him a similar one for free. The fact that the money was for cancer research soothed her guilt over Alex's bid—but just barely.

Charley's thoughts were spinning. She needed to tell Alex that she was Ce Ce Kane. But how could she tell him now, after all the time they'd spent together talking about photography and she'd failed to mentioned it? He might think she had purposely hidden the information from him, but one thing was for sure: he would feel like a fool and blame her for it. He had spent thirty thousand dollars on a photograph, and the photographer was sitting quietly by his side. He had told her earlier that he didn't trust his judgment where women were concerned, and this incident would not reassure him that his judgment had improved.

The event wrapped up not long after the auction ended. Alex and Charley said goodbye to Mrs. Maitland and thanked her for the wonderful evening. Alex became unusually quiet as they left the Maitland estate and drove through Charleston. Each time Charley tried to engage him in conversation, while not rude, his comments were brief and to the point, before falling back into his private thoughts. Was he regretting bidding so much for the photograph?

The auction house would deliver the photo to Alex's office on Monday. She needed to tell him she was the photographer before then. But how should she broach the subject? The best way, she decided, was to invite him in for a nightcap when they reached her house and tell him then.

Do it! Quit stalling! You know you should, Charley's inner voice silently lectured her as they neared the beach house. Yes, but how? She was formulating the words and how to begin her confession when her attention was diverted by a car parked beside hers in the driveway. She immediately recognized the black SUV with New Jersey license plates.

"Aunt Beth!" Charley cried as she opened the car door, barely giving Alex time to stop. She raced up the steps. Two figures rose from the rockers on the dimly lit front porch. "Aunt Beth! Uncle Lance! Why didn't you tell me you were coming?"

"We called earlier this evening, but got your voice mail," Aunt Beth said. "We apologize for popping in on you uninvited. Lance had a business meeting in Richmond that wrapped up early, so it was a spur-of-the-moment decision. Since we were close, we decided to come down and visit you." Aunt Beth looked behind Charley at Alex. "Hi, I'm Beth Rainier, Charley's aunt. This is my husband, Lance."

"Sorry," Charley said. "I'm forgetting my manners. I'm just in shock over finding you here on my porch." Charley turned to Alex. "This is Alex Morgan. We just came from a charity ball and fundraiser."

Alex stepped forward and shook their hands. He peered closely at Lance in the dim light. "You're *the* Lance Rainier? The famous football player? I used to watch you as a kid."

"As a kid, huh? Boy, that makes me feel old. But yes, I once played football. I don't know how famous I am, since I've been retired for over twenty years. You're pretty famous too, Alex. We've heard a lot about you from Charley."

"He lives next door. We're neighbors," Charley said as color rose in her cheeks. She was certain that talking about a close neighbor wasn't unusual, so why was she blushing?

"I see," Beth said with slight smile. "Neighbors." Aunt Beth didn't sound convinced that being neighbors was the reason why Charley mentioned Alex every time she called them. Well, he was the one she had spent all her time with lately, so naturally she'd bring him up.

Alex talked with them for a few minutes, then excused himself. "I'll go and let you visit with your aunt and uncle," he said to Charley. He then turned to Beth and Lance. "I'll see you tomorrow, if you're around."

"Sure thing," Lance replied as he took the house key Charley handed him. He unlocked the door, and he and Beth went inside, leaving Charley and Alex alone on the porch.

Alex turned to leave, and Charley walked down to the bottom of the steps with him.

"Thanks for inviting me. Your family is wonderful. I had a great time," Charley said.

"Thank you for going. My family has their good moments," Alex replied with a slight smile. He reached out and placed both hands on Charley's arms. She leaned toward him, but Alex paused, ignoring her invitation for a goodnight kiss. Charley had a momentary urge to ignore his hesitancy, pull his head down and kiss him. That would be the perfect ending to her perfect evening. She quickly dropped the idea, though. Alex didn't appear to be thinking along those lines.

"Goodnight. I'll see you tomorrow," Alex said quietly. He squeezed her arms lightly then dropped his hands to his side. He turned away, and walked to his car.

Charley stood at the foot of the steps and watched him walk across the sandy yard to the driveway. He waved one last time, got into his car, and backed up.

That was odd, Charley thought as she watched Alex drive the short distance to his house. And, *poof*, just like that, the magical evening was over. Alex had made a 180-degree turn from the attentive partner he'd been at the ball less than two hours ago. Now, he was an aloof man that left her abruptly standing in the driveway. What had changed his mood? Charley stood at the bottom of the steps for a moment longer and gazed up into the star-filled sky. It was a beautiful night, but the universe didn't offer any explanation for Alex's behavior, either.

Charley had her disappointment well hidden by the time she climbed the steps and entered the house. Uncle Lance stood near the foot of the stairs with their luggage. Charley directed him up the stairs and to the guest bedroom.

"Charley, we're sorry if we interrupted your evening," Aunt Beth apologized from where she sat in the living room. "We did try to call."

"You didn't interrupt anything. We didn't have further plans. We're just neighbors. I'm going to change out of these clothes, and then we can catch up."

"Charley," Aunt Beth said as Charley turned to go to her bedroom. "Alex seems very nice. And he's *very* handsome."

"He is all that, but honestly, Aunt Beth, we're friends, nothing more. I'm still trying to get over Daniel, and Alex may not yet be over his ex-fiancée."

Charley left the room, but heard an "Uh-huh" from Aunt Beth as she went down the hall to change her clothes.

Charley stepped out of her dress, then pulled a pair of denim shorts out of the drawer of the armoire and angrily pulled them on. She was mad at herself. She'd had her relationship with Alex all sorted out after the kiss in the marsh. But then, tonight, she's felt all these crazy emotions and longings after just one dance with him. She'd let her imagination run wild and misconstrued Alex's friendliness as romantic overtures.

She grabbed a T-shirt and pulled it over her head. The shirt caught on her braided hair. She sat down on the side of the bed and untangled her hair before pulling the shirt over her head fully this time. Why was she acting like a teenager who was miffed that the hottest guy in the class didn't kiss her on prom night? Alex had been the perfect escort this evening and hadn't given her any indication that they were anything other than friends and neighbors. What she felt had been *her* fantasy. What she felt now was foolish!

But she would have liked more warmth on the drive home and less stiffness in his goodbye in the driveway. Even friends expected that. And although the evening hadn't ended exactly as she expected, the night had still been magical.

And as for her comment to Aunt Beth about her still getting over Daniel, that was an obvious lie. Daniel was rarely in her thoughts lately, while her *neighbor* seemed to be constantly on her mind.

CHAPTER ELEVEN

Charley, Aunt Beth, and Uncle Lance were having their coffee on the front porch the next morning when Alex came by on his way to his beach run with Rex.

"Alex," Charley called from the porch railing, "come have coffee with us."

Alex didn't break his stride, but changed directions and very quickly was at the top of the stairs. He stepped onto the porch with Rex right behind him.

"Don't be afraid." Charley smiled as she poured a cup of coffee from the thermal carafe on a nearby table and handed it to him. She pointed to the cream and sugar on the table. "Aunt Beth made the coffee this morning."

Alex's brow wrinkled as he accepted the cup of coffee from her, and he looked at her with a question in his eyes. He added cream and stirred the coffee.

"Don't pretend you don't know what I'm talking about! I know why you vigorously refused my offer to make coffee and insisted on buying it from the Island Café before our photo shoots last week." Charley touched Alex's forearm and laughed.

"I spotted real fear in your eyes the first time I suggested I'd make it."

"Oh, that! I was just hoping to avoid 'death by coffee.' And I was being nice by saving us both the effort of making it." Alex chuckled as he playfully reached out and tweaked a tendril of Charley's hair near her cheek. His eyes sparkled as he looked at her over the top of his coffee cup and took a sip. "But this is good."

"'Death by coffee'? That's your idea of nice? What made you think I make bad coffee?"

"My first clue was when we were grocery shopping at Whitaker's Market and you asked me how many *cups* of ground coffee were needed to make a pot. I figured you were entering brand-new territory in making your own coffee."

"Point taken," Charley replied with a shrug as she sat back down in her chair. "I'm used to stopping at a coffee shop every morning. But you exaggerate. I meant how many *spoonfuls* of coffee were needed to make a pot, but thanks for pointing out the directions on the can. I admit, my coffee sometimes resembles mud, but I'm learning."

"It's not hard, but make sure to have lots of cream and sugar on hand," Alex countered. He leaned casually against the porch railing and smiled broadly at Charley. His coolness from the night before was gone, and he was back to teasing and bantering with her. Charley definitely preferred the man who smiled warmly at her now over the quiet man from last night.

"Come here, Rex," Alex said. "Lie down." Rex ignored Alex's command and stood by Charley as she scratched behind his ear. "Come, Rex. Lie down." Rex ignored Alex's command again and plopped down at Charley's feet.

"I guess he knows who has the treats." Charley took a treat out of the bag on the table and gave it to Rex.

"I think it's more that he likes beautiful women." Alex met

Charley's eyes, gave her a half smile, then looked away.

Charley looked down and patted Rex's head as a flush crept over her cheeks. Normally, she wouldn't be embarrassed by an inferred compliment, but it was the speculation in Aunt Beth's eyes as she looked on from across the table that caused Charley's blush. Charley avoided her aunt's eyes and focused on giving Rex another treat.

"I'd better get back to my run, or it'll be too hot soon," Alex said, standing up from the railing. "Thanks for the coffee. I look forward to trying a cup you make, Charley. Come, Rex. Let's run." This time, Rex heard the magic word "run," and he rose and trotted toward Alex, eager to get to the beach.

"Count on it. It'll be good!" Charley assured Alex. "You said yourself that it wasn't that hard to make."

"We'll see," Alex laughed. With a wave, he ran down the porch steps.

"Alex, would you like some company?" Lance called as he stood up from his rocker and placed his coffee cup on the table. "I need to get some kinks out from our drive yesterday."

"Sure. I'd love the company," Alex replied as he paused in the yard below. He waited for Lance to join him, then both men began trotting across the road and toward the break in the seagrass-covered dunes. They followed a worn path to the beach.

Charley's eyes followed them. Alex's arms were waving around as he pointed down the beach, an obvious indication to Lance of the route he usually ran.

"Aunt Beth," Charley said as soon as the men had disappeared down the beach, "Alex doesn't know about my pseudonym. He has one of my photos, and well, now he has two. He bid thirty thousand dollars for one last night at the auction."

"Wow! He liked it that much?" Beth's eyes grew round in surprise over the amount.

"I think there's some animosity between him and the other bidder. Alex was the last man standing when the bidding stopped. Plus, Alex and Annabelle were at my last showing in New York."

"What? Really? What a coincidence! Why haven't you told him that you're the photographer?" Beth asked.

"I don't know. Habit, I guess. As you know, I always kept my business life separate from my artistic life, so when I first met him, it didn't seem like something that mattered. I figured I'd be gone soon and that would be that. I never imagined he'd be bidding on my photo at an auction. And now that so much time has gone by, if I tell him, he'll think I intentionally hid my identity for some reason."

"You need to tell him, but you already know that. Is what he thinks about you important?" Beth asked quietly. She looked intently into Charley's face and waited for the answer. "You know, we've always been truthful with each other."

"I don't want him to think I'm a fraud. We're friends, and I don't want him to think I purposely hid it from him. I met his family last night, and they were very kind and welcomed me as though they had known me for years. They're very nice people, so yes, it does matter what he—and they—think of me." Charley picked apart the paper napkin lying on the table, then gathered the pieces into a pile.

"Charley," Beth started, then paused before continuing, "is Alex becoming more than a friend to you? The way you look at each other as you spar and banter is... well... it indicates to me that there's affection between you."

Charley took a moment before she answered. She searched for words to explain her relationship with Alex. This was her Aunt Beth. She could always spot a lie, even if Charley only thought about telling one. After a long pause, she said, "Honestly, I don't know. We haven't known each other very long, but I'm comfortable with him, and we have fun together. But it's a different feeling than I had with Daniel. I was all shaky and breathless when I first met Daniel. He swept me off my feet without much effort. My feelings for Alex are more… uh, elemental, more basic. Maybe that's the word I'm looking for: elemental. I have a deeper, more stable feeling toward Alex. I'm not all 'schoolgirl giddy' around him. That's friendship, isn't it?'

"It can be friendship," Aunt Beth replied, "but it can also be more. Is that all you feel?"

"Alex respects who I am and what I do." Charley began rambling as she examined out loud, how she felt when she was with Alex—on their photography shoots, on their trip to Pawleys Island, and again last night. "I don't feel like he'd demand that I change. I'm my own person with an equally important job, yet I feel connected to him. I feel important when I'm with him." Charley suddenly stopped. "Oh, I can't believe I'm saying this." She had momentarily forgotten that she was speaking out loud as she sorted through her innermost thoughts. She quickly backtracked. "Forget what I said, Aunt Beth. I'm still caught up in the magic of last night."

"Oh, Charley," Beth said as she reached across the table and clasped Charley's hand. "An 'elemental' feeling, as you put it, is the basis of real love. 'Giddy and breathless' is just infatuation. You were young when you met Daniel. Deeper, more solid, and mature feelings are what you build a lasting relationship on."

"Well, I don't know if he feels anything more than friendship for me. And we're still just getting to know each other. You of all people know how I sometimes let my imagination run wild. Alex hasn't given me any reason to think that he feels more for me than simple friendship. I even wondered last night if he's still hung up on his ex-fiancée. I let myself get carried away just now. Please forget what I said."

"Your imagination is what makes you such a good artist. Well, if Lance gets the chance, I'm sure he'll pump Alex for information on what he feels for you." Aunt Beth laughed. "I can see Lance saying, 'What are your intentions toward my niece?' But Alex looks like a man who can handle your overprotective uncle."

"I don't want to know what Uncle Lance finds out. If he finds out anything. And don't tell Uncle Lance what I just said. I'm just caught up in a fairy tale after the ball we attended last night. Hanging out with beautiful, powerful people can make you see and think things that aren't really there."

"But you've been to many events with beautiful and powerful people in New York," Aunt Beth reminded her.

"But this was different somehow," Charley said. "The historic plantation house with the sweeping staircase that's been owned by the same family for generations; the warm, friendly, genteel people; the music; the food; seeing my print put up for auction—they all combined for a surreal evening." Charley's expression had turned dreamy again.

"It sounds like quite a night," Aunt Beth agreed.

"Yes, it was. There was something truly magical about the whole evening. See? My imagination is off and running again."

"Maybe the person you were with made the difference," Aunt Beth pointed out. "But I won't tell Lance about our conversation. It's our secret."

The Rainiers decided to stay with Charley for a couple of days, since neither Beth nor Lance had pressing business to return to. Alex volunteered to act as tour guide again. He took them to some of the neighboring islands; to see the famous Rainbow Row on East Bay Street in Charleston where houses here were painted in a variety of pastel colors and had been featured in the famous musical *Porgy and Bess;* to see the seawall, called the Battery, its name derived from its origin as an artillery battery built to defend Charleston Harbor during the Civil War. While in the city, they visited a few historic mansions

that were open for guided tours. They drove to Middleton Place
Gardens, and walked through the historic landscaped garden
known for its sculptures, shrub-lined walkways, a lake in the
shape of a butterfly, and a large collection of blooming trees and
plants. Charley took more pictures that she might include in her
book.

On Monday night, they ate dinner at Manny's restaurant.
Beth and Lance were leaving the next morning, so Alex wanted
them to experience "the best seafood in the South." Beth chuckled when she noticed the restaurant's name, The Tides of the
Marsh. Since Manny was a transplanted New Yorker, he spent
several minutes at their table, visiting with Beth and Lance and
reminiscing about the many places in New York and New Jersey
they had in common. After they finished dinner at The Tides,
they returned to Charley's front porch for a glass of wine.

"I could get used to sitting here and watching the ocean
waves," Aunt Beth remarked. "It's so peaceful, it could easily lull
one to sleep." She turned her gaze from the ocean and addressed
Charley and Alex, "I can see why both of you love living here—
and why Annabelle loved it so much."

Aunt Beth's comment reminded Charley that she would
soon need to decide what to do with the beach house—and
about her career. Her editor at the magazine had agreed to her
request for the summer off, but by August or September, they
would need to know whether they could count on her for future
assignments. The magazine wanted her back, but they kept an
active list of freelance photographers that they could call upon
if she didn't return. Someone could easily fill her spot. Hearing
that she could easily be replaced was a jolt, but her editor cush-
ioned her words with the compliment that Charley brought a
uniqueness to her photographs. She didn't want to lose her.

Charley pushed these thoughts aside and decided to just
enjoy the moment. The night was too perfect to worry about

anything that wasn't immediate. She had about two months before she would be forced to decide what she wanted to do.

Aunt Beth and Uncle Lance left early the next morning, saying their goodbyes to Alex and Charley in the driveway. Charley hated to see them go. She would miss their company and activity of the last few days.

Alex was preparing to go into Charleston to his law firm that morning as well. Some problem with the case against Dawson Construction had come up. Charley would have the day to herself, so she asked if Rex could keep her company while Alex was gone.

"I hope your involvement in the Dawson case won't cause trouble between Robert and Corine," Charley commented when Alex walked Rex over to her house.

"It doesn't seem to have affected them thus far. Corine doesn't live at home, so she may not even know what her father's doing. As an architect, Robert doesn't have much contact with Charleston legal proceedings unless it involves his job directly. He may not know much about it, either. But he does know that I won't file a case unless I'm on sound legal grounds. If anyone causes problems in their personal relationship, it won't be me."

As Charley settled in for the morning, she decided to review the photos she had taken during their visit to Pawleys Island. She analyzed the quality of each photo, creating a file for those she might potentially include in her book and rejecting any that were similar or not quite up to her standards. When she came to the one of Alex leaning against the pickup truck and watching her walk toward him, she paused, letting her eyes rove slowly over the photo.

"I think I'll title this one 'Masculinity in Repose.' What do you think, Rex?"

At the sound of his name, Rex raised his head from his

paws. He turned to look at her, but didn't move from his position at her feet.

"I get it. The masculinity of your master doesn't interest you—only the treats and attention he gives you. Your affection is easily bought, huh, Rex?" She bent and scratched Rex behind the ear, then gave him a pat on the head. "But trust my expert opinion, Rex. He does strike a very masculine and handsome pose. That he does! My book would be an instant bestseller if I put this picture on the front cover."

Charley had finished reviewing a large portion of the photos when she finally stood up and stretched. It was now late afternoon, and she had been sitting for some time. She had taken a break only to eat lunch and feed Rex. She decided to make a quick trip to The Tides to get takeout for dinner that evening. Alex still had not returned to the beach house when she arrived back home.

"You want to go to the beach, Rex?" she asked.

They spent about an hour on the beach. Rex chased seagulls while Charley took off her shoes and casually strolled along the water's edge, letting the cool water wash over her feet.

She and Rex had just returned to the beach house and were relaxing on the porch when Alex drove into his driveway, parked, and walked back to her place. He had already removed his coat and tie. He climbed the stairs, then sagged into one of the rockers beside Charley on the porch. Tired lines creased his face, but he smiled at her as he reached down and patted Rex's head.

"Tough day?" Charley asked.

"A little." Alex stretched out his long legs in front of him. "Dawson's lawyers are using any argument they can to stall and deny Dawson's involvement in the illegal dumping. The sheriff caught Dawson's men in the act of moving the contaminates to the island, but Dawson claims the men were doing this on their own and not at his direction. According to him, he told his men to dispose of the chemicals properly. He's blaming his men." Alex mouth twisted in a grimace. "The judge shot that argument down quickly. After the court session, I spent some time at the firm convincing Mrs. Maitland that she shouldn't acquire a company she has her eye on. It has terrible financial projections. She wouldn't take anyone else's advice about the company and wanted my opinion. I think she just likes to annoy me."

"She must trust you a lot."

"She wants everyone to do her bidding—on her schedule. And we do." Alex sighed. "She has power, and she's not afraid to use it."

"Have you eaten?" Charley asked as Alex leaned his head back against the rocker and closed his eyes. "I have chicken parmesan—enough for two."

Alex opened one eye and gave Charley a suspicious look.

She added, "You're hurting my feelings, Alex Morgan. Trust me, it's good."

Alex still looked skeptical.

Charley decided he was too tired to be teased. "It's takeout from The Tides. Manny has a good selection of Italian on his menu, too. I figured we needed something other than seafood for a change."

Alex visibly relaxed.

"Don't look so relieved. My cooking isn't that bad."

"I'm sure it's delicious," Alex replied with a smile, but his words held little conviction. "I'd love to join you for the chicken parmesan. I barely have the energy to make it home, much less cook."

Charley warmed up their food and brought it out to the table on the porch, along with plates, silverware, a bottle of wine, and two glasses. As the moon began to rise over the ocean, Charley and Alex relaxed and shared stories of the day's activities. Charley couldn't help but compare this relaxed evening with the evenings she had shared with Daniel. They were rare to begin with and were often interrupted by phone calls that Daniel said couldn't wait until later. She never had Daniel's undivided attention as she had now with Alex.

"I've been meaning to ask if you know how Annabelle obtained this sign?" Charley nodded toward the sign at the edge of the porch. She stacked her empty plate on top of Alex's and pushed them to the back of the table. "'*Leig Anail.*' Did it mean something special to her?"

"After Annabelle's husband passed away, she spent more and more time here on the beach. She had me put up the sign for her. It seemed important," Alex explained as he refilled their wine glasses. "Before he passed, they traveled a lot. I imagine she picked it up on one of their trips, probably in Scotland or Ireland. It's Gaelic, isn't it?"

"Yes," said Charley. "In Gaelic, it means 'to rest' or 'to breathe.'"

"Ah, I see," Alex said. "South Carolina has two state mottos, one of which is 'While I breathe, I hope.' The sign may have reminded her of home when she saw it."

"It's very appropriate for here, the beach house, isn't it?"

"It is," Alex said as he relaxed and leaned back in his chair. His eyes closed to smoky slits as he gazed out toward the ocean and the endless darkening horizon. "I always rest and breathe better when I'm here." He closed his eyes completely for a moment.

"I can see that," Charley pointed out with a chuckle. "Tell me more about your day in court before you fall asleep."

Alex went over the major details of his court case as they sipped their wine. The case wasn't concluded yet, but Alex expected that Dawson would have to pay for the cleanup of the damage he'd done to Kings Island, plus a hefty fine. He was also likely to get five years' probation and be subject to a prison term if he was caught dumping hazardous material again.

"I've appeared before Judge Davis before. He doesn't take environmental cases lightly," Alex added. "Judge Davis is fair, but he gets particularly angry when someone sneaks around, trying to hide what they're doing, and then lies when they get caught. So, what about you? How did you fill your day… other than spoiling my dog?"

"Rex is my buddy, aren't you?" Charley reached down and patted Rex on the head. He nuzzled her hand. Charley shared the details of her review of the photos for her book. Still teaching Alex the fine art of photography, she explained what she was looking for as she eliminated certain shots, and outlined the criteria she used for deciding on those that were acceptable for publication.

They were both yawning when Alex stood up.

"As much as I like the company, I think we both need to get some sleep. Come, Rex." Alex hugged Charley goodbye. "Thanks for dinner." He kissed her on the forehead, then turned and walked down the stairs and across the yard toward his house. Rex obediently trailed behind him.

Charley remained on the porch and watched him until he climbed the steps and entered his house.

"A brotherly kiss," she mumbled into the night air. "But that's better than the almost-handshake on the night of the fundraiser." Since the night of the charity ball, Alex had not been the cool and aloof man who had left her standing alone at the foot of the steps, but was warm and friendly as before. He didn't give an explanation for what had been bothering him, or give any indication that after their magical night he now wanted anything more from her than friendship. They were neighbors, nothing more.

CHAPTER TWELVE

Charley pulled into a parking spot in front of a small, un-
assuming brick building on Broad Street in Charleston.
She climbed the short flight of stairs to the second floor
and stopped in front of an office. 'Lynn Calhoun, Historian and
Genealogy Researcher' was printed in gold letters on a name-
plate beside the frosted-glass door.

Charley took a deep breath and pushed open the door.
She had hired Ms. Calhoun a couple weeks ago to research the
Mathews family and find out if she had relatives living in the
area. The city librarian had recommended Ms. Calhoun and
promised Charley that she was one of the best researchers of
family genealogy in Charleston. If there were lost family connections to be found, she could find them.

"Have a seat." Ms. Calhoun invited. She was a tall, sparse
woman that Charley guessed to be in her mid-fifties. She indicated the chair in front of her desk. "I've gathered some information for you."

"I'm anxious to hear it, Ms. Calhoun." Charley clenched her
hands together in front of her, opening and closing her fingers

nervously. She was both excited and apprehensive about what
Ms. Calhoun would reveal about the Mathews family history.

"Call me Lynn. Can I call you Charley?" At Charley's nod,
Lynn continued, "You can relax. I didn't find any ax murderers
in your past. A few pirates, maybe, but many people in Charleston have connections to the thieves who once used the marshes
to hide their contraband. Some even amassed fortunes that
way. It's an old city with a long, proud history. But like most old
cities, some parts of its history aren't as pretty as we'd like, especially when viewed according to today's standards."

Despite Lynn's words, Charley was unable to relax. She shifted in her chair and leaned forward. "What did you find?"

"I'm sorry," Lynn said. "I'm getting off-topic, and my come-
dic attempt to lighten the mood is not what you're here for. I
do realize how important this is for you. So, let's get to it." She
pulled some documents toward her. "Your Mathews line came
to Charleston from England in the late 1700s. They were mostly
rice and cotton farmers. A few served in the city government.
They weren't as wealthy as some other families, but they weren't
poor, either."

"That's interesting." Charley tried to hide her impatience.
"But do you have anything on my father and more recent generations?"

"I'm getting to that. I have your linage and family tree all
mapped out. I saved it for you on this flash drive." Lynn pushed
a flash drive toward Charley.

"Sorry," Charley apologized. "I'm just anxious to learn about
my father and any living relatives."

"Let's skip forward, then." Lynn pulled another document
from a folder. "As you know, your paternal grandparents are
both deceased, having died within two years of your father's
death. Your father, an only child, was born at Moncks Corner
about thirty miles north of Charleston. I've included a picture

of the house he was born in. It still stands, by the way. Your grandfather had only one sibling, his sister, Annabelle. She had one son, but he was killed in the Vietnam War. He was unmarried and didn't have any children. It appears that living descendants of the Mathews family are few."

"So there's no one alive who is related to me through the Mathews line?" Charley asked, disappointed.

"I didn't say that. But the nearest relative I found is a fourth cousin. And this is a bit apropos: his first name is Mathew, last name Kirkland. He lives near Hilton Head Island. That's only a day trip from here, if you ever want to look him up. I'm sorry I didn't find anyone closer."

"No, that's okay," Charley replied. "You can't create family when there isn't any. A fourth cousin is at least a connection to my father's family, even if only distant."

Charley exited Lynn Calhoun's office feeling only slightly let down. The fact that Lynn found no living relative closer than a fourth cousin was, in a way, a positive outcome. It meant the Mathews family had not willingly abandoned her after her father's death. Natural attrition in an already-small family was what had left her without close relatives on her father's side. Her mother's anguish and vitriol were what drove her Mathews grandparents away, and they both died not long after Aunt Beth took Charley to live in New Jersey. Before she left the area for good, she would at least visit her father's birthplace and also seek out Mathew Kirkland. Maybe he'd want to meet a long-lost cousin. He might even have pictures and could fill in personal details missing from Lynn's genealogy charts, especially about her grandparents.

Charley's next stop in Charleston was the art gallery located on Lower King Street—the one that had donated her photograph to the charity auction. She parked in the Charleston Visitor Center parking garage and walked toward King Street.

She stopped frequently to browse the antiques and home décor displayed in store windows. Soon, she reached her destination: the Lower King Street Art Gallery.

Charley entered the gallery and walked around, looking at the paintings displayed on easels and on the wall. One painting immediately caught her eye. In it, two women and a young girl knelt on the beach next to an open pit in the sand. One woman was pulling a leathery-looking egg from inside the pit. A pile of eggs lay on a burlap bag next to the pit, while the other woman was placing them in a Styrofoam cooler nearby. The young girl looked on with her eyes widened in awe.

"A lovely painting, don't you think?"

Charley turned toward the voice. A woman about her age stood at her elbow. "It's beautiful," Charley replied. "What are they doing?"

"They're moving a loggerhead turtle's nest."

"Doesn't that destroy the nest? Sorry for the questions, but as you can tell, I'm new to the area."

"No problem. I don't mind sharing what I know. Moving the nest does quite the opposite—if done properly—and this painting captures the process beautifully. Look closely. See how close the water comes to the nest? High tide would eventually wash away the sand and expose the eggs to predators. The nest is also in the path of beach walkers and sunbathers. The tide and humans are two of the biggest threats to turtle nests."

"Where do they move them to?" Charley was intrigued by the process as depicted by the painting.

"Higher on the beach and hopefully out of the way of human traffic. But it can sometimes be merely a hopeful endeavor. If they move the nest too far from the ocean, the hatchlings will be lucky to make it into the water before seagulls and other predatory wildlife grab them. Once the nests are moved, they're marked with orange tape tied to stakes driven into the ground."

"Fascinating." Charley nodded.

The dangers that Alex and his band of environmentalists tried to prevent was now a little clearer. Alex said they needed to get Kings Island cleaned up before the turtle-nesting season began. And since it was hard to predict when instinct would send the females to the beach, the cleanup needed to happen right away.

"Is this painting for sale?" Charley asked. She was suddenly struck with an idea. She knew the perfect place to hang it.

"It is. It's here on consignment from the artist, Gena Middleton. I think she signed the back."

Of course! The rich colors and the brush technique were similar to the paintings she had seen at the Harrison house on Pawleys Island. The painting was done by Mrs. Harrison's daughter, Gena.

"I'd like to buy it." Charley wanted to purchase it even more, now that she knew who the artist was.

She left the gallery with the painting in her possession. She couldn't wait to show Alex. He had invited her over for dinner—the rain check for the night she had declined his invitation after her return from Costa Rica. She had received a text from him earlier, updating her on their dinner plans: "Rain coming. Double rain check on my 'fabulous' steaks. Pan-seared blackened salmon okay?"

"Only if the salmon is also 'fabulous,'" Charley had texted back.

A thumbs-up emoji was Alex's reply.

Charley arrived back at the beach house with just enough time to shower and change before she walked across the yard to Alex's house. Rex met her at the door and danced in circles around her, happy to see her. She pulled a treat from her pocket and gave it to him, along with a hug.

"You're spoiling my dog again," Alex accused as he accepted

the bottle of wine she offered. He hugged her warmly. His arms lingered around her for a long moment before he released her. Then, he noticed the other object in her hand.

"What's this?" Alex indicated the painting in her hands.

"I brought you a present to fill that blank spot on your wall." She indicated the wall behind the arm chair in the living room. A hanger was already there, but it was empty. Charley wondered if a picture of Alex and Rebecca had once hung there. She stepped forward and hung the painting on the wall behind the chair. It fit the space perfectly. She stood back and waited for his reaction.

"Beautiful!" Alex exclaimed. He stepped closer to take a look. "The sand looks so real, and the artist captured the process of moving a nest perfectly. The look on the child's face is priceless."

"Do you recognize the artist?" Charley asked. "Look at the brilliance of the colors in the sky and the white-capped waves of the tide coming in."

Alex studied the painting a minute longer. "Gena Harrison."

"Almost correct. Gena Middleton—her married name."

"It's beautiful," Alex said again. "And that's the perfect spot to hang it." He placed his hands on both sides of Charley's face, pulled her close, and gave her a long, slow kiss. Not brotherly at all. "Thank you," he said quietly.

He started to pull away, but Charley obeyed her sudden urge and wrapped her arms around his neck, pulling him back. She rose up on her tiptoes and kissed him—a soft but lingering kiss. "I should bring you presents more often," she whispered when the kiss ended.

"The kiss is present enough," Alex answered with a smile. The timer on the oven went off. "I absolutely want to continue this later," he added softly, "but right now, if I don't get that timer, we'll have blackened herb-roasted potatoes to go with our blackened salmon."

"Okay," Charley agreed, dropping her arms from around his neck. One kiss from Alex was apparently enough to crumble her earlier resolve to avoid a summer romance and stay focused on her life plan. She would inspect this new development later.

"Is there anything I can do to help?" Charley asked. "Alex, don't look at me like that!" Charley reprimanded with a laugh when he looked at her skeptically. "I didn't mean I'd cook. I meant I set a 'fabulous' table."

Alex removed the roasted potatoes from the oven and set the pan on the stovetop burner. He pointed to the cupboard. "You should find plates in there. Silverware's in the drawer below." He opened the bottle of wine she had brought and poured two glasses before turning to the stove to prepare the salmon. The patter of rain began to echo on the tin roof of the beach house. It fell gently at first, but as the storm moved closer, the noise reverberated through the room.

"That's a squall coming in off the ocean," Alex yelled over the din of the storm. "Small ones come in frequently during the afternoon at certain times of the year. They usually don't last long, but this one sounds like it might be stronger than usual."

"I love the sound of rain," Charley yelled back. "The sound on the tin roof makes it cozy in here—where it's dry, of course."

It didn't take Alex long to prepare their dinner. He held Charley's chair out for her, then placed a plate of blackened salmon, roasted potatoes, and steamed green beans in front of her. He sat down in the chair across from her. The storm slowed enough that they could hear each other speak. Their dinner conversation soon turned to the painting Charley had bought for Alex.

"Moving the turtles' nests was a project originally started by just two women," Alex informed her. "They noticed that the nests were becoming threatened as more and more humans were visiting the area. Their original efforts have since grown into a variety of coordinated programs all across the beaches on the Atlantic coastline in the South and the Gulf Coast."

"Some of the most impactful programs start at the grass-roots level, led only by a handful of dedicated people," Charley acknowledged. "Are the turtle programs successful?"

"Moving the nests is mostly successful, but the turtle population is under constant threat. Some threats are from accidents like oils spills that poison the water, but the polluters who don't care for anything other than their bottom line are what angers me the most—like Dawson Construction. With more and more people coming to the area, the push for hotels, houses, and condos is never-ending." Alex frowned, then added, "And even when the eggs safely hatch, the lights from the cities and buildings confuse the hatchlings, so they need assistance in finding their way to the water."

"I guess people don't understand that they're destroying the very thing that draws them here," Charley commented.

Alex reached across the table and took Charley's hand in his. "I get it. I understand why people want to live on the beach and even in a condominium. I love this beach house. But we have to find ways to coexist and save the islands so future generations can enjoy them, too."

"This is your niche, Alex," Charley said as she returned the pressure on her hand. "What are you doing practicing corporate law and not environmental law?"

"It's a long story, but mostly, I didn't know what kind of law I wanted to practice when I graduated from law school. I followed my father and joined his firm, but once I took my first pro bono case for the Save Our Islands organization, I knew that my passion was for environmental law."

"Why didn't you change specialties?"

"Rebecca didn't want me to change. She liked the idea of

being the wife of a corporate attorney. She preferred to social-
ize with the rich and powerful, rather than suing them," Alex
said with an ironic smile. "An environmental lawyer seemed so
'gauche'—her words—so I stayed in mergers and acquisitions at
Winton, Morgan, and Gilbert."

"Speaking of Rebecca," Charley said, then hesitated a moment. It wasn't any of her business, but she was curious. "Was
she the redhead I saw you dancing with at the charity ball?"

"So, you were watching me?" Alex teased. He smiled,
pleased by the flush that spread across Charley's face.

"I, well, I was looking for an escape from my partner at the
time."

"Eric Winston. He can be a bit much, and he's definitely
full of himself," Alex said, nodding in sympathy. "But to answer
your question, yes, that was Rebecca. She asked me to dance
so we could talk." Alex rose from the table and began clearing
away the dishes. "She wanted to apologize for the way our wedding fell apart, and I accepted her apology. It was odd seeing
her and dancing with her again. It brought back memories, but
I agreed with her that we did the right thing. We didn't actually
have as much in common as we thought—or I thought. I see
that now. I don't know where my head was at the time."

"She's beautiful, so maybe that's where your head was—in
love with the idea of a love that came wrapped in a beautiful
package," Charley said as she rose and carried her dishes to the
sink. She rinsed them before placing them in the dishwasher.
She then picked up a dish towel and wiped up the water she had
splattered on the counter.

Alex smiled. "Maybe. I'd hate to think I'm that shallow, but
you may be right. A package can be beautifully wrapped and
still not be the item you thought you ordered. My parents' marriage is the only model I had, and they're so happy that I guess I
thought all marriages were like theirs."

"Rebecca missed out on having a great cook, that's for sure. The dinner was delicious, Alex. I promise to learn more about cooking and return the favor."

"Humph!" Alex said with a smile. "You either have it, or you don't."

Charley slapped him on the arm with the dish towel. "How did you learn to be such a good cook? Did your mother teach you?"

"Hardly," Alex replied. "My grandmother lived with us for a while after my grandfather died. My mother worked, so Grams was there when Robert and I got home from school. She cooked dinner each night. She started out by asking me to peel vegetables or do some other small task. Then, the jobs became bigger and more complicated. I discovered that I liked cooking—turning raw ingredients into something tasty. It was challenging. I could either cook or do my homework."

Charley laughed. She had a hard time picturing Alex as a young teenager in an apron. "What type of food did she cook? Did she have a specialty?"

"Grams could cook almost anything, but her dishes were primarily Southern, Creole, and Italian. She would lay out the ingredients for whatever she had planned for dinner, then ask me what we could add that would make the dish extra special. I would come up with different cooking methods or a new combo of spices and change up the recipe. When Grams passed away, I continued cooking dinner for the family until I graduated from high school and went off to college."

Alex wiped up the stove top, then looked at Charley. "Didn't your mom teach you anything about cooking? I realize she didn't teach you to make coffee, but maybe something else?"

"No," Charley replied, "and stop picking on my coffee." Charley smiled, but a sadness settled inside her.

She didn't want to talk about her life after her father's death.

Her situation until she went to live with Aunt Beth still bothered her. At eight, she hadn't been very creative with cereal, crackers, and peanut butter that she found in the cupboard. But she was resourceful and managed to hide her situation from her teachers and others she came in contact with.

"My mother wasn't the domestic type," Charley replied. "Or, at least, she wasn't after my father died. I mostly lived with Aunt Beth. She didn't cook much, either, but that was because she started her own company shortly after I came to live with them. Uncle Lance was retired by then, so he did the cooking." Charley wanted to change the subject. That was all a lifetime ago, and she didn't want to bring it into the conversation tonight. "Did Robert cook after you went to college?"

"Nah, but he was good at ordering takeout, though. He'd get lost in drawing up architectural designs on his computer and forget the time." Alex paused, then added, "He's a good architect now, so I guess it paid off."

They worked companionably as they cleaned up the kitchen, laughing whenever they bumped into each other as they moved around the small space. The rain had slowed to a steady hum on the roof by the time they finished. They settled down together on the sofa in the living room. Rex emptied his bowl of food, then plopped down in his bed in the corner and was soon fast asleep. Charley settled back against the cushions and relaxed. Alex leaned over and brushed her lips with his, then picked up their wine glasses to refill.

"I found three possible wide-angle lenses online that will work with your camera," Charley said. "You know, the lenses I was telling you about the day we went to Pawleys Island? I wrote down the name of the company and the item numbers in my phone. Do you have a piece of paper and a pen? I'll copy them down for you."

"There should be some in the desk. Middle drawer," Alex

directed as walked toward the kitchen with their wine glasses. He filled the glasses, capped the bottle, then turned to pick up the filled glasses.

Charley walked to the desk and pulled open the drawer. She shuffled through the contents, looking for a pad of paper and a pen. She stopped suddenly when her hand knocked against a folder and the contents slipped out into the drawer.

"What's this?" Charley asked as a familiar portrait slid partially out of the folder. She pulled it all the way out. The face in the photograph was none other than her own. It was a headshot done by the magazine she worked for. "What's this?" Charley repeated.

She picked up the folder and opened it. "Oh my god!" She numbly flipped through the other documents in the folder. Her face blanched, and her breath stopped. There were candid photos of her on the streets of New York. One was of her having dinner with her friends. In another, she was going into her divorce attorney's office. The words on the papers were blurred by the tears in her eyes, but she could read most of them: "Rainier... Phillips... age twenty-eight... birthplace, Atlanta, Georgia... photographer."

"Alex, what *is* this? You've been spying on me?" She couldn't believe what she was seeing: private details of her life in a folder in Alex's house. "Oh my god!" Charley's voice caught in her throat. She turned and looked at Alex as angry sobs clogged her throat. Her hands trembled. "Why? Why would you spy on me?"

"No! It's not what you think." Alex moved from his frozen position and quickly approached her. He reached out and tried to pull the folder from her hands. "I wouldn't spy on you. I don't even know what's in this folder."

Charley pulled the folder out of his reach. Her face twisted in anger. "These photos and documents tell a different story."

The heat from her anger had dried her tears, but the anger now turned into rage. She steadied her voice. "Even a photo of me on the day of my divorce? This is who you are! Spying on me at my most vulnerable time? You pretend to care about me? About other people? You're a fraud!"

"Charley, please, don't! Let me explain." Alex reached out to touch her, but she shrugged out of his reach. She threw the folder at him, hitting him in the face. Papers and pictures bounced off his cheekbone and spread across the floor.

"Don't touch me! You're despicable!" Charley yelled as she pushed past him and stormed toward the door. "Don't speak to me! You're a fraud! I never want to see you again!"

"Charley, wait! I can explain!" Alex ran after her. He reached her at the edge of the stairs and tried to stop her.

"Get away from me!" Charley screamed, slapping at his hands. The rain was coming down hard again, but Charley didn't stop. She ran down the steps, across the soggy yard, and up the steps to her house.

Alex hurried after her, pleading for her to listen. "Charley, please, let me explain," he begged as Charley slammed the door in his face. The loud click of the dead bolt followed.

"I said, leave me alone!" Charley yelled through the door. Her voice choked with a new wave of tears. "Go away! Just leave me alone! I never want to see you again!"

Charley's clothes were soaked, and rain streamed down her hair in rivulets. She fled to her bedroom. Ignoring her wet clothes, she fell face-down on her bed. Charley's sobs and the rain on the tin roof drowned out the pounding on the door as Alex begged her to let him explain. By the time she had exhausted all her tears, the pounding on the door had ceased.

Charley's anger resurfaced again. She pounded her fists into the mattress. "I knew it! I never should have trusted him." She punched her pillow. "I knew he was too good to be true—always offering to help and using his sweet dog to get close to me. It was all a trick just to get me to trust him. A con game! All the time he was nice to me, he was collecting information on me."

Charley gulped back a fresh sob. She should've known how this would turn out. She couldn't trust anyone. First her mother, then Daniel. Alex was Daniel all over again, selfish and conniving! She had thought he was different. He'd claimed that business took him to New York when he attended her art exhibit with Annabelle. Ha! Another lie. He had also used Aunt Annabelle to spy on her. The proof was plain and in his possession: the pictures hidden in his desk drawer. The thought of the folder full of her private information set off a new round of tears.

After a few minutes, the tears ceased, and her anger was back. She was done with crying. Alex wasn't worth her tears. He was just another deceitful man. She seemed to have a knack for finding them, no matter where she lived. She would go back to her original plans. She'd finish her book, and at the end of the summer, she'd put the beach house up for rent. She'd return to her familiar life in New York and forget the Alex Morgan phase of her life. Another hard lesson learned. With her future plans decided, an exhausted Charley fell into a restless sleep in her soggy clothes.

Her dreams were filled with island scenes featuring her and Alex laughing together as they roamed the marshes and beaches, taking photographs. Hovering in her subconscious mind were nagging questions that didn't fit the happy images in her dreams. *Why would he spy on her? Why had he compiled a folder on her? And for what purpose?*

Charley woke as dawn was lightening the eastern sky over the ocean. She rolled over onto her back. Her anger renewed itself as she thought about last night.

"What underhanded game are you playing, Alex?" Charley asked out loud. She rubbed her eyes to unstick her lashes from where they had dried as she cried herself to sleep last night. She sat up in bed. Her eyes were fully open now—in more ways than one.

Charley was done with crying, and she was done with trusting anyone. Charley Mathews was once again on her own, just like she had been when she was eight years old and later when she had divorced Daniel. She had survived those heartbreaks, and she would survive this one, too.

CHAPTER THIRTEEN

Alex's father had summoned him to an urgent meeting with Mrs. Maitland at the law firm in Charleston this morning. He was tired and in a black mood—an angry black mood—and it didn't improve as his pickup got closer to the office. This meeting with the Gang of Three was particularly ill-timed, since all he could think about was Charley throwing the folder in his face and storming out of his house last night. He was primed and ready to unload on all three of them.

What a mess he had made in everything concerning Charley.

The romantic evening he'd planned for last night had come crashing down around his head. He'd thought that he and Charley might get over distrust left from their past relationships and explore something beyond casual friendship. Screwing up was becoming a habit with him where Charley was concerned.

He had messed up the night of the charity ball. After seeing Rebecca and being reminded of all the hurt and humiliation she had put him through, he had combed through their relationship, looking for any signs he had missed that should have warned him that a breakup was coming. His behavior that night had nothing to do with Charley, but he hadn't bothered to explain it, either. How could he explain when he didn't completely understand himself? After he dropped Charley off, he spent the night examining his breakup with Rebecca. Alex finally reached a conclusion. It was the shock and his bruised ego, more than the loss of Rebecca, that had soured him on love at the time.

As Alex's sleepless night dragged on, Charley became all he could think about. The feeling of her in his arms as they danced at the charity ball had sparked a longing for something that was missing in his life, and that longing centered around Charley. It had snuck up on him after their impromptu kiss in the marsh. After the night of the ball, Charley had taken over almost all of his waking thoughts.

Alex had wrestled all of his fears of loving someone again into submission by the time dawn arrived the morning after the fundraiser. He was over the past. His talk with Rebecca had closed an old wound left raw by the way things had ended, not *because* things had ended. When Charley called to him from her porch the next morning as he took Rex on his run and they bantered about her coffee-making skills, memories of his life with Rebecca were not even a blip on his radar. Only thoughts of Charley had filled his head. And, he thought he saw a few glimmers suggesting that she might feel something for him. If her aunt and uncle hadn't been there, he would have tested his theory that very morning. Charley might have pushed him over the porch railing, but it would have been worth the effort.

Their romantic evening last night was intended to make up for his previous behavior. And then, it had been ruined by the three people he was now on his way to meet. Mrs. Maitland was primarily at fault, but she had been aided by his father and Mr. Winston. They were all in it together.

Charley had refused to let him explain. But, really, what

could he have told her? He hadn't known himself what was in the folder. His handlers hadn't even told him *why* there was a folder on her in the first place. It was stupid of him to think that the hands-off approach he had adopted could save him from negative fallout from his "mission."

Alex had spent the night sitting on the front porch as the rain, aided by a strong sand-laden wind, blew in over him. His clothes became soaked, his hair plastered to his head, and the sand stung his eyes, but he didn't move. At one point, a brief thought that he should get drunk wormed its way into his mind, but he quickly discarded that idea. That would just give him another headache in the morning, and he needed a clear head to decide how to fix the situation with Charley—if he even could. But before he could begin fixing anything, he had to find out what the situation was and what he was even trying to fix.

The only solace Alex found as he sat brooding on his porch was when Rex nudged his hand, then placed his head on Alex's knee and looked soulfully up at him.

"I know, Rex," Alex said as he rubbed Rex's head. "I really messed up this time. Will you still be my friend if we've lost Charley forever?"

Rex tilted his head to the side, a question in his eyes.

Alex had to laugh in spite of his brooding. "I can't believe she's gone either, buddy."

Alex continued to rub Rex's head as all the what-ifs continued to tumble through his mind. What if he had refused to participate in this scheme? What if he had refused the folder his father had given him? What if he had left it at his home in Charleston, rather than taken it to the beach? What if he hadn't put it in the desk? What if he'd told Charley to just text him the information about camera lenses instead of sending her in search of paper and pen in the desk drawer?

It gave him something to think about as the hours dragged

on, but that was about all it accomplished. It was too late for what-ifs. It was time for "What now?"

He wanted to be anywhere but at the office this morning, but the office was where the information he needed would be found. He was angry with all of them for roping him into whatever harebrained scheme they had going on. They had robbed him of... something. He wasn't sure exactly what that something was, but they had definitely robbed him of the chance to find out.

"It's her! I know it is!" Mrs. Maitland stated excitedly as Alex opened the door to Mr. Winston's office and walked in.

He was on time for the meeting, so the discussion must have started early. He took a seat next to his father on the sofa facing Mr. Winston's desk. Mrs. Maitland paced back and forth on the carpeted floor between the sofa and Mr. Winston. Alex's plan had been to just sit, listen, and stubbornly refuse to participate in the meeting, but that wouldn't get him the answers he needed. No more going along with only knowing bits and pieces of the scheme they had conceived.

"What do you mean by 'It's *her*'? Who is '*her*'?" Alex addressed Mrs. Maitland. "And how do you know it's 'her'?" He scowled.

Mrs. Maitland stopped pacing and leaned her arms against the back of a chair in front of Mr. Winston's desk. "I'm talking about Charley. I spoke with her at the charity ball. Her looks and mannerisms leave me certain that she's who I'm looking for," Mrs. Maitland replied as she turned toward Alex. "Her DNA will prove it."

"Well, don't look to me to get a DNA sample. I'm done," Alex stated.

Mr. Morgan gently elbowed Alex in the ribs. Alex got his father's unspoken message: "Watch what you say and how you say it to our biggest and most important client."

"You don't have to get a DNA sample, Alex. I have the wine glass Ms. Mathews used the night of the ball. Typically, the DNA results take a couple weeks, but I've asked the lab to put a rush on it." Mrs. Maitland spoke as though asking a lab to rush a DNA test was no big deal. For her, it wasn't.

Alex's mouth fell open. He rubbed both hands over his face as he groaned inwardly. He wanted to be respectful to Mrs. Maitland, but she was pushing him over the edge. It wouldn't take much more to make him explode, in spite of her being their biggest client. He cooled his anger. He needed answers, and pissing off his handlers wouldn't help him get them.

"Alex," Mr. Winston spoke up in Mrs. Maitland's defense, "we were getting nowhere, otherwise. You hadn't uncovered anything. You obviously got distracted by Ms. Mathews' pretty face."

Mr. Winston's comment was like nails scraping across a blackboard. "She is who she says she is. That was what I was asked to find out. Only that! Was I supposed to come right out and ask, 'Is Charley Rainier your real name? Are you an imposter?'"

Now that he had started, Alex found that he had a lot to say even to Mr. Winston, his boss and the majority owner of the firm. "I can't believe you three! You'll do... Wait! What? You called her 'Mathews.' I thought her name was 'Rainier.'" God, he was confused. So much for Charley's accusation of him spying on her! Mr. Winston was right: he wasn't very good at it. Apparently, there were things he still didn't know about Charley, including her real name.

"I spoke with the county clerk," Mrs. Maitland replied. "Ms. Mathews legally changed her name the same day she recorded her inherited property—the beach house. To be specific, her name now is Charlotte Christine Rainier-Mathews. At least she's dropped Phillips, her ex-husband's name. Mathews was the name I was looking for."

Alex sighed heavily. He'd had his fill of subterfuge and dishonesty. He'd never fully understood what he was involved in, but something more was going on beyond simply finding out Charley's last name. He didn't understand why her last name mattered so much to Mrs. Maitland. That he was part of the charade while not understanding what the charade even was had his nerves stretched to the breaking point. He wanted answers, even if his father punched him in the gut to keep him quiet.

"What's going on? Why all this mystery and secrecy? It's time you told us—or me—what this is all about." Was he the only one who didn't know why Mrs. Maitland was desperately searching for Charley?

Mrs. Maitland positioned her chair in front of Mr. Winston's desk so that she faced them all, then she sat down. "I think you're right, Alex. It's a story that has been hidden long enough. My husband, may he rest in peace, will forgive me, I'm sure, since our daughter's life depends on Ms. Mathews being who I hope she is—and upon her agreeing to help us."

Mrs. Maitland relaxed back in her chair and began her story.

"It all began in the mid-1990s. Arthur and I had been married for ten years, and we'd tried to have a baby for about eight of those years. I had several miscarriages, and the doctor ultimately advised me that it was unlikely I'd ever have a successful pregnancy. This development put a lot of strain on our marriage. I was a failure in both my eyes and Arthur's. Although he didn't overtly blame me, I felt that he was disappointed in me. I wanted to adopt a baby, but Arthur wouldn't hear of it. He was from a long line of men who had fathered lots of children—and fathered them without much effort, it seems. To Arthur, adopting a baby would make our problem public. More importantly, his buddies at the country club would question his virility—or at least might tease him about it. It's silly, I know, but this was very important to Arthur. The crowd he associated with were having babies at will. Sometimes, it seemed like it was a contest to see who could produce the fastest."

Mrs. Maitland shifted in her chair and included them all in her look. "I know how awful this makes Arthur sound. He wasn't a bad person. He was just trapped in seventeenth-century thinking. He didn't want the family lineage to stop with him, and he didn't like any of the options we were faced with. He had built a successful international company by beating back anything that stood in his way. He was now presented with a problem that he couldn't solve. And it was all my fault… or so we initially thought."

Mrs. Maitland took a tissue from the box on Mr. Winston's desk, wiped her eyes, then twisted it in her hands. She offered a weak smile. "My story is about female and male reproductive disorders and infertility. Close your ears if you don't want to hear details on that subject."

"I think we can handle it," Alex replied. "Go on."

No one else in the room commented, so Mrs. Maitland continued her story. "We decided to explore in vitro fertilization. My eggs and Arthur's sperm would be fertilized in the lab, then implanted in my body. We were tested to see if we were good candidates for the procedure. Put simply, we were not. I had a diminished egg reserve—not enough eggs—and Arthur couldn't produce viable sperm. He couldn't fertilize my eggs, even if I had them. These were both medical conditions without a workable treatment. I won't bore you with the medical jargon that described the severity of our conditions, but this was the end of our dream of having a biological child. I didn't take any pleasure in the fact that our childless life was as much Arthur's fault as mine. We had hit an insurmountable brick wall."

Alex looked at the faces of the other men in the room. They sat listening in rapt attention, hanging on to every word Mrs. Maitland said. Obviously, they had not been privy to this information, either. They had agreed to help her without knowing these details. But how did any of this involve Charley?

"Even though we now knew the reasons behind our childlessness, it still put a heavy strain on our marriage. It was even worse for Arthur, because now our situation was as much his fault as mine. The acrimony in our marriage became so unbearable that I suggested divorce even though that wouldn't solve his sperm problem. He didn't like that option, either. He was a very unhappy man. I persuaded him to go to marriage counseling. Our counselor was the one who told us about frozen embryo adoption."

Alex, Mr. Morgan, and Mr. Winston all straightened in their chairs, their attention riveted on Mrs. Maitland. Alex had expected her to say that Arthur had come around to the idea of adopting a baby, but embryo adoption? He had heard of the procedure, but wasn't familiar with the details of the process.

"I was reaching my late thirties by then, so time was running out even for this option. Arthur agreed to explore this new avenue. If I became pregnant this way, we could keep it quiet. The outside world would never know the baby wasn't Arthur's biological child. I would experience pregnancy, and Arthur could brag about his pregnant wife to his buddies at the club. It was a win for both of us. Arthur was still thinking like a seventeenth-century man, but he was willing to use a modern medical procedure. The counselor put us in touch with a lawyer who found a fertility clinic in Atlanta. They had two frozen fertilized embryos from one couple that were up for adoption. I had never heard of such a thing, but the lawyer assured us that this was a new technique but had been successful for other couples and recommended we try it."

"The clinic provided us with the medical history of the couple and their physical descriptions, which turned out to be similar to ours—though a difference wouldn't have dissuaded me from the adoption. The donor already had one successful pregnancy through in vitro, so there was an excellent chance that, once transferred, at least one of the frozen embryos would result in another pregnancy. The woman's pregnancy had been difficult, and she had to have a hysterectomy afterward, which is why the couple didn't use the additional embryos themselves. But they didn't want them destroyed, either. Instead, they put them up for adoption. The donors asked not to be identified and instructed the clinic to not give them any information about the adoptions—not even if one or both embryos resulted in a child. The woman was adamant that she didn't want to be contacted once the donation was complete."

"Wait. Wait just one minute," Alex interjected again, holding up his hands to stop Mrs. Maitland. She kept adding details that confused the situation. In this case, illegal details. "This woman didn't want to be identified? Yet it sounds like you've identified her. Isn't that illegal? How did you do that? And how exactly does Charley fit in?"

"If you grease enough wheels, Alex, and have the right connections, you can uncover anything. You should know that. A large donation to the right people can unlock most doors." Mrs. Maitland looked Alex squarely in the face. "I know you think I'm crazy. We hired the best doctors in the field, and the embryo donation worked. We had a beautiful child. You've met Dorsey, Alex. One day when you have a child of your own, you'll learn that you'll do anything for that child. But to answer your question, my investigator believes our embryos belonged to George and Debra Mathews of Atlanta. Charley is the biological sister of my Dorsey."

"I don't believe this," Alex said in exasperation. "You invaded these people's lives when they specifically asked for anonymity." *And I helped you*, he added to himself. His help had been minimal, but he was the one who took Charley to the charity event where Mrs. Maitland obtained Charley's DNA.

Mrs. Maitland was not offended by Alex's accusation. She waved it off and went on with her story. "George Mathews was killed in a horrible auto accident shortly after they donated the embryos, and Debra has moved around a lot over the years. We stopped looking for her a while back. By that time, we had a lead on Charley. And despite what you say, Alex, we stopped searching for Debra *because* she asked not to be contacted. As you point out, there are legal issues here. And Debra is difficult to keep up with, according to the investigator."

"She lives in Miami," Alex said without thinking, then pointed out the obvious, "and yet, you had already identified her when you stopped looking. You think Charley's okay with being investigated? Having her privacy invaded?"

Alex looked at his father, then turned toward Mr. Winston. "You two are being very quiet. Did you get involved in this scheme without asking for the details? You've involved the firm in something illegal."

Mr. Winston brushed away Alex's concern. "We didn't know. But don't worry about it. Our only involvement was in getting you to help."

"I'm you fall guy?" Alex asked angrily, exasperated by the lack of concern over what they had involved him in.

"No," Mr. Morgan replied firmly. He placed his hand on Alex's arm. "I won't let that happen."

Alex ignored his father and turned back to Mrs. Maitland. "So you've found her," Alex stated. "You think she's the one you're looking for. Now what? Why is it so important that you find her? You wanted Dorsey to have a sister, so you just went out to find her one?"

"Dorsey, Charley's biological sister, has myeloid leukemia." Mrs. Maitland took a deep, shaky breath. Her knuckles whitened as she gripped the arms of her chair. She had been as stiff as iron through most of her story—until she spoke of her daughter. "We've tried chemo and radiation, but those treatments have failed. She needs a stem cell transplant, and since she has cancer, she can't use her own stem cells. The doctors warned us in advance that chemo didn't always work, so I started searching for Charley as a backup. I always hoped we wouldn't need it. And yes, I also wanted Dorsey to meet her sister."

"Your wanting something doesn't mean that's the only consideration," Alex pointed out. "And you could have found another way to bring them together without all the scheming and skulking around." Alex was the only one challenging Mrs. Maitland. The others were happy to sit back and let him take the lead.

"Charley is most likely a perfect match for an allogenic transplant—a transplant using a matching donor. Dorsey will die without it. What would you have me do, Alex?" Mrs. Maitland asked, ignoring the points he had made. Her annoyance with him was apparent.

"Oh, I don't know," Alex replied sarcastically, equally annoyed with Mrs. Maitland. "Ask her outright if she's who you think she is. Why haven't you asked her before now?"

"At first, I had no idea where she lived, so I hired someone to find her. When she fell into our laps by moving to Turtle Island, right next door to you, I thought you'd be the best one to find out for sure." Mrs. Maitland paused and took a deep breath. Her voice was uncharacteristically shaky when she continued. "Quite frankly, I was afraid. I was afraid to ask and find out that she wasn't Dorsey's sister after all. Dorsey could die without her help. I didn't want to hear or accept that."

Alex almost felt sorry for Mrs. Maitland. No, he was sorry that she was in this situation. Normally fearless when dealing with her businesses, she had now encountered a problem that no amount of money or dogged determination could overcome. She had hit a brick wall that she couldn't plow through or run over, just like her late husband had when confronted with his inability to father a child. Alex now understood why Dorsey had not been at the fundraising event.

"Alex, the reason I wanted you here this morning is to ask if you would speak to Charley for me. Ask her if—should her DNA prove she's Dorsey's sister—she would consider being a stem cell donor. If you don't want to do this, then bring her to me. I'll ask her myself." Mrs. Maitland, the formidable business-woman, was back in full bulldozing mode. She was now convinced that Charley was who she was looking for, and she was determined to see her plan through to the end. The shakiness and fear she had demonstrated moments before were gone. She stared at Alex, not blinking an eye or moving a muscle.

As Alex stared back at a reinvigorated Mrs. Maitland, a thought occurred to him—one he'd had many times since she had become his client: he was glad that he never had to face her in a courtroom when her steely eyes were set on something she wanted very badly. She didn't take no for an answer. And she really wanted Charley to be Dorsey's sister. She would just find someone else to do it if he refused. Her latest request had the ring of another gangster edict, but this time, she wanted the whole body. As much as he'd like to agree to take Charley to see her, things were now complicated by the blowup with Charley last night.

"Well, that'll be a bit difficult, since she probably will never speak to me again," Alex replied.

"What did you do?" his father asked as he frowned at Alex.

Alex's simmering anger finally boiled over. "It's not what *I* did." He raised his voice. He was normally respectful when dealing with his dad and Mr. Winston. He was always deferential to Mrs. Maitland, even when she was ploughing through a business deal and he had to point out that something she wanted to do wasn't legal or wasn't feasible. But his father's accusation pushed him over the edge. He wasn't the one who had screwed up this charade. "It wasn't me. It's this cloak-and-dagger scheme you three cooked up and that dossier the private investigator complied. Charley found it, and now, she thinks *I'm* the scum that's been spying on her. How would you feel if someone had a file on you that contained every little detail of your life?"

Alex got up from the sofa and stalked to the window, hoping to cool down before he said something he might regret. He focused on the traffic below on Broad Street. It had thinned to only a few cars, but pedestrians filled the sidewalks and milled around in front of store window displays. The nice day had brought out the summer tourist. Some were lined up below to board excursion buses, while others casually strolled along the sidewalk, enjoying the beautiful morning. Alex normally enjoyed the clear mornings that followed an ocean squall like the one last night because they were always bright and sunny. This morning was no exception, but it could be black outside for all he cared right now. The influx of people below happily going about their business, while he was stuck neck-deep in something he wanted no part of, just added to his foul mood. But the normalcy outside the window did help calm him somewhat.

Alex took a deep breath and slowly turned from the window to speak to Mrs. Maitland. "I understand your need to speak with Charley. I really do. But do you realize what you're asking me to do? You want me to inform Charley that she has a sister she knows nothing about. And you want me to then ask if she would undergo a medical procedure and donate stem cells to a virtual stranger."

188   TIDES OF CHANGE

"Yes," Mrs. Maitland replied bluntly. "That's exactly what I want."

Alex shook his head. The plan sounded even crazier when he detailed it out loud. He was tired and worn down by hearing about the lengths Mrs. Maitland had gone to over the years—from finding a solution to her and her husband's inability to have a child to finding Charley. Even though Charley was mad at him, he would rather be the one who spoke to her than have her exposed to some other scheme Mrs. Maitland might dream up. She wouldn't give up.

"Alright, I'll try to talk to Charley. I'll relay your request." Alex gave in. It seemed to be the best solution at the moment. Charley may slam the door in his face again, and who could blame her? "I don't know if she'll listen or if she'll let me bring her to see you, but I'll try."

Alex walked away from the window and faced the group. "I'll try to do as requested, but there's only one thing I'm certain of this morning: Charley has lost all trust in me. She'll quickly leave this crazy town and return to New York, where even brash New Yorkers would never stoop to invading her life the way you have." Alex walked toward the office door leading to the hallway. He didn't say anything more as he opened the door. He'd had enough of all three of them.

"Thank you, Alex," Mrs. Maitland said. "I know it's asking a lot, but..."

Alex slammed the office door, cutting off the rest of her sentence as he stepped into the hallway.

Alex had just reached the bank of elevators at the end of the corridor when his father caught up with him.

"Alex, I'm sorry I got you into all this. I didn't expect you to fall in love with Charley, and now, I've made a mess of any chance you might have with her. I wanted to help Mrs. Maitland and, at the same time, get you to see that there are other women in the world. I only wanted you to stop mooning over Rebecca."

Alex scowled at his father. "I'm not mooning over Rebecca. I have—or had—a friendship with Charley that was very important to me. It's never progressed beyond that. Now, thanks to you and your little cabal, even that friendship is over."

"I really am sorry," his father said. "Do you want me to talk to Charley?"

"No!" Alex almost shouted. "Look, I agreed to try to talk to Charley and get her to meet with Mrs. Maitland. *Try* is all I can promise."

"That's all anyone can ask of you," his father said as Alex stepped into the elevator. Mr. Morgan caught the door to keep it from closing. "You aren't the only one who's in trouble here. Your mother really liked Charley, and she thought she spotted a budding romance between you two. When she finds out the mess I've made of things, she's going to be very angry at me." Mr. Morgan shrugged. "I'll be in the doghouse with you. That should make you feel better."

"It doesn't," Alex replied shortly. The buzzer on the door went off. Alex rudely pushed the 'Close' button, and the elevator door closed on whatever else his father was going to say.

Alex left the law office and immediately drove back to Turtle Island. He usually enjoyed the drive across the West Ashley River, but today, his swirling thoughts overrode the picturesque beauty of the river. The sound of a commercial ship's horn in the distance as it came into Charleston's port didn't interrupt his thinking.

Alex sifted through everything he had just learned in the meeting. He needed a plan that would persuade Charley to hear his explanation… *and* convince her that he had nothing to do with the information Mrs. Maitland's private investigator had gathered on her. Advice his father had given him when he was in law school replayed in his mind: "The best way to get a jury on your side, Alex, is to be direct, look them in the eye, and tell them straight out why you believe in the case you just present-ed. No great oratory is needed, no fancy words—just be honest, direct, and sincere."

Alex had used that advice in the courtroom, but would it work with Charley? He didn't have any other ideas, so that was his only plan: the truth as he knew it.

Alex parked his truck, let Rex out of the house, and walked back to Charley's beach house. He climbed the stairs and knocked on her door. "Charley, I need to talk with you." He paused to listen. No sound came from inside. "Charley, I can explain. The folder you saw wasn't complied by me." Still no sound.

Charley's car was in the driveway, so maybe she was taking a walk on the beach. Alex looked out toward the ocean. The pil-ings under the house elevated it enough that he had a long view of the beach. She was nowhere in sight.

"Charley, I have something you need to hear."

She still didn't come to the door.

Alex played his last card. She'd have a hard time ignoring Rex. He motioned for Rex to approach the door. Rex barked twice, then began sniffing around the door. He whined and whimpered and scratched at the crack under the door.

Rex's reaction indicated Charley was in the house. She was just ignoring them.

"Charley, please talk to me," Alex called, but she still didn't open the door.

"Come on, Rex. She doesn't want to talk to either of us," Alex said. "Let's go for a run on the beach." Alex turned, walked down the steps, and took the path to the beach with Rex at his heels.

His plan didn't work. So, what could he try next?

CHAPTER FOURTEEN

Charley relaxed when she heard Alex and Rex leave the porch. She had almost caved when Rex started whining and scratching at the door. But she still seethed with anger at Alex. She had been very gullible and had so easily fallen into his trap. She had believed all his lies, while all along, he had been gathering information on her. But why? That was a very good question for which she didn't have an answer. She was a lowly photographer from New York and not some part of an international ring with illegal funds hidden in an off-shore bank account or buried in a sand pit on the beach. What was he after?

Maybe Alex was the criminal, and he was stalking her for some dark, nefarious purpose.

No, even in her anger, she didn't believe that. Alex? A criminal? He didn't fit the profile. She had witnessed the respect that people like Mrs. Harrison, Bowen, and Manny felt for Alex. But then, why? Why had he spied on her?

Charley's plan to avoid a summer romance had crumbled into dust by the time she reached Alex's house yesterday. So the evening started out full of possibilities. Good food, good wine, soft music that mingled with the sound of the rain hitting the tin roof, and a handsome man who made her laugh and was focused only on her. Yet all the trappings of romance had come crashing down thanks to a blue folder in a drawer.

Charley shifted her reflections on last night to reality. *Trappings of romance? No, change "trappings" to "trapped."* She was now trapped in a nightmare she didn't understand.

Of course, Alex had been focused on her. That was the plan. His interest was all about fishing for information on her.

When she had pulled the folder out of the drawer and the story of her life stared her in the face, a white-hot rage seized her. When she threw the folder at Alex, every tiny detail of her life spread out over the floor. What hurt her the most was the picture of her going into her attorney's office to finalize her divorce from Daniel. She and Daniel had mutually agreed to the divorce, but it had still been a difficult day—an admission of a colossal failure and the loss of three years of her life. To see a picture reflecting the sadness and strain on her face was a painful reminder of that day.

Charley tried to summon the anger she had felt last night when she discovered the folder. But on this bright, sunny day, washed clean by last night's rain, her anger had turned to hurt and deep disappointment over the loss of a friendship she had come to enjoy and rely on. She was reminded that she had again trusted someone who had let her down.

"You should have known that you can't count on anyone," Charley cynically reminded herself. "After what happened with your mother and then with Daniel, you should've expected and prepared for disappointment."

Charley picked up her phone and went to the back deck to call Aunt Beth. She looked around to make sure Alex wasn't lurking nearby. Even in her hurt and anger, she had a hard time picturing him lurking and sneaking around. But she needed to

face the facts. Her personal information he had in his possession showed that anything was possible. From her view on the
back deck, Alex was nowhere in sight.

Aunt Beth answered Charley's call immediately. She was
always the first one Charley turned to when she found herself
hurting or in trouble. She poured out the whole story to Aunt
Beth.

"Charley, that doesn't sound like the Alex we met when we
were down there. Are you sure you saw what you think you
saw?"

"Yes," Charley answered emphatically.

"I'm surprised," Aunt Beth said. "Have you asked Alex for
an explanation?"

"No. He's tried to talk to me, but I don't want to talk to
him right now." Charley looked over at Alex's house. He wasn't
anywhere around that she could see. Maybe he hadn't returned
from his run with Rex yet.

"You know that the best thing to do is talk to him," Aunt
Beth advised.

"I know, but I'm afraid he'll reel me back in with more lies.
You know how I fell for Daniel's lies." At the moment, Charley
didn't trust her ability to separate truth from lies.

"That was different," Aunt Beth replied. "You were trying
to avoid divorce. This could all be a simple misunderstanding.
And quite frankly, the Alex I met doesn't fit the picture you're
describing."

"Maybe," Charley replied, unconvinced. "But I don't know
how he can explain this away."

"Uncle Lance wants to know if you want him to come down
and threaten Alex."

"No," Charley laughed. "I'm not eight years old any more. I
have to solve my own problems. But thank him for the offer."

"He'll be disappointed until I remind him that Alex is as tall as he is and almost twenty-five years younger."

Charley ended the call soon after. Her mood felt lighter—but only a little. Aunt Beth was a good sounding board and usually helped her sort things out. Charley's world always seemed a little better after a talk with her aunt. But as she'd just said, her problem today was one she had to solve on her own.

Charley's mother was never the person she thought about calling when she was confused and upset. Her mother had relinquished that right when she stopped providing a home for Charley, many years ago. And Debra's problems were always bigger than Charley's, at least to her. Her mother had finally asked for forgiveness, though, so maybe a call to her today would be a good way to further their renewed relationship. She wouldn't ask for advice on her current situation with Alex, but she would check in and see how her mother was doing. With Debra, one could never predict what might have happened in the course of just a few weeks.

Charley dialed her mother's number in Miami.

"It's so good to hear from you," Debra exclaimed. "Kenneth, it's Charley," Debra excitedly yelled to her husband in the background.

So, she was still married to Kenneth. That was progress. They had been married almost a year now—a record. Charley immediately felt ashamed. Her mother was who she was, and Charley had accepted that. She had only good wishes for her mother, and she hoped Debra had turned a corner toward real happiness.

"Charley," Debra said after they had exchanged greetings and caught up briefly, "someone called here a little bit ago. They were asking about you."

"Was it a man?" she asked. *Alex, you don't give up, do you?*

"No, it was a woman. I didn't catch her name. She was asking about your father—about his accident, where he was born, when he moved to Atlanta—and when and where you were born. I couldn't talk about his accident, but she said she was just verifying dates, not the details. Then she said she was looking to hire you for some portrait photography and was checking out your background."

Charley slumped against the deck railing. Her gullible mother would be the perfect victim for a scam like this—or any scam, for that matter. Debra believed everyone and never thought anyone was out to con her. Maybe that was where Charley got her own trusting nature. He inner voice chose this moment to speak up and pile on. *Ha! You're too cynical to fall for something like this. You only fall for untrustworthy men.*

"Did I do something wrong, Charley?" Debra asked, worried by Charley's silence.

"No. It's alright. I hope they didn't upset you too much. I'm sure I'll hear from this person if she follows through." Charley had never done portrait photography, but her absentee mother wouldn't know that.

She said goodbye to her mother, went to the kitchen for a glass of sweet tea, and returned to the deck. She avoided the front porch, just in case Alex and Rex walked by on their return from the beach. She didn't want to see him now—maybe never. And yet, even though she was still mad at Alex, the thought of never seeing him again filled her with sadness.

As Charley sipped her tea, she thought about her conversation with her mother. Who, she wondered, would go to the trouble of tracking down her mother to wheedle information out of her about Charley father? An uncaring person, obviously. If this person knew about her father's death, but was brazen and callous enough to badger her mother about the most tragic event in her life, she was not someone Charley wanted to associate with, let alone work for. That someone was pumping her mother for information just added to her sense of unease.

People were spying on her. Why?

Charley finished her tea and went inside. She had more photos that she still needed to review. Mostly, she needed something to occupy her mind.

The next morning, Alex and Rex made their way back to Charley's house. Alex carried two cups of coffee—a peace offering, if only a small one. This was the time when he usually took Rex for a run, but he thought he might surprise Charley and catch her when she wasn't expecting him to be around. He started to climb the steps to the front door when Rex stopped, his ears pointed toward the back of the space beneath the house.

Alex looked around the steps and saw Charley struggling to pull the vacuum cleaner around several boxes filled with yard tools that were blocking the doorway. He placed the coffee down on the steps and walked toward the storage space.

"Hung up again, are you?" Alex asked from close behind Charley's back. She yelped and dropped the vacuum. "You seem to have a thing with doors, don't you?"

"God! And you have a knack for sneaking up on me. Do you always have to scare me like that?" Charley turned away and tugged on the vacuum again. "But that's what you do best, isn't it: sneak around and spy on people?"

"I didn't sneak up on you. I don't sneak or spy, Charley." Alex reached around her, lifted the vacuum up and over the boxes to free it, and then pulled it through the door. "If you'd let me explain, you'd know that." Some people might technically call his plan to surprise her and catch her unawares a form of sneaking, but he had no other choice, since she refused to talk with him.

"I don't want to talk to you, and I don't need any more lies. I saw everything I needed to see in that folder you have—evidence of your spying. You can't deny it. You spied on me." Charley repeated her accusation.

His sudden appearance behind her had obviously startled her and caught her off guard—which had been his intent. But at least she hadn't run from him, as he had feared. He watched her face as she searched for some new insult to hurl at him.

"Did you call my mother in Miami, fishing for more information?"

"Call you mother?" Alex repeated. "Why would I do that?"

"I don't know. But you've lied to me and deceived me about everything else." She grabbed the vacuum and started walking away from the storage space and toward the porch steps.

Alex quickly followed her and touched her arm just as she started to climb the steps. "I don't want to do this in this way, but since you refuse to listen to me, you give me no other choice. Charley, you have a sister," he blurted out. "You're forcing me to tell you point-blank. I don't want to hurt you or frighten you, but it's true. You have a sister."

"What? What did you say? Is this some kind of sick joke, Alex?" Charley asked as she turned and faced him. Her mouth tightened in a straight line and her green eyes shot fire at him. "I don't have any siblings."

"I said, you have a sister. I also said that I didn't want to tell you this way, but you won't talk to me. I'm serious," Alex explained, his voice raised so there would be no doubt that she heard what he was saying. Shouting seemed to be the best way—the only way, really—for him to get her attention.

Charley sank down onto the steps leading up to the porch and stared up at Alex. Her mouth worked as she tried to find the right words. "You're crazy. I'm an only child. Is this some nutty scheme of yours to make me forget what you did?"

"It's not a scheme. It's true, Charley. Or, at least according to Mrs. Maitland, it's true. I'm only the messenger. And I repeat, I didn't spy on you."

Charley looked taken aback, but it was obvious she still didn't believe him. She absently picked up the cup of coffee Alex had placed on the steps and took a long swallow. "I don't believe you… on any count. And what has Mrs. Maitland got to do with any of this?"

Alex paused before answering. Mrs. Maitland was so desperate to get help for her daughter that she may have jumped to the wrong conclusion, which would complicate things even further. Alex needed to verify a few things for himself. He sat down on the step beside Charley.

"First, tell me, were you conceived through in vitro?" Alex asked. "Do you know?"

Charley's head swerved around to stare at Alex. Anger hadn't left her eyes. "Your spying didn't uncover the answer to that? You aren't a very good spy, are you, Alex?"

"That's what I've been trying to tell you. I'm not a spy." Alex smiled at her, hoping to soften the news, but that just made her angrier.

"I've seen the results of your spying, remember?" Charley spat back at him. "So why should I believe your story about my having a sister—a sister I've never heard of?"

"Just answer me. Do you know if your parents used in vitro?" Alex repeated bluntly.

"Yes! Yes, they did!" shouted Charley. "What does that prove?" She clenched her hands around the coffee cup.

Alex hated being an inconsiderate heel for dropping the bombshell news about her sister in this way, but her anger hadn't given him any other choice. She wouldn't listen if he tiptoed around the truth. Now, he had her full attention.

"Mrs. Maitland and her husband adopted the frozen embryos that your parents put up for adoption after you were born," Alex explained. "They had a daughter whom Mrs. Maitland says is your sister. She wants you to meet with her to discuss it. Will you go with me to meet her?"

Charley's mouth dropped open. She gulped and tried to speak, but nothing came out. Alex saw the wheels turning in her head as she processed what she just heard. First shock, then wonder moved across her face. Never in a million years could she have anticipated the news he had just given her. She was interested now, and she hadn't thrown anything at him. He was making progress.

"But I need to caution you that I'm getting this information secondhand from Mrs. Maitland," Alex said. "I don't know if it's one-hundred-percent true. Mrs. Maitland may be wrong in her assumptions, but she thinks it's true."

"What do you have to do with this, Alex? And what game is Mrs. Maitland playing? What game are *you* playing?" Her scorn had returned to her voice, though it had decreased slightly—but only slightly. "I can't trust you," Charley whispered. Her voice weakened and trailed off. She was having a hard time denying outright what he had told her. Was it shock, or was it hope he heard in her voice? Alex wanted to take her in his arms, assure her that things would be alright, and remove the confusion in her eyes. But she was still suspicious of him, and a move like that would get a wildcat's response for sure.

"Yes, you *can* trust me, but I'm only the messenger," Alex said softly. "I wish you would believe that. A messenger, not a spy. There's something else."

"I knew there must be more to this story, since you're involved," Charley accused. "Nothing with you is ever as simple as it might appear on the surface."

Alex ran his hands through his hair in frustration, leaving it standing on end. He ignored Charley's comment, smoothed his hair back down, and pressed on. "Your sister has leukemia. She needs a stem cell transplant. A biological sister like you would be a match."

"What? Oh no!" Charley temporarily forgot she was angry with him. "I'm so sorry. That's terrible! Even if this person is a stranger, there's no way I won't help her if I can."

"I expected you would say that." Alex breathed a sigh of relief, happy to see that she at least believed him on that much.

"But first, I need to meet with Mrs. Maitland to find out if all this is true," Charley said, turning to face Alex. She was curious, but she needed to know more. "I can't just take your word on it."

"I can take you to see her," Alex offered, ignoring her insult.

"No, I'll meet with her," Charley said. "I don't need you to escort me. I can go by myself. You spied on me. I haven't forgotten or forgiven that. I thought we were friends, and friends don't do that."

"Listen to me," Alex replied loudly. He turned toward her and faced her on the step. "I never spied on you."

"I saw proof at your house that you did." Charley looked at Alex, her lips tightening in a straight line. She hadn't given up that belief.

Everything in Alex's life was backward today. Charley agreed to meet with Mrs. Maitland, the one who had actually spied on her, but she'd have nothing to do with him, the one who was basically tricked into the whole affair.

Charley rose from the step, turned her back on Alex, picked up the vacuum, and started climbing up to the porch. Alex stood up, motioned Rex to follow, and turned to walk back toward his house. The sound of a car pulling into the driveway made both Alex and Charley stop and turn. A silver Porsche came to a stop behind Charley's car and a tall, lithe man with blond hair exited the vehicle, stretched, spotted Charley and

Alex, and began walking towards them.

"Daniel," Charley whispered as she came down off the steps. She took a couple steps, then stopped. She didn't move forward to greet him.

Alex looked from Charley to the man. Daniel—the ex?

"What are you doing here?" Charley demanded.

Daniel stopped a short distance away and looked up at the house behind her, assessing its weathered and imperfect painted exterior.

Rex left Alex's side and came to sit down next to Charley. He studied the intruder.

"It's okay, Rex." Charley reached down and patted Rex's head.

"I need to talk to you. I drove all night to get here."

Yes, this is Charley's ex-husband, Alex thought.

Daniel turned and looked around the area, taking in Alex's property nearby, the beach, and the dusty road that ran in front of the houses. His eyes swept over the large dunes that were covered in sea oats and unruly stands of grasses. It wasn't neatly manicured, but that was purposeful. The thick grass and dunes separated the cottages and the road from the beach and blocked surging storms.

Alex stood quietly and watched Daniel assess the landscape, the beachfront, and the cottages. *Being a New York City boy and a Wall Street banker, he likely thinks this is all tacky and beneath him*, Alex surmised.

He wasn't wrong in his assumption. Daniel' turned disdain filled eyes at Charley—a clear sign he was not impressed with any of it. He waved his hand to encompass the landscape around them and smirked. "You left New York for *this*? I can't believe the great, world-famous photographer Ce Ce Kane is living here, on this desolate, rundown island, in a shack," Daniel's voice was laced with contempt. "What's happened to you,

Charley? You've gone low-class."

Alex, who had been waiting for an opening to excuse himself, felt a gut punch as the meaning of Daniel's words sunk in. He whipped around stunned and stared angrily at Charley. "Ce Ce Kane? *You're* Ce Ce Kane? Did he say you're Ce Ce Kane?" Alex repeated his question, unsure if he'd heard right. "We discussed her photos many times, yet you failed to mention that you're Ce Ce Kane. I even bid on your photograph at the auction! And not a word from you!" Alex stood with his hands balled into fists on his hips. His voice, louder with anger, he spit out the accusation, "You hid your identity from me? Why?"

"No! Alex, listen to me, please," Charley begged as she stepped toward Alex. Rex moved between them. He wagged his tail, but looked from one to the other, confused by the raised voices and anger.

"Charley! My god! What other secrets have you kept from me? Is everything I know about you a lie?" Alex started to turn away.

"No! Listen, Alex! I meant to tell you, but I didn't know how to bring it up. So much time had passed."

"You have a lot of nerve, accusing me of deceiving you." Alex turned, then took a step closer, and pointed his finger at her. He had felt guilty about his part in the folder debacle. But not anymore. "I don't even know your last name. Since I met you, it's been Phillips. It's been Rainier. It's been Mathews. Now it's Kane?" Alex shook his head in disbelief. "Ha! And you say *you* can't believe me? Well, I damn sure can't believe you—not even on your name!"

"You don't understand, Alex. Let me explain," Charley protested. She grabbed Alex's arm as he turned to walk away.

He yanked it out of her grasp, turned, and scowled at her. Anger turned his eyes a bright blue. "No, Charley. You don't like explanations, remember? Mine weren't good enough for you. I don't want to hear yours, either. I'll leave you two alone so you can plan your next lie. Come, Rex. Let's go home." Alex stalked off, with Rex trailing along behind him.

Alex turned back for a parting shot. "It's clear I don't know you, and apparently, Annabelle didn't know you, either. I hope your low-class beach hiatus was all you expected."

"That's not fair. Please listen," Charley begged. "I'm sorry." But Alex didn't turn around.

Alex stalked to his house and quickly decided. He would put the West Ashley River between himself and Charley whatever-her-name-was as fast as his pickup could drive. He was a fool to trust Charley. You'd think he would learn.

He entered the beach house and immediately went to his bedroom, where he began rummaging through the drawers of his dresser and throwing a few items on the bed. The closets were stocked with beach clothes, athletic shoes, running clothes, and a couple pairs of pants for dressier occasions. He wouldn't need any of them once he got back to the mainland. His closets there were filled with jeans, work attire, and casual dress clothes. He moved back and forth between the beach house and the house in Goose Creek with minimal packing. It wouldn't take him long to pack up any personal items he'd need.

Alex cleaned out the fridge and cupboards, removing any leftover food items that might attract bugs, then set the trash out by the road for collection. He locked the door and windows. If a severe storm was forecasted, he would return and board up the windows to prevent damage from strong winds and flying debris. The start of hurricane season was still a few weeks off, so he didn't need to worry about that yet. He loaded Rex into his pickup truck. As he drove past Charley's, she and Daniel were sitting on the steps, engaged in conversation. Maybe they would work out whatever had gone wrong between them, though it seemed to Alex that a lot of time had passed since their split, making a reconciliation unlikely. But what did he, Alex Morgan, know about marriage or women? Absolutely nothing.

"I'm a fool," Alex muttered to himself. Rex whimpered from the back seat. Alex adjusted the rearview mirror so he could see Rex clearly. "At least I have you, huh, Rex?" Rex answered with a short bark, then lay down in the seat.

Early the next morning, Alex was back at work at the law firm on Broad Street. He stopped in the doorway of his father's office before going to his own office down the hall. His father looked up from the documents he was reading and waved Alex into the room. Alex sat down in the chair in front of the desk and slumped back into the leather-covered seat.

"More sleepless nights? They're catching up to you, Alex. You look like hell," his father said as he gave Alex the once-over.

"I feel like hell, too. And thanks for pointing that out." Alex rubbed his hands over his face, straightened, then leaned forward with his chin resting on his clasped hands.

"Charley still mad at you?"

Alex turned an obstinate look upon his father. He wasn't going to spill his guts on the latest blow up with Charley, regardless of his father's prying. "I can see the answer to that question written all over your face. If Charley wasn't still mad at you, you wouldn't be here, looking like you've been pulled backward through a knothole."

"Yep, she's still mad at me, but I'm furious with her." Alex relented and shared that much. He then fell silent again. He didn't feel like providing more details. He was tired of thinking about his last conversation with Charley and the name she had hidden from him, and he definitely didn't want to talk about it. Being played for a fool once again didn't sit any better than it had with Rebecca. It was a different woman, but the same outcome.. His lingering question about his judgment had been answered. It hadn't improved.

"Is she still at the beach house?" his father asked, prying for more information.

"I guess," Alex replied sullenly. "She was there yesterday. So was her ex. I guess he's her ex. I don't know what's true and what isn't anymore—not even her real name."

Alex pulled a piece of paper from his pocket and pushed it toward his father, hoping to distract him from further interrogation. "She agreed to meet with Mrs. Maitland, but I want you to set up the meeting. That's her cell number, but don't give it to Mrs. Maitland. I don't want her badgering Charley if she doesn't agree to go along with Mrs. Maitland's plans."

"Charley is mad at you, you're mad at Charley, and you aren't sure what her name is. Her ex—or maybe not her ex—is at the beach house on Turtle Island," his father recapped. "My son, you do have a complicated life right now."

"And she said she would drive herself to the meeting," Alex said, ignoring his father's comment. "She wouldn't give me a chance to tell her that the unmarked roads make the drive to Oak Lane Plantation a little tricky for someone not familiar with the area. I guess she'll find that out for herself. Let me know when the meeting is scheduled to take place. I plan to be there."

"Why would you need to be there? This is Mrs. Maitland's personal matter."

Alex looked at his father and frowned. "Personal matter? Yet, you and Mr. Winston are knee deep in it and dragged me in with you."

"Yeah, well, that's over now." His father shifted in his chair, obviously uncomfortable with the reminder. "I'm sorry about that."

"I may be mad at Charley, but I'm not about to let her meet alone with someone as ruthless as Mrs. Maitland."

"She's not *that* bad," his father laughed. "She's tough, but

Charley can probably hold her own."

"I plan to be there to make sure. Marietta Maitland will do anything to get what she wants. After I slipped up and mentioned that Charley's mother lives in Miami, I think Mrs. Maitland called her to fish for additional information on Charley. I know her, and I don't trust her when she wants something this badly."

"She's a tough woman, but she's had to be that way to become successful in an industry dominated by men. But I don't think she'd do anything underhanded," his father asserted.

"By 'underhanded,' do you mean doing something like hiring a PI to investigate Charley? Bribing a fertility clinic for information on an embryo donation? Getting Charley's DNA sample without her consent?" Alex looked skeptically at his father.

"Okay, I see your point. She did do all that. But I think her desire to save her daughter's life was driving those decisions. Any parent might do the same if they were in her shoes."

"Just let me know when you have the meeting set up. By the way, where are we on the Thompson acquisition?" Alex was ready to get his mind off of Charley and back on business.

"Representatives from Thompson and Cordon Manufacturing are meeting today. They should have something worked out by the end of this week. You really don't have to be here for that. It'll all be preliminary, and one of the interns can handle that."

"I want to be here. Get my mind back on something concrete, something I can understand. It's obvious I don't understand women," Alex replied.

"If you're hopeful that one day you'll suddenly understand women, you can forget about it. They're just more complicated. We men are simple—or, as women might say, simpletons."

"Well, I'm done trying to understand Charley." Alex ignored his father's attempt to make him smile. He opened and closed his clenched fists, then ran his hand over the back of his neck. He shrugged to release the tension that had been steadily building for two days.

"I said something similar after every argument I had with your mother before we got married. Now, thirty-six years later, I still don't understand her sometimes. But she feels the same way about me."

"She has reasons to feel that way about you." Alex couldn't pass up the opening his father had given him. He could still throw a dig at his father, so maybe there was a kernel of humor buried somewhere deep inside, underneath the anger and disillusionment he was feeling now. He stood up and started toward the door.

"Alex, just remember: you should always find a way to talk it out, iron out the misunderstanding. It's part of the challenge of a successful merger. You learned that in law school, didn't you? A relationship is a merger with benefits."

"And I learned that a merger isn't successful unless both parties are honest with each other. I also learned—more than once—that once burned, you shouldn't try again," Alex replied.

"Someone as smart as you are should recognize when your hurt pride is calling the shots," his father advised. "You mean it right now, but a week from now, you might see things in a whole new light."

Alex looked at his father and frowned. He reached for the doorknob. He was suddenly tired of listening to his father's fatherly advice. "I'd like to think you're right, but this time, there's too much deceit on both sides—deceit on my side that I had nothing to do with, I might add."

Without waiting for a reply, Alex left his father's office.

CHAPTER FIFTEEN

Charley stopped, reversed, and turned her car around in the middle of the two-lane road. She had chosen the wrong road to the Maitland estate, Oak Lane Plantation, twice. She hadn't paid attention to the route the night she and Alex had traveled this same way to attend the charity ball.

"You were caught up in a fairy tale," she grumbled, "and a handsome escort. Now you're lost because of it."

Two days ago, Bob Morgan had scheduled an appointment for her with Mrs. Maitland at Oak Lane Plantation. Charley had no idea what to expect from the meeting. Alex's news that she had a sister had shocked her, and it took a while for the shock to wear of. At first, she didn't seriously consider this to be true. But why would Alex make up something like that? Or Mrs. Maitland? Finally, as she started to accept it might be true, she became intrigued and excited by the prospect of meeting her.

A sister! Imagine that! Even her overactive imagination couldn't have dreamed up this scenario when she left New Jersey and traveled to South Carolina. If this woman really was her sister, fate was orchestrating her life in ways no one would believe. Everything that had happened since she received the letter from Mr. Lewis had been surreal. Not only had she moved to the city of her father's birthplace, but she might also have a sibling. And it was all happening because Great-Aunt Annabelle—whom she didn't know—had left her a beach house on a tiny island—which she had never heard of—off the coast of Charleston, South Carolina. Her whole life of late was like a movie script.

Charley had made the drive toward the plantation without any problems until she came to a stop sign at a crossroads. There weren't any markings or road signs at the intersection to indicate which road was Oak Lane. That was weird. The local highway department must believe that everyone who had business out this way knew where they were going. Why waste money on signs? That decision was as dumb as her plan: pick a road and begin the process of elimination to find the correct one. Her GPS had chosen this time to become confused, too. It had gone mute, refusing to help her. It was a good thing she had left early for the meeting.

She first drove straight through the intersection, but soon realized she'd made the wrong choice. Nothing looked familiar, and she didn't see any sign of the oak-lined driveway to the Maitland estate. The driveway was the one thing she remembered from her previous visit. Charley retraced her route back to the crossroads and turned onto the left fork. After driving several miles in that direction, she still hadn't spotted the oak-lined driveway. Once again, she'd gone the wrong way.

"Damn! Wrong choice—just like many of my other decisions." Her only recourse was to turn around again and take the remaining fork, the one that branched off to the right. If that wasn't the correct route, then she was truly, horribly lost.

Choosing the wrong road reminded her of one of her biggest mistakes, and her discussion two days ago with Daniel. To say his arrival had surprised her was an understatement. They had sat on the steps of the beach house and had a long talk. She owed him that much, and she was curious as to what he wanted. What was so important that he had driven all night to find her?

"Charley, I'm sorry," Daniel said, getting right to the point as soon as they sat down. "I was wrong to let you go. I don't know why I did that."

"You didn't *let* me go. You *left* me for someone else. You made the first move, but our marriage had died long before, when you cheated on me. I wasn't interested in keeping it going any longer. A divorce was the best thing to do.," Charley replied, shocked that Daniel thought an apology would wipe away his infidelity. After all this time—after all he had done and said? "Tell me, Daniel, why are you here? Did you break up with your little friend?" Charley couldn't keep the bitter sarcasm out of her voice. She didn't want to get back together, but it still smarted that he had been so cavalier about their marriage.

Daniel flushed slightly, but he was always one to try to bluster his way through something, even when caught red-handed. "I left her. I realized we had nothing in common. She never meant as much to me as you did. I made a mistake." Daniel had cut and run again and left his mistress—his usual way of handling things.

"Our mistake was in spending over a year trying to save a marriage that couldn't be saved," Charley said. "The marriage died the first time you cheated on me. In fact, our biggest mistake was getting married in the first place." Charley couldn't look at Daniel. She didn't want him to see the pity in her eyes for a man who couldn't commit to anything other than his own selfishness. She turned away and looked out toward the ocean. In the distance, two porpoises sliced through the ocean waters, their backs glistening in the sun each time they rose above the waves. Too bad she didn't have her camera with her.

Charley breathed in deeply, taking in the dampness and the fresh, clean smell of the ocean breeze. She was calmed by the normalcy of the ocean waves that reminded her that life went on in perfect rhythm. The morning tide was coming in, bringing nutrients to the salt marsh, then flowing back to the ocean, just as it did every day. She and Daniel had made the right decision, even if he said differently. And with Daniel, he'd forget his apology as soon as she gave in and he got his way. He would never change.

Alex drove by in his pickup truck. Rex looked out the back, passenger seat window at her, but Alex didn't look her way. Alex, Alex, Alex. So much of her life since coming to the island had revolved around him. He had deceived her and she wasn't ready to let that go. But she had also kept her pseudonym from him. That was a mistake that had gotten away from her. The friendship they had would be hard to get back because of distrust on both sides. One lesson Daniel had taught her was how hard it was to get over the hurdle of distrust.

"Charley, are you listening to me?" Daniel bumped her arm with his elbow, interrupting Charley's thoughts. "Surely you remember the good times we had. You can't throw all that away. Come back to New York. We can have all that again,"

"I didn't throw our marriage away. You did. Good times? You cheated on me—twice."

"But you can't be happy here. Look around you. It's practically a desert. There's no people or restaurants or theaters. Don't you miss all that?"

Charley smiled and pointed to the ocean. "I don't think you could call this place a desert with all that water."

"Please, I need you to come back," Daniel begged. "Sell this place. Come back with me. I know we can make it work."

Charley turned and looked Daniel in the face. He was sincere and believed what he was saying—now. He was always sincere when there was something he wanted. But it only lasted for a short time—until he found something else to be sincere about. And his comment about selling the place rankled Charley. Once again, Daniel was jealous that she had something she could call hers alone. He'd been that way about her career. Her job was never as important as his. Now he wanted her to give up the beach house, just like he wanted her to give up her career.

"I'm actually happy here," Charley said. "I don't miss my old life at all. The people here have been warm and friendly. They are kind and genuine, and I've felt welcomed by everyone."

"Is it that guy who just left? I can't believe you'd fall for someone like that—a beach bum. And he was angry and rude to you," Daniel sneered. Stereotypes were Daniel's fallback position. No one was ever as good as Daniel, and nothing anyone had was as good as what Daniel had. Charley couldn't believe she had been stupid enough to stay with him for three years.

"He's not a 'beach bum,' as you call him. He's a successful attorney. We've had a recent misunderstanding, but he has nothing to do with my decision about us. We're over and done." Charley pointed to the wooden sign hanging over the porch. "'*Leig Anail*,'" she read to Daniel, "'to rest' or 'to breathe.' That's what I've been able to do since I came here. Why would I give that up?"

Daniel continued to argue and try to persuade her to return to New York. She steadfastly refused. She was clear-eyed in her belief that Daniel didn't have a place in her life anymore. And it had nothing to do with Alex or anyone else. Time and distance had cleared up a lot of things for her.

"It's over, Daniel. You can spend the night here, in the guest room, if you want, but we are not getting back together again. Going our separate ways was and still is best for both of us. As far as I'm concerned, this is the end of this discussion."

Daniel had refused her invitation to stay at the beach house, preferring to find a hotel on the mainland before driving back to New York. He had peeled out of the driveway, scattering crushed shells all over the yard, just to show his displeasure with her. Charley sighed, relieved to see him go. That chapter of her life was closed—finally.

As she watched Daniel drive away, Charley's attention turned to the news Alex had given her. She didn't completely believe it just yet, but she would go meet her maybe-sister. She couldn't pass up the chance to meet her if it was true.

And Alex? Well, that chapter of her life seemed to be closed before it fully opened. She had messed up by keeping her pseudonym a secret, but she couldn't forget that he had invaded her life and photographed her most private moments. Had his business trip to New York with Annabelle been a trip to spy on her? How long had he been sifting through her life and tracking her? All good questions, and since she wasn't speaking to him, the questions wouldn't be answered anytime soon, maybe never.

Charley spent the night tossing and turning and thinking, but that was a waste of time. By the next morning conclusions about everything that had kept her awake were still elusive. She fixed breakfast was almost finished eating when her phone rang. It was Mr. Morgan, calling with a request to schedule a meeting with Mrs. Maitland. Charley had agreed.

So now, here she was, on her way to the appointment with Mrs. Maitland—and possibly lost in the South Carolina countryside. She followed a curve in the road and immediately spotted a sign that that read, 'Oak Lane Plantation, two miles,' and pointed straight ahead. She breathed a sigh of relief and relaxed. She followed the right lane as it took her around a large oak tree growing in the middle of the road, separating the two lanes. Another South Carolinian quirk? Apparently, they didn't cut down their trees for any reason, especially for something as trivial as a road. But it was a nice scenic touch.

Charley soon came to Oak Lane Plantation and turned into the long driveway. The oak trees on either side of the road overlapped each other, creating a shaded corridor leading to the main house. Charley parked her car in front of the house and sat there for several minutes, gathering the courage to face Mrs. Maitland—and possibly, her sister. Her heart was racing as she got out of the car, walked to the house, and rang the doorbell. She was greeted by a maid who led her down the hall and into a sitting area.

At first, Charley thought she was alone in the room, but then, she spotted a familiar figure standing by the bank of windows. Alex stood looking out the windows at the manicured gardens along the back acreage. His suit coat was unbuttoned, and his hands were casually stuck in the pockets of his trousers, but there was nothing about him that spoke 'casual'. Charley chewed her lip as she tried to decide if she should be the first to speak.

Alex turned from the window and nodded briefly to acknowledge her presence. Then, he turned back to resume staring out the window. He frowned, his hostility toward her obvious in his tensed, squared shoulders. His business suit and tie meant he was here in a professional capacity.

Charley stared at his back. Why was he here and dressed as though this was a court proceeding? Did Mrs. Maitland feel she needed her attorney present? What was she afraid of? That Charley would make some sort of financial demand in exchange for the stem cells? Was Alex here to make sure that didn't happen? He had made a wasted trip, if that were the case. Charley didn't voice any of her questions. He didn't want to speak to her, and she didn't want to speak to him. Charley walked to a sofa and took a seat to await Mrs. Maitland's arrival.

Mrs. Maitland soon swept in and sat down across from

Charley. She nodded to Charley, then turned to Alex and said, "Alex, come sit with us."

"No, ma'am. I'd rather stand," Alex replied shortly. He didn't turn from his place at the window and continued to stare at something in the backyard.

"Charley… can I call you Charley?" At Charley's nod, Mrs. Maitland continued, "Do you know why you're here?"

"Your daughter might be my sister?"

"Yes. Let me explain how that came about. My husband and I couldn't have a baby of our own." Mrs. Maitland leaned back in her chair, then continued, "And we desperately wanted a baby. We had almost given up hope until we found out about the frozen embryos your parents had put up for adoption. Did you know about the embryos and the adoption?"

"No," Charley replied. "I knew that I was born through in vitro and that my mother couldn't have more children, but I didn't know there were extra frozen embryos. So, what makes you think I'm who you're looking for?"

"Just by adding up everything I know about your life. The timeline of events line up perfectly. But now, I'm certain. I just received the results of your DNA analysis. And it confirms it," Mrs. Maitland said.

"My DNA? You have my DNA?" Startled, Charley glanced at Alex. He closed his eyes and a soft groan escaped his lips. His mouth tightened as he looked over at Mrs. Maitland.

Apparently, Mrs. Maitland didn't believe in easing into a topic. She was everything that Mr. Morgan had warned Charley about when he set up the meeting—a shrewd businesswoman who didn't let anything slow her down when she was set on an objective. She frequently forgot or ignored the effect her words and actions might have on other people. That was a useful trait in the business world she thrived in, but her lack of empathy was jolting to Charley. Her objective was to help her daughter, and that didn't require being sympathetic to how Charley might feel about having her DNA secretly collected and tested.

They had her DNA. Charley was shocked as she slowly processed what that meant. Alex had spied on her, but collecting her DNA? That was a new low. He had to be involved in some way.

"Mrs. Maitland used your wine glass from the charity ball," Alex answered Charley's unasked question.

Charley narrowed her eyes at him. A sharp pain went through her. Tears pooled behind her eyes as knowledge of what her magical night with him at the ball had really been about. Alex had taken her there just to get her DNA. Charley's disappointment in him got more painful by the minute.

Alex started to say something else, but Mrs. Maitland barreled ahead with her story. "You're a perfect match. The DNA indicates that you and my daughter are biological siblings. I would never have tracked you down or asked for your help, were it not for the fact that my Dorsey, your sister, has leukemia. She needs a stem cell transplant."

"I have a sister," Charley whispered softly in awe. What had only been a possibility was now confirmed by their DNA. Charley's voice was low as she slowly repeated the words, "A sister? I have a sister?" Like many only children, she had always longed for a sibling. But she had given up on that wish years ago, when her mother explained that she couldn't have more children.

Mrs. Maitland pressed forward, "Yes, but we need—"

Alex interrupted her. "Mrs. Maitland! Please!" he said sharply. "Slow down. Give Charley a chance to absorb what you just told her. This is not a board meeting."

Mrs. Maitland opened her mouth to continue, but stopped when she saw the frown on Alex's face. She switched tactics. "Would you like to meet her?"

Charley's mind settled and cautioned her to proceed slowly.

She didn't want to be played for a fool by only accepting Mrs. Maitland's version of the story. Mrs. Maitland would do anything to help her daughter. "First, I need to find an attorney and make sure what you're telling me about our DNA is true. On the surface, learning that I have a sister is wonderful news, but I won't be duped, Mrs. Maitland. Not by you—or anyone." Charley looked accusingly at Alex.

"It's true. I checked with the lab for you," Alex said softly.

"Why should I believe you—Mrs. Maitland's attorney? I'll get my own attorney." Did Alex really think she was stupid enough to accept his word? He had been knee-deep in the affair from the beginning.

"I'm here as *your* attorney," Alex replied firmly. "I know the suspicions you must have, but you can call my father and verify. I'm here to represent you. You can fire me if you want, but first, hear me out. It's entirely *your* decision whether to meet Mrs. Maitland's daughter or agree to any other requests she makes of you, including stem cell donation."

"Of course, you would say that. Isn't that a conflict of interest? Representing both sides in a case?" Charley's comment was spiteful, but her mind was racing as she sorted through conflicting emotions. She wanted to accept the possibility of a sister, but she was trapped between the two of them. Mrs. Maitland wanted something from her, and Alex had represented Mrs. Maitland's interests for years. He would want what she wanted. She couldn't trust him. He had again inserted himself in her business without asking her permission. The only thing keeping her from bolting from the room was the thought that somewhere nearby was her sister. She couldn't pass up the opportunity to meet this woman and find out if they were indeed related.

"Mr. Gilbert, another partner at the firm, has taken over as my attorney," Mrs. Maitland stated. "It seems Alex here doesn't want to represent me anymore."

"It's not that simple. Charley deserves legal representation, and she's right. I can't represent both sides," Alex said. He turned and looked at Charley, but didn't smile. Up until a few days ago, she and Alex had been friends. But that was over now. This was purely business. "I'm here on your behalf, but I can leave, if you want. Do you want me to leave?" Alex asked as his gaze locked with hers and held real concern. He waited for her answer.

"No. Please stay," Charley replied softly. There couldn't be that many legalities involved in any of this, and Charley could read documents as well as Alex. She could fight her own battles, too, but Alex might be useful. Based on Mrs. Maitland's behavior, it was clear that someone was needed to handle her and Alex had experience with that. And deep down, she was glad he was here. Even though she was angry at him, his presence gave her the courage to meet the woman who might be her sister.

Mrs. Maitland waved away both Alex's and Charley's comments and quickly went back to the main topic. "Do you want to meet Dorsey? Once you meet her, you'll be convinced that all I've told you this morning is true. You're sisters."

"Yes. Of course, I want to meet her." Charley couldn't leave without meeting the person who was purported to be her sister. She was confident she could spot an imposter.

Mrs. Maitland picked up a device the size of a cell phone and spoke into it: "Louisa, please bring Dorsey into the drawing room."

A modern twist on the silver bell the mistress used to summon a servant, thought Charley. But this wasn't a nineteenth-century drama on BBC. This was real life. Her life.

Charley clasped her hands tightly together, held her breath, and waited. Only a few minutes passed before the door opened, and a young woman came into the room. She hesitated for a moment as fear mixed with anticipation played over her face. Charley felt much the same way: confused and nervous. Charley clenched her hands even harder to keep them from shaking.

She rose from her seat and stepped forward to greet the woman. She stuck out her hand and said, "I'm Charley." She smiled, hoping to help the woman relax, while also trying to ease the tension that had her own knees shaking.

"I'm Dorsey," the young woman replied with a smile. She wore a scarf wrapped around her head that hid her hair. Her face was pale and drawn, but the smile, cheekbones, and bright green eyes matched those Charley saw each time she looked in the mirror. They were similar in build and height, though Dorsey was lighter in weight—possibly a result of her chemo and radiation treatments. Instantly, Charley knew this was her younger sister. She reached out again, but this time, she wrapped her arms around Dorsey and hugged her.

"It's good to meet you, Dorsey Maitland. I'm Charley Mathews, your older sister."

With shaking hands and tears in her eyes, Dorsey hugged her back.

Dorsey led Charley back to the sofa. They sat down with their hands still clasped together. They stared at each other as an instant unspoken connection passed between them.

Mrs. Maitland interrupted the silence. "I was preparing to ask Charley if she'd be willing to donate stem cells, but then decided she should meet you first." Mrs. Maitland looked at Charley with a question in her eyes.

"Of course I will," Charley said. "If I can." She didn't know much about the process of donating stem cells, but she did know that it was a common medical procedure. She frowned at Mrs. Maitland. She wasn't so callous that she wouldn't help someone if she could—even if that person wasn't related to her. "What do I need to do?"

"Excuse my mother's brusqueness. Her attorney—or former attorney—often calls her a 'bulldozer.'" Dorsey looked at Alex, and they exchanged smiles.

"Well, I have names for him, too," Mrs. Maitland replied. "'Cocky' is my favorite. He sometimes disagrees with my decisions and thinks he knows more about legal matters than I do. You'd think he was a lawyer or something." Mrs. Maitland looked at Alex and laughed. Charley's agreement to donate stem cells had removed much of the worry from her eyes. Relief had softened her manner, and she sounded almost giddy.

Alex ignored Mrs. Maitland's comment and answered Charley's question. "First, you need to get tested to make sure you're actually a match. Then, you'll be asked to sign various consent forms. And Charley, that's *informed* consent, so make sure the medical staff tells you exactly what is expected of you. They need to explain the procedures in detail."

"She's a match," Mrs. Maitland stated firmly, "and I can tell her all about the process."

"No, you can't," Alex replied sternly. "You'll let your need for a match run roughshod over her. I'm here to see that that doesn't happen."

"Oh, Alex. You can be such a fuddy-duddy sometimes. 'Fuddy-duddy' is another name I call you behind your back," Mrs. Maitland replied good-naturedly. "You're right. I do want Charley to do the transplant, but I wouldn't lie to Charley or Dorsey."

"I'm holding you to that," Alex replied, sounding unconvinced. "And this 'fuddy-duddy' has kept you out of jail, hasn't he? But the authorities would probably pay me to keep you out of their jail."

"I love a good fight with you, Alex," Mrs. Maitland laughed. "Sometimes, it's the fight more than the victory. You're a worthy opponent. That's why I kept you on as my attorney for so long."

"Humph! You're pushing too hard with this one," Alex replied sternly. He wasn't smiling. "This cocky fuddy-duddy isn't going to let you bulldoze Charley into doing something she doesn't want to do."

"It's alright, Alex," Charley said. "I appreciate your concern, but I can take it from here. I want to help Dorsey in any way I can."

Charley turned to Dorsey. She had a million questions she wanted to ask her. The two women were soon deeply engrossed in conversation.

Dorsey was twenty-one years old—seven years younger than Charley. Charley steered the discussion away from questions about her own early childhood, not yet ready to share those details, even with her sister. During a pause in the conversation, Charley glanced toward the window. Alex was gone. He had quietly slipped out of the room while she and Dorsey caught up on the twenty-one years they'd been apart. A packet of information with Charley's name on it lay on a table next to the sofa.

Charley accepted an invitation to stay for lunch with Dorsey and her mother. As they ate, personal details worked their way into the conversation. Charley briefly told them about her marriage to Daniel and her divorce, and Dorsey explained that she'd been in a serious relationship, but her boyfriend had cut and run when she received her cancer diagnosis.

"That just shows what weak character he had," Mrs. Maitland commented. "You can judge the character of men by whether they stick with you when times are bad."

"I know, Mom, but he wasn't that bad. Not everyone is as strong as you."

"Well, they should be. You should find yourself someone like Alex. He would stick by you even if hell froze over. Don't you think so, Charley?"

Charley didn't answer. Was Mrs. Maitland probing for information about her and Alex, or was she suggesting that Dorsey consider Alex as a potential suitor despite their age differences? If the question was about her and Alex, it was off the mark.

"Mom, hush," Dorsey said. "You're meddling again."

"I know, sweetie. I'm just trying to get your mind on something besides your illness." Mrs. Maitland's face showed real fear and concern. Underneath her hard, businesslike exterior, this was a worried mother fighting for her daughter's life.

Mrs. Maitland was the exact opposite of Charley's mother. Whereas Debra Mathews caved under the pressure of tragedy and adversity, Mrs. Maitland fought until she had exhausted all available options. Charley admired that trait, even as she resented being the target of some of Mrs. Maitland's tactics.

Soon, Dorsey excused herself to go lie down. She was tired, and the strain from the excitement of meeting Charley was beginning to show on her face. Charley hugged her goodbye and promised to come visit again the next day if Dorsey felt up to it.

Before Charley left, Mrs. Maitland gave her a slip of paper. "I called and set up an appointment for you with Dorsey's doctors at the cancer center tomorrow at nine a.m. You can go there first, then come visit Dorsey once you're done."

Charley nodded and took the paper. She could see how Alex had come up with the nickname 'bulldozer.' Mrs. Maitland was full steam ahead—a mixed metaphor, but appropriate.

When Charley arrived home, she sat on the front porch of the beach house with a glass of sweet tea and read over the information in the packet Alex had left for her. Once she had finished, she understood the process of stem cell collection and donation a little better. She would find out more tomorrow when she met with the doctor at the cancer center.

Charley's eyes wandered toward Alex's beach house. Nothing moved there today. Nothing had moved at the house for the last two days. He had gone back to the mainland and back to work. She couldn't lie—she missed him—and Rex. Her anger at him over the spying and prying into her life had softened somewhat. Now that she had spent some time with Mrs. Maitland, she realized who the driving force behind the spying had been. And now, he was mad at her. Hiding her professional identity had been an innocent mistake, but Alex wouldn't see it that way. If only he would let her explain. That thought echoed Alex's pleading at her door a few days ago. But her mistake hadn't invaded his life so it was his actions that had destroyed their relationship.

Relationship? Was that what she had with Alex? Well, they had a *friendship,* at least. Charley's gaze turned toward the ocean, a calming force whenever she felt confused and conflicted. But not this time. Two container ships, one inbound and one outbound, were barely visible on the horizon. They were a symbol for her and Alex's current situation—two ships passing each other and heading in different directions. Charley smiled at the trite cliché.

Face it, Charley Mathews, she thought, *these sad musings are because you're lonely. You miss Alex, and you want to talk about your sister with him.*

After a restless night, which seemed to be normal for her lately, Charley rose early and got ready for her drive into Charleston and her appointment at the cancer center. She arrived at the hospital promptly at nine a.m. Her blood test showed that she was indeed a match for Dorsey. Next, she underwent a complete physical exam. That done, Charley got dressed and awaited the results.

Dr. Baker soon arrived and pronounced Charley strong and healthy. She was a good candidate for donation and could become a stem cell donor if she wanted to.

Charley took the consent form from her purse that Alex

had included in the packet of information. She let Dr. Baker look over it before she signed it. He affirmed that it was the exact same form they gave to all donors. Knowing that Alex had looked over it already made Charley more confident that there weren't any hidden details or misunderstandings lurking in the medical jargon it contained. Alex had signed the top of the form in the upper right-hand corner.

"I see by your attorney's signature that he's advising you during this process. That's good," Dr. Baker said as he looked over the form. "We want all our clients to be well-informed and confident in what they're doing. Your attorney also called me this morning."

"Alex? He called?" Charley asked. "Why?"

"He had some general questions about the donation procedure. He had read up on it, but wanted me to verbally go over it with him. He's straight to the point," Dr. Baker said with a smile. "I wish my personal attorney was that thorough."

Charley blushed. "He's definitely thorough and takes his job seriously."

"He does," Dr. Baker agreed. Then he leaned back, rested his elbows on the arms of his chair, and began the explanation he gave all stem cell donors. "I'm giving you a general description of stem cell donations. Feel free to stop me and ask any questions you may have."

Charley nodded as Dr. Baker began. "There are two types of stem cell donation that can be used in Ms. Maitland's case: peripheral blood stem cells and bone marrow cells. In peripheral donation, the donor—you—would be required to take injections for five days before collection in order to increase your cell count. Once we finish the injections, the collection of the stem cells will be done on an outpatient basis. Collection takes two-to-four hours. This type of collection often needs to be done more than once, until enough stem cells are collected."

Dr. Baker paused. "Do you have any questions?"

Charley shook her head, and he continued, "The second method is bone marrow harvest. Collection is done in an operating room under anesthesia. A needle is inserted into the back of the hip bone, into the marrow, and the cells are withdrawn. The collection takes about one-to-two hours, with the objective of withdrawing about two pints of marrow. After collection, the donor is taken to the recovery room or, if needed, to a hospital room until fully alert."

"How long does the donor remain in the hospital with the bone marrow method?" Charley asked.

"The donor is usually allowed to go home within a few hours or by the next morning, at the latest. Dorsey is young, so either type of donor cells will work for her. Which method you choose is up to you. Any questions?" Dr. Baker asked as he finished.

"No," Charley replied. "I believe I understand both methods. Alex, uh, my attorney, also gave me some pamphlets that describe the procedures. I can refer to them if I think of something."

"Good, good," Dr. Baker said, nodding.

"I've gave it some thought, after reading the pamphlets, and it seems like the bone marrow harvest is less involved and easier to do," Charley said. "It's the best method in my case. I live out on one of the islands, so a daily trip into the mainland would be harder. Let's go with the bone marrow method."

"That makes sense," Dr. Baker agreed.

"I can ask my aunt to come down from New Jersey, just in case I need to have someone with me after the collection." Charley didn't expect to need help, but Aunt Beth would insist that she and Uncle Lance come down anyway.

"That's good," Dr. Baker agreed. "Serious complications are rare, but you probably shouldn't be alone for a couple days afterward. The effects of collection are usually mild: just muscle soreness and some aching in the back and hip. This can be treated with ibuprofen. Most donors are back to their regular schedules in two or three days."

Before Charley left the cancer center, Dr. Baker's nurse scheduled the bone marrow collection for the following Monday. They would store the bone marrow until Dorsey was ready for the transfer. Dorsey would start prepping for the procedure a few days after the collection.

Charley left the cancer center and drove to the Maitland estate. Mrs. Maitland was not at home, so Charley and Dorsey were able to have a nice visit with just the two of them. When Dorsey became tired, Charley hugged her goodbye and left for home. She called Aunt Beth as soon as she arrived back at the beach house. Charley bypassed the usual greetings and blurted out, "Aunt Beth, I have a sister."

"What?" Shocked, Aunt Beth took a moment to digest Charley's declaration. "What? A sister? Are you sure? But... I don't understand. How?"

"Did you know that my parents donated frozen embryos for adoption after I was born?" Charley asked.

"No, I didn't know that. I knew they had some left over after Debra became pregnant with you. I completely forgot about them. At the time, I assumed they either paid the storage fee to keep them or opted to have them destroyed. Adoption was a relatively new option at the time, so it never occurred to me that they would do that."

"It's true. I have a sister. Our DNA proves it."

"I'm truly shocked," Aunt Beth said. "I vaguely remember your mother insisting that she wanted nothing to do with the embryos once she couldn't use them herself, but she had trouble deciding what to do with them. George must have convinced her to donate them."

"Dorsey looks just like me. I still can't believe I have a sister."
Charley launched into the full story, recounting the events of
the last few days and the details of Dorsey's leukemia. "I'm
doing the bone marrow collection next Monday," she added at
the end.

"My goodness! Things are moving so quickly! Are you sure
about all this, Charley? You're sure that she's your sister and that
you aren't being tricked?"

"Yes, I'm sure. You'd only have to meet her to see that it's
true. Alex was at the meeting with Mrs. Maitland. He's not
speaking to me personally, but he's acting as my attorney. He
verified the DNA and looked over the forms before I signed
them."

"What? Alex is mad at you? I thought you were mad at Alex.
I'm having a hard time keeping up with you, Charley," Aunt
Beth replied, confused.

"Daniel was here. He let it slip that I'm Ce Ce Kane. Now,
Alex is angry with me for not telling him."

"Daniel was there? My goodness!" Aunt Beth exclaimed
again. "Slow down. My head is spinning. I did warn you that
you should tell Alex before he found out on his own."

"I know. I intended to tell him, but things got a little crazy
after I found he had been spying on me," Charley replied.

"The spying is old news compared to everything else you
just told me. Lance is away on business right now, but he gets
home tonight. We'll be down there no later than the weekend."

Charley assured Aunt Beth that the donation was a routine
procedure. Still, she was happy to have her aunt and uncle with
her, if for no other reason than for moral support. Plus, she was
anxious for them to meet Dorsey.

Before Charley ended the call, she asked, "Do you think I
should tell Mom about Dorsey?"

There was a short pause as Aunt Beth considered the question.

"No. Not yet, anyway. She may not like the idea of meeting a daughter that she can't claim, and she was very adamant that she didn't want to be involved with the frozen embryos."

"That's true," Charley agreed. "I don't have any idea how she'd react."

"And just think," Aunt Beth added, "if she does get to know Dorsey, and Dorsey then loses her battle with cancer, what would that do to your mother? I don't want to see her fall apart again. She seems to have finally found a bit of happiness. I think it's best to wait. We can decide later, once we see how this all plays out."

Charley hadn't considered the possibility that the stem cell transplant might not work and that she might lose Dorsey so soon after finding her. She couldn't let herself even think about that prospect. But Aunt Beth's reasoning where her mother was concerned made sense. Charley was still getting used to the idea herself that she had a sister, so it might be too much to spring on her fragile mother.

CHAPTER SIXTEEN

Uncle Lance drove Charley and Aunt Beth to the cancer center early on Monday morning. She was scheduled to check in at nine a.m., and the collection would start at 10:30 a.m. Charley was nervous, even though she was confident that the stem cell collection was a safe and fairly routine procedure. But it was reassuring that she had her family with her during the collection.

Aunt Beth and Uncle Lance had arrived on Friday, as promised. They had always supported her through everything she did since she came to live with them. There was never a school function or sporting event that she participated in where at least one of them was not in attendance. Accompanying her today was just routine for them.

Charley had visited with Dorsey several times over the past few days. Dorsey tired quickly, and their visits were brief. Aunt Beth and Uncle Lance had joined Charley for dinner at the Maitland Estate on Saturday night. They quickly agreed that Dorsey was indeed Charley's sister, even without DNA confirmation. Not only did they look alike, but their mannerisms and gestures were also similar. They laughed similarly, and just like Charley, Dorsey slanted her eyes and quirked her left eyebrow when she questioned or disagreed with something that was said. The eye rolls Dorsey directed at her mother were identical to the ones Aunt Beth had received from Charley over the years.

Shortly after her arrival at the cancer center on the day of the collection, Charley was prepped for her procedure by the nurses. Aunt Beth and Uncle Lance came to see her before she was wheeled off to the operating room.

"We'll be here waiting for you when you get back. Just relax and know that you're helping your sister," Aunt Beth said as she kissed Charley on the forehead.

"I know. Thank you," replied Charley. She squeezed Aunt Beth's hand.

Beth and Lance returned to the waiting room to wait for notification that the stem cell collection was finished. They took their seats and were checking their phones when someone stopped in front of them.

"Alex!" Aunt Beth looked up to see Alex standing before her. "What are you doing here?" She rose and hugged him.

Lance stood and shook his hand. "Sit with us," he invited.

"I wanted to check on Charley and make sure things are going as planned," Alex said as he took the chair beside them. "Mrs. Maitland let me know the collection was this morning."

"She just went back," Beth said. "The doctor assured us that complications are rare, though the procedure will take a while."

"I know," Alex said, nodding. "I talked with Dr. Baker. One-to-two hours, he said." He leaned forward, clasped his hands together, and rested his elbows on his knees.

Beth put her hand on Alex's shoulder. "She'll be alright."

"I know," Alex said again. He fidgeted in his chair. "You want a cup of coffee?" At Beth's nod, he stood and went to the coffee stand in the corner. He soon returned with three cups of coffee. "It looks strong but still might be better than Charley's." He smiled as he handed them the warm beverages, then took his seat again.

As they sipped their coffee, they chatted casually about what Beth and Lance had done since their return to New Jersey. No one mentioned the status of Charley and Alex's current relationship.

Not long after Alex finished his coffee, he was up and pacing around the room. He stopped to read the flyers and announcements on the bulletin board before moving on to the window. There, he stopped and gazed out at the parking lot.

"Hey," Lance said as he walked up to Alex. "Waiting is hard for those of us who are used to calling the shots. Do you suppose it's a flaw in the male species?"

"It's one among many," Alex replied with a smile. He seemed to have something more than worry about the stem cell collection bothering him this morning. "I just wish Charley had let me explain that I had nothing to do with the folder she found. You do know about the folder, don't you?" At Lance's nod, he went on, "Well, nothing other than accept it from my father and stick it in the desk drawer. Lance, I didn't even look at it."

"I believe you, Alex, but I'm not the one you have to convince. Did you let her explain why she didn't tell you about the name she uses for her photography exhibits?"

"That's different. She had plenty of opportunities to say something. I bid thirty thousand dollars for one of her photos and didn't hear a peep from her about being the photographer." Alex warmed to the subject. "And her husband was the one who spilled her secret!"

"Daniel is her ex-husband. 'Ex,' as in, 'used to be and never will be again.'" Lance placed his hand on Alex's shoulder and gently shook it. "My advice? You both made mistakes, and you need to talk. Clear the air." He turned and walked back to his chair beside Beth. "Young people!" he muttered to her as he sat down.

"You're so ancient—an old wise man—aren't you, Lance?" she teased gently.

Lance picked up Beth's hand, kissed her knuckles, and smiled. "I'm just trying to impart lessons I've learned the hard way, my sweet."

It was almost 1:30 p.m. when Dr. Baker came into the waiting room. Beth, Lance, and Alex all rose to meet him.

Before he could say anything, Alex stepped forward and stuck out his hand. "Dr. Baker, I'm Alex Morgan."

"Her attorney?" Dr. Baker asked somewhat nervously. "I can assure you—"

"I'm here as a friend, not as an attorney," Alex said, cutting the doctor off. "How is she?"

"The collection procedure went according to plan. We got started a little late, but didn't have any problems. She's in recovery now, but she's having some trouble with nausea."

"What do you mean?" Aunt Beth asked in a chorus with Lance and Alex.

Dr. Baker held up his hands in a calming gesture. "Don't be alarmed. This sometimes happens with anesthesia. It's not from the collection. She's nauseated and has thrown up a couple of times. We're going to watch her a little longer and hope the nausea goes away. If it doesn't, and she can't keep anything down, we'll move her to a room and keep her overnight. It's just a precaution, nothing to be alarmed about. A nurse will keep you posted one way or the other." With that, he went back behind the swinging doors to the surgery wing.

"Go grab some lunch," Alex suggested to Beth and Lance. I'll call you if there's news." They both nodded and walked toward the hospital cafeteria. They had just returned to the waiting room and taken their seats when the nurse appeared.

"We've moved Ms. Mathews to a room—Room 305," she said. "She's still nauseated, so Dr. Baker has ordered some medication to help with the nausea. The meds will make her sleep, and sleep will also help. But you can go on up to her room and see her, if you like."

Aunt Beth picked up her purse and phone. She and Lance started toward the bank of elevators located just around the corner from the waiting room.

"I'm going to go grab a bite to eat," Alex said from behind them. "I have a deposition at 3:30, but I'll be back tonight. I'll also update Mrs. Maitland and Dorsey. Make sure you call me if there's any change." Alex turned and quickly strode toward the automatic doors that led outside.

Aunt Beth watched him go, then quirked an eyebrow at Uncle Lance.

"Maybe he doesn't want to see Charley in a hospital bed," Lance said. "And he's probably on a tight deadline. I hope they will talk soon and clear the air."

When Beth and Lance walked into Charley's room, the nurse was injecting a medication into her IV. She looked up as they entered the room.

"This will make her sleep," the nurse said, "so if you want to chat, you need to do so quickly. This will work very fast."

"How are you feeling?" Aunt Beth asked as she sat down in a chair next to the bed and took Charley's hand. Uncle Lance sat in a chair across the room.

"Like I'm going to barf," Charley replied with a weak smile. "I don't barf gracefully."

After only a few minutes, Charley began to get groggy, and

very soon, she closed her eyes. Aunt Beth and Uncle Lance settled into the visitors' chairs in the room.

Alex returned to the hospital around nine p.m. and called
Beth and Lance into the hallway. After getting an update on
Charley's condition, he handed a set of keys to Lance. "Here's
the keys to my house. The address in on the key chain. It's not
far from here. You and Beth go get some sleep. I'll stay here. I'll
call if you're needed."

Beth and Lance objected, but Alex was persistent. "It doesn't
make sense for all of us to stay here. You've been here all day.
I'm not leaving, so you two go and get some rest. You don't need
to go back to the island. I just changed the sheets in the guest
room about an hour ago. It's the room with the covers turned
down. Help yourself to anything you find in the kitchen."

Beth and Lance gave in when it was clear that Alex wasn't
taking no for an answer. With assurances that he would call if
there was any news, they left the hospital.

Alex pulled a chair up to Charley's bedside. He leaned
forward, with his elbows resting on his knees and his hands
clasped together beneath his chin. He lost track of time as he
sat beside the bed with his eyes closed and his head bowed. He
dozed off some time during the night.

Suddenly, a hand touched his head. He looked up. Charley's
eyes were closed. She was still asleep, but her free hand had
reached out and was roving gently over the side of his head.
She touched his ear, then moved down the side of his face, then
crossed his face. When her hand brushed his lips, Alex placed a
soft kiss on her palm. Her hand lingered on his mouth.

Charley mumbled something unintelligible, then pulled

back and dropped her hand onto the bed. Alex picked it up, gently held it a moment, and then covered it with the sheet.

Alex sat unmoving for several minutes as he watched Charley sleep. Lance was right: he and Charley needed to have a long conversation. Would she be open to a discussion about all the things that had gone wrong between them? In view of everything that had happened—Dorsey's cancer, Charley finding a sister—their issues with each other seemed trivial. But their disagreements, simple or not, were what was keeping them from a friendship and the possibility of more.

More than friendship? Is that what he wanted with Charley?

Yes. Meeting Charley had made him realize that the life he'd been living—working constantly and remaining closed-off like a monk—was *not* what he wanted.

Alex's workload was heavy right now. He had the Thompson merger that was entering its final phase, and he had just taken on another case for Save Our Islands. As soon as he had his workload under control and Charley had recovered, they were going to have that talk. He had to convince her of his innocence in the collection of her personal data.

Beth and Lance returned to the hospital the next morning around six a.m. Alex motioned for them to follow him into the hall. "She had a peaceful night," he said. "The nurse said she should be waking up any minute now."

Alex accepted his keys back from Lance, but then removed the house key from the ring and handed it back to Lance. "They'll probably release her this morning. I'd like you to take her to my house."

"That's not necessary," Beth said. "We can take her home to the beach house"

"No, listen. If she has any further problems, she might need to return to the hospital. I don't expect that'll be necessary, but if you're on the island and the bridge shuts down for some reason—which does happen—you'll be marooned on the island for who knows how long."

"Good point," Lance agreed. Beth nodded.

"According to everything I know about the collection procedure, she should be in the clear in a day or two. Put her in the master bedroom. I'll be working late tonight—a business meeting—and I'll use one of the guest bedrooms," Alex advised.

"Are you sure? We don't want to put you out," Beth said.

"It's no problem. The kitchen is well-stocked, but there's a bunch of takeout menus in a kitchen drawer if you want to go that route." Alex looked at his watch. "I have to run. Just make yourselves at home."

Beth and Lance watched Alex rush down the hallway toward the elevators.

"No wonder he stays so fit," Lance commented as they watched him practically run down the hallway. "He's always on the go."

Dr. Baker discharged Charley later that morning with instructions to take ibuprofen for her pain and call his office if it got worse. Around ten a.m., she climbed into Aunt Beth's car, thankful that the procedure was over and that she was going home.

Uncle Lance had driven for about ten minutes when Charley noticed he wasn't taking the route to Turtle Island. "We need to go back that way and take the Maybank Highway," she said, pointing behind her.

"We aren't going home today. We're going to Alex's place," Uncle Lance said.

"What? Why?" Charley asked. "I'm confused."

"Alex cautioned that if you need further medical help and you're on the island, if the bridge shuts down, you'd be stranded." Aunt Beth turned and looked at Charley in the backseat. "We agreed. Spending another day on the mainland is a good idea, just in case."

"I'm glad you and Alex are making my decisions for me," Charley grumbled. "Alex won't speak to me, but he'll lend me his house? I don't need his help. I have a house of my own."

"I could point out that you aren't speaking to him, either—but I won't," Uncle Lance, said. "Beth and I think it's best to take his advice on this. He knows more about the islands than we do."

"Spoken like a man! Just take his side," Charley argued grumpily.

"I'm not taking sides, just pointing out the obvious," Uncle Lance replied. "Don't worry. I doubt you'll see him. From what I've observed, he's been working some very long hours."

"Hmph." Charley crossed her arms over her middle in the stubborn stance she'd used since she was a toddler when she didn't get her way. What Uncle Lance said made sense, but she was tired and crotchety and maybe still a little disoriented from the anesthesia. Mostly, she was mad at Alex for being so considerate. Being mad at someone for being nice to her sounded strange, even in a her grumpy mood.

Charley's sullen mood had improved by the time they pulled into the driveway of a ranch-style house located on a large corner lot. The house was large and rambling, but modest from outside appearances. No columns or turrets adorned the red-brick single-story home. Rows of red blooming azaleas separated the front of the house from a tree shaded, well-manicured lawn.

A homey home, Charley thought as she emerged from the car.

Uncle Lance opened the front door and let Charley and Aunt Beth precede him into the foyer. A red and white bundle of fur came racing through the kitchen and across the living room, then came to a screeching halt at Charley's feet.

"Rex! How are you, buddy?" Charley bent down, hugged Rex, and kissed him on the head. "I've missed you at the beach." Rex danced around and returned Charley's kisses.

Charley walked into the living room and sat down on a sofa. She patted the space beside her, and Rex jumped up. He settled down with his head in Charley's lap. She looked around the room. A bank of pictures was displayed nearby on a side table. She eased out from under Rex's head and crossed the room to get a closer look. There were photos of Alex's parents, his brother, and two couples whom she assumed were his grandparents. Toward the back of the photos was one of her. Charley picked it up to examine it. It had been taken not long after the baby egrets had taken flight. She hadn't realized he took it.

"Alex Morgan, you learned your lessons well," she whispered. Her face was framed perfectly, and he had captured the wonder and joy on her face from witnessing the young birds taking their first flight. She could not have taken a better photo herself.

Aunt Beth came in from the kitchen with a steaming cup of coffee and handed it to Charley. "Don't drink it if it makes you ill," she cautioned. "Do you feel okay? Do you want something to eat?"

"I'm fine, Aunt Beth," Charley replied. "And yes, I could eat some lunch, but don't go to a lot of trouble."

"There's deli meat in the fridge. Would you like a sandwich?"

"Sounds good. I could make it myself, but you seem to know your way around here." Charley took a large gulp of coffee and closed her eyes. "Yum. So good. No one makes coffee like you, Aunt Beth."

"You're just coffee-deprived this morning," Beth laughed. "Lance and I stayed here last night. Oh! By the way, we went to the beach house last night for a few things, and I brought you some toiletries, just in case you'd have to spend another night in the hospital." She handed a cosmetic bag to Charley. "Sorry, but you'll have to wear what you have on."

"Thank you! I definitely need to brush my teeth and wash my face. My clothes and hair will have to wait."

"Follow me. I'll show you where you can clean up." Beth led Charley down the hall and into a large bedroom. A king-sized bed sat in the middle of the room, which was lit by sunshine that streamed through the floor-to-ceiling windows in the back wall. A door opened to a patio and a sparkling pool surrounded by pots of blooming pink hydrangeas and red bromeliads.

"I'm pretty sure this isn't a guest room," Charley said as she looked around. The décor was classic and traditional, neither overly masculine nor overly feminine, but she instantly knew whom the room belonged to. She started to back out of the room.

"This is the master, but it's where Alex said to put you."

"I don't want to take his room," Charley objected. "I can use a guest room."

"It's just for one night. The bathroom's this way." Aunt Beth turned, and Charley followed her into the bathroom. "I'll let you clean up while I make us some lunch."

Charley followed Aunt Beth's instructions and laid out her toiletries on the double vanity. She noticed a pair of pajamas and a T-shirt on a bench next to the whirlpool bathtub. Her name was written on a piece of paper lying on top.

Charley's eyes widened in surprise at the pajamas. A girl-friend's? Rebecca's? Was he clueless? She'd much rather sleep in her own clothes than the pajamas one of his girlfriends had left behind.

Charley brushed her teeth, washed her face, applied moisturizer, and combed the tangles from her hair. She still wore yesterday's clothes, and her muscles ached as though she had just finished a strenuous workout, but she felt better after freshening up.

"Let's go find some lunch. What do you say?" Charley said to Rex who had followed her into the bathroom.

Together, Charley and Rex left the room and walked down the hall toward the kitchen. Aunt Beth and Uncle Lance were making sandwiches in a large, sunny kitchen. All the appliances were new and modern—an obvious upgrade from the original kitchen. As an amateur chef, Alex would naturally have the best tools in order to hone his cooking skills.

Charley sat down on a stool next to the bar. "Ouch," she said. "I keep forgetting to sit down carefully."

Aunt Beth passed her a bottle of ibuprofen and a glass of water, then placed a plate with a sandwich and a small pile of potato chips beside it. Charley's stomach rumbled in appreciation as she bit into the turkey sandwich.

"Do you know when Alex will be home?" she asked, keeping her voice casual. It wasn't that she was anxious to see Alex; she just didn't want to be surprised by his sudden appearance.

"He said he had a late business meeting. I think he's doing more than just his job at the law firm," Uncle Lance replied.

"He sometimes does pro bono work for an environmental group," Charley supplied. "Maybe that's it." She took another bite of her sandwich, then looked up at Aunt Beth and Uncle Lance. "I see you two! Stop with those knowing looks! I was just curious to know if you knew when he'd be home."

"Uh huh," Uncle Lance said, making an exaggerated expression of disbelief. He rolled his eyes at Auth Beth.

"I'll leave you two mimes alone," Charley said as she picked up the rest of her sandwich. "I'm going to finish this out by the pool and call Dorsey and her mother. Come, Rex."

Rex didn't follow behind her, but instead hit the doggie door in the mudroom off the kitchen. He was waiting for Charley when she stepped through the kitchen door onto the patio.

Charley finished her lunch, settled in the sunshine, and dialed Dorsey's number. Alex had already called them, so they knew about Charley's extra night in the hospital. Charley assured them that she was fine and there was nothing to be concerned about. Obviously, Alex had appointed himself her guardian as well as her attorney. Deciding where she should spend the night and acting as a go-between with her relatives should have made her angry, but knowing that someone other than Aunt Beth and Uncle Lance was looking out for her gave her a warm feeling. Still, she planned to ask him to back off. This New Jersey/New York girl by way of Atlanta now living in South Carolina could take care of herself.

That thought reminded her of the circuitous route her life had taken. In her twenty-eight years, she had almost come full circle. Or maybe, more accurately put, she had been running in circles all this time. Both scenarios described her life of late.

Dorsey updated Charley on her own scheduled treatment. She would start the conditioning process later that week, getting herself ready for the stem cell transplant. She would undergo intense chemotherapy, which would kill the cancer cells and also suppress her immune system. This procedure would prepare her bones for the infusion of new cells.

"Some patients are permitted to go home after a transplant," Dorsey said, "but my mother has convinced the doctors that I should stay in isolation for a few days before going home. A precaution, she says, against infection of any type. She's treating me like a baby."

"It's just for a few days," Charley said. "I'd also feel better knowing you're there and safe."

"Well, you know my mother, the bulldozer," Dorsey laughed. "She didn't give me a say in the matter."

Once the transplant was complete, Dorsey would need to undergo regular tests at the hospital to check the levels of her blood cells and platelets. Patients sometimes needed blood transfusions to help with the platelet level, but she was hopeful she wouldn't need that.

"I can give blood, if you need it. And I know that the rest of my—or now it's your—family will help in any way they can," Charley said.

"I know you would," Dorsey said. "I can't thank you enough for what you did yesterday."

"What are sisters for? But stop! I should thank you. I have the sister I've always wanted. I'm thrilled about that," Charley assured Dorsey. "I'll come visit as soon as your doctors clear you for visitors."

"It's my mother, not the doctors, you'll have a problem with on that," Dorsey chuckled. "The challenge will be keeping her from putting me on a leash or locking me in my room."

"We'll find a way to manage your mother," Charley promised. Soon after, she finished their call.

Charley spent the rest of the afternoon playing fetch with Rex and taking him for a walk around the neighborhood. Maybe if she kept moving she would work out the soreness in her muscles and joints. Alex's neighborhood was upper-middle class, with most of the houses looking similar to his—not ostentatious, but homey and comfortable. A memory niggled at the edge of Charley's mind as she walked, and a picture of another house from long ago came into focus. The houses in Alex's neighborhood reminded her of the one she had lived in for the first eight years of her life.

After the walk with Rex, Charley took a short nap on the

patio in the shade of a large oak tree. Even with the nap, she was ready for bed early that evening, not long after she had finished the spaghetti dinner prepared by Aunt Beth and Uncle Lance. Alex had not returned home when she went to bed around eight p.m.

Charley pulled back the covers and crawled into bed. The sheets were fresh and clean, but there was a pleasant lingering masculine scent in the room, one she had come to associate with Alex. Comforted by the familiar scent, she nestled deep into the softness of the bed and was soon fast asleep.

Charley was awoken by the sound of the bedroom door opening later that night. Through the crack in the opened door, she saw Alex standing just outside the bedroom. A nightlight in the hallway lit his silhouette. He was dressed in jeans and a T-shirt. Charley pretended to be asleep as she watched him through partially closed eyes.

"Rex, you want to go out?" Alex whispered. "Come on, boy. Let's go outside for a minute." Rex didn't rise from his position on the floor by the side of the bed. He turned his head and looked away from Alex.

"Okay. Don't say I didn't ask." There was a slight bump as Alex pulled the door shut. Charley looked over at the bedside clock. It was 1:30 a.m. Alex had worked very late. Or maybe he'd been on a date?

Charley forced thoughts of Alex's late night from her mind, rolled over and quickly went back to sleep. She didn't wake up again until daylight lightened the drapes and blinds in the bedroom. She heard noise and movement somewhere in the house, and then, a loud sound came from the kitchen. Charley came fully awake. She was ready to get up anyway, as her back and hip were in need of some movement and stretching. Charley got out of bed, ran her fingers through her tangled hair, straightened her clothes as best she could, and with Rex at her heels, made her way to the kitchen.

Alex stood at the counter, pouring coffee into a cup. His hair was damp from his morning shower. Freshly shaven, he was dressed for work with his tie loosened around his neck, and his suit jacket hung over the back of a chair nearby. Charley paused near the entrance to the kitchen, leaned against the door, and silently watched him. The clock on the microwave showed that it was six a.m. *To bed late and up early*, Charley thought. *How long could he keep that up?*

Rex, who had followed her down the hall, gave away her position when he dashed through the kitchen and outside through the doggie door in the mudroom. Alex turned toward her. His eyes moved over her, then came back to rest on her messy hair. He stared at her for a few seconds before he spoke.

"Sorry if I woke you. I knocked over a pan, and it hit the floor before I could catch it. How are you feeling this morning?" He opened the fridge, took out a carton of cream, and poured some into his cup of coffee.

"Don't worry about it. I was ready to get up anyway," Charley said. "I'm feeling better. I felt like a truck had run over me yesterday, but the ibuprofen seems to have helped the muscle soreness." Charley relaxed, happy to have a normal conversation with him, one similar to those they'd had before their falling-out. It took more energy than she had in her this morning to be as angry as she had been when she found the blue folder. But she still hadn't forgotten or forgiven what he'd done.

Alex's smart looking business suit made Charley suddenly self-conscious of her wrinkled jeans and shirt. She tried to smooth out some of the wrinkles in her T-shirt with her palms.

"I see you didn't use the pj's that were left you," Alex said as he took a sip of coffee. His eyes never left her face.

"No, I didn't. I didn't feel comfortable sleeping in your girlfriend's pj's." Charley badly wanted a cup of coffee, but she wouldn't get any closer to him. She could spar with him better from a distance.

"What makes you think my girlfriends sleep in anything?" Alex asked, stressing the plural in *girlfriends*.

The image of Alex in bed with some unclothed female leaped into her imagination. Charley couldn't stop the blush that spread across her cheeks.

Alex's eyes sparked, and his gaze remained fixed on her face. "My mother will be insulted that you compared her to my girlfriends. She's quite sure she's a cut above all of them," Alex added. "I asked her to bring the pajamas by yesterday, just in case you needed them."

Charley blinked, taken aback. She hadn't considered the pj's were his mother's. His comment threw her for a second, but it eliminated the earlier visual of him in bed and loosened her tongue. "How is it you know I didn't use them? Did you sneak into my room last night while I was sleeping?" Her question was a weak counterpunch, but the flush on his face signaled he was surprise that she saw him at the door. "Just imagine," she teased, "Alex Morgan sneaking into my bedroom. My, my!"

"Actually, it's my bedroom. And yes, I did peek in last night, but I was just trying to get Rex to go out for a tinkle. Don't worry. I was too tired to jump your bones—even if that had been my intent. Which it wasn't," Alex replied.

He rinsed out his coffee cup, then put it in the dishwasher and turned toward Charley. "I'd like to stay here and trade barbs with you, but I have to get to the office. By the way, if your next question is about where I was last night, Conner and Mary got arrested, and I had to bail them out."

"What? What happened?" Charley asked. Her concern for the two environmentalists had made her momentarily forget her contest of words with Alex.

"They found some construction runoff at a building site on

James Island. They were there taking pictures when the construction site manager caught them. He had them arrested for trespassing. This wasn't chemicals, just construction debris that wasn't properly secured—along with some pollutants. I waited until the manager left the site, then went to see for myself. I'm meeting with another attorney this morning who's offered to help me decide our next step."

"I… uh, what you do is not my concern," Charley replied, turning back to their verbal sparring. "I'm not interested in your whereabouts last night. If you're out fooling around after midnight, it's your business."

"If I fool around any time, *you'll* be the first to know," Alex returned. He grinned, and as much as she tried to stop it, color again rose in her cheeks. "Pink is a good color on you, by the way." He didn't laugh outright, but Charley could see that he was holding in a chuckle, pleased that she got the meaning of his remark.

Charley was suddenly tongue-tied again and without a comeback. Alex argued for a living, so it wasn't much of a contest between them. Her reservoir of clever zingers suddenly dried up as he slowly approached her.

Alex placed one hand on the doorframe above Charley's head, then leaned closer. He was close enough that she could smell his aftershave—a slight hint of citrus, mixed with the same masculine smell she had noticed in his bedroom. "Ms. Charlotte Christine Rainier-Mathews… Phillips… Ce Ce Kane… when I get through with the craziness that is my life at the moment, we need to talk. I think I'm ready for that explanation you promised me."

"Well… I…" Charley paused, searching for a reply. Without smiling, she said, "Just to remind you, I didn't compile a file on you and spy on you."

"Neither did I," Alex insisted. He removed his hand from

the doorframe, ran it across the back of his neck, and shrugged away her accusation. He remained quiet for a moment, but mischief quickly returned to his eyes as they settled back on her face. Alex reached out, gently placing warm hands on either side of her face, and stared intently into her eyes. She didn't move.

"Yep! That many aliases must mean you're hiding something," Alex whispered softly, his lips close to hers, as his smoky-blue eyes probed her face. "A dark secret? A hidden life? Are you running from the law, Charlotte Christine?" For a moment, Charley thought he was going to kiss her, but instead, he withdrew his hands and dropped them to his side. He still didn't step away.

Charley wanted to deny his accusation, but his nearness had her thinking of other things. She struggled to hide her disappointment that he hadn't kissed her. Alex ran his forefinger down her nose, then straightened and walked away.

"I have to go. See you later, Miss Whatever-Your-Real-Name-Is," Alex said as he picked up his suit jacket from the chair, draped it across his forearm, and walked into the hallway. He stopped, picked up his briefcase from the hall table, and turned toward her. "If you go back to Turtle Island today, just leave the key under the mat by the front door. And Charley?" Alex paused by the front door, his hand on the knob. "Don't even think about stealing my dog. I know where you live."

Charley couldn't hide her own smile as she watched him pull open the door. Without looking at her again, he stepped outside and pulled the door shut behind him. Charley stared at the closed door for a few minutes before leaving the doorway and making her way to the coffee pot in the kitchen.

Charley filled her coffee cup, then sat down at the kitchen table with one of the muffins she found stacked on a plate on the counter. Rex came through the doggie door and sat down at her feet. The thrust-and-parry argument with Alex had taken her mind off of any lingering pain she felt from the stem cell collection procedure. Alex's nearness had caused her more discomfort than any pain in her hip. But was it *discomfort* she felt this morning, or was the feeling more akin to *anticipation* of what he might say or do next? He'd managed to stay one step ahead of her during their verbal sparring.

Alex kept insisted he hadn't compiled the folder of information on her she'd found at the beach house. It was an invasion of her life so it wasn't close to the same as her not telling him her pseudonym. The evidence of spying she'd found was hard to explain away.

"Whatcha think, Rex? Will your master and I ever get back to trusting each other?" Rex sat silently and stared up at her. "You don't know? Neither do I. But it's a crazy situation, isn't it?" Rex barked once.

Before leaving Alex's house, Charley, Aunt Beth, and Uncle Lance straightened and tidied the house. Charley scrawled a note for Alex and left it on the kitchen counter, letting him know the extent of the tidying they had done. Aunt Beth added a thank-you for his help over the last three days. They locked the door behind them and hid the key under the mat, then climbed into the car to drive home to Turtle Island.

As they pulled into the driveway of the beach house, Charley couldn't suppress a sigh of happy relief. The sign "*Leig Anail,* that Annabelle had left hanging on the edge of the porch welcomed her home. The squeak of the weathered board on the porch was a comforting sound after being away for three days. Charley appreciated Aunt Annabelle's gift more than ever this morning.

Daniel had called the house a 'shack,' but he was always chasing shiny new objects. He could never appreciate the beauty Charley found in this aged house or feel the history left behind by her ancestors. She pictured them gathered at the house for summer holidays or crouched in fear as they waited out powerful storms that came roaring in from the Atlantic. Her father had likely spent time here, too. Family history was what made the beach house important to her. It was a Mathews home, with a Mathews legacy. No, Daniel would never understand that. It would take someone like Alex to appreciate the history of this house.

Charley's gaze swung across the yard toward Alex's house. How long would he remain at his house in Goose Creek? Would the pull of the ocean soon bring him back to the beach? He loved the beach, but with his workload at the moment, he obviously didn't have time to commute back and forth to the island. But what about his summer off? What had that been about? Their argument over her pseudonym had made him flee the island and his anger had kept him away for days. But now he seemed ready to talk. Was she ready to hear his explanation?

"He was there, you know," Aunt Beth said at Charley's elbow. She nodded toward Alex's house.

"What? Who was where?" Charley asked.

"Alex. He spent Monday night by your bedside at the hospital," Aunt Beth replied. "He insisted on staying there with you while Lance and I spent the night at his house."

Vague pieces of memory floated to the surface. She hadn't been dreaming after all. She *had* reached out and touched someone, and they *had* touched her back. The contact had been warm and reassuring.

"He's taking his job as my attorney very seriously." Charley tried to keep her response bland. "You'd think we were friends or something."

"He wasn't there as your attorney. But you know that." Aunt Beth said quietly.

"I... uh... I remember thinking someone was there, but I

thought that I was dreaming or that it was one of the nurses," Charley admitted to Aunt Beth.

She looked wistfully toward Alex's house, and sincerely hoped his explanation for spying on her was a good one.

CHAPTER SEVENTEEN

After leaving Charley standing in his kitchen, Alex drove to his office on Broad Street. Some might call their conversation this morning an argument, but not him. He liked the back-and-forth, point-counterpoint debates with Charley. He liked to see the fire in her eyes when she had a quick retort, or her bewilderment when she couldn't come up with a good comeback. He just wished their debate concerned something different than the current topic.

Alex logged onto his computer and began documenting what he had witnessed at the construction site the night before. By the time Greg Bennett, the attorney Alex had asked to help him with the case, entered his office, Alex had transferred the pictures and his write-up of the incident to a thumb drive. They introduced themselves, then Greg sat down in a chair in front of Alex's desk.

"You should find all the info on this drive," Alex said, pushing the thumb drive toward Greg. "I really appreciate your help in this and for answering my call last night. Marlowe Aiken, whom I met at the jail last night, is a friend of my client,

Conner. Conner called him when he was arrested and couldn't initially reach me. Marlowe said you have experience with the company that had Conner arrested."

"Yeah, he's right. Granger Properties keeps pushing the limits of what the regulations require of them," Greg said as he picked up the thumb drive and put it in his briefcase. "You'd think they would learn that a building permit doesn't give them carte blanche to do whatever they feel like. They could save themselves a lot of trouble—and court costs—if they'd just follow some simple rules."

Alex nodded in agreement. "By the way, how did you get into environmental law? And how are you able to do it full-time for underfunded groups? It's not exactly the most lucrative field for an attorney."

"I manage." Greg shrugged. "I don't do it to make a profit. You only need so much money, right? It helps that my grandmother left me a small trust fund, and I've been lucky with my investments. But I made this my life's work because my father grew up in California at a time when the smog and haze were so bad, you could barely see a city block some days. He was born into a dirty climate, and he had asthma as a child, and it was made worse by the air quality where he lived. By the time he was grown and his company transferred him to Charleston, the damage had been done. The lung disease led to heart disease and he died four years ago. That's when I decided to take up this fight for others like him."

"I'm sorry, Greg," Alex said, thankful his father and mother were still around and both in good health. "That's definitely an admirable reason for choosing a career."

"How about you, Alex? I know you're a successful attorney at this firm, so why the pro bono work chasing polluters in the dead of night? It can't be easy doing two jobs at once."

"I grew up here," Alex replied. "I've loved these islands all my life. I can remember times before the construction boom, when the wildlife and plant life had some of the smaller islands all to themselves. I understand that everyone wants a beach house. I have one myself, but we need to develop the islands in a smart and controlled fashion. The big chain hotels that move in and block public access to the beaches, well…" Alex paused and leaned back in his chair. He was letting his personal anger at the companies who abused the privilege of developing the islands color his remarks of what was legal and what was illegal. "It's just not right," he finished.

"I hear you. But aren't you getting stretched a little thin with your work here at the firm, chasing polluters in your free time, and then taking the most abusive cases to court? When do you relax? Your private life has got to suffer."

"What private life?" Alex shrugged and laughed. "Say 'non-existent,' and you've nailed it."

"But I saw you at the Maitland fundraiser. You looked pretty cozy with the woman you were with that night," Greg replied.

"Yeah, well, that ship hit a sandbar," Alex replied. "I'm afraid it may have sunk."

Greg's comment brought the image of Charley to the forefront of Alex's thoughts. She had stood in his kitchen earlier that morning looking beautiful even with her messy clothes and wild hair. He had almost kissed her despite the fact that she probably would have slapped him. But had he seen a softening in her eyes as he leaned toward her? Or maybe he was just seeing what he hoped to see. His father thought he was still brooding and brokenhearted over Rebecca—and that may have been the case initially—but by and large, he hadn't been involved with anyone since her because he hadn't met anyone that interested him—until Charley.

His argument with Charley over her hiding her identity as Ce Ce Kane seemed more trivial with each passing day. He had stewed over the situation and poked and prodded at his anger so many times that he'd worn holes in all his reasons to be angry. Was she ready to hear his explanation about the folder filled with her private information? He had to carve out some time in his work schedule to see if she was at least willing to talk about it. Which brought him back to the idea he wanted to discuss with Greg.

"I have an idea I'd like to run by you," Alex said as he forced his attention back to the current conversation. His plan, if it worked, might give his life some balance. "What would you think of a merger between several of our small groups into one large umbrella group? Your group is better funded than Conner's ragtag team of about ten people, but what they lack in funding, they make up for in passion for the cause and skills in ferreting out polluters."

"You mean merge Save Our Islands with my group, Citizens Against Island Pollution?" Greg asked. "We'd have to get all the members on board for a change that big."

"I know. And we could invite other loosely organized groups to join us, too. You know, the turtle helpers, the bird watchers, and that group whose specialty is saving the dunes and plant life."

"Strength in numbers? That might work better than each group going off in all directions. Fundraising would be easier, too. We'd need to draw up rules so that everyone would know their specific lanes and avoid infighting." Greg leaned back in his chair, a thoughtful look on his face as he assessed Alex's proposal.

"Yes," Alex replied. "It could be called something like Coalition to Save our Islands for the Future, or CSIF—or something similar."

"Speaking of fundraising, that reminds me." Greg straightened in his chair. "Evelyn Pinckney's, Garrett's widow, who's one of our major donors—actually our only major donor—just offered to increase her donation for our cause. If she comes through with the amount she mentioned and we pool our other smaller donors, we could afford to hire another attorney. Would you be interested?"

"Maybe, but I might have a better plan. I don't have a trust fund to fall back on, so if my plan works out, it would be perfect for me. It's a long shot, but if Mrs. Pinckney is involved with our new organization, Mr. Winston might actually listen."

"What's your plan?" Greg asked.

"I haven't worked out all the details yet, and we first need to see if the various groups are even interested in forming the coalition. But I thought I'd pitch the idea that this law firm take on our new organization as a client—put the power of Winston, Morgan, and Gilbert behind our cases. The firm would handle the cases free of charge—pro bono."

"That's a big request. Do you think they'd go for that?" Greg seemed skeptical.

"If we're fair and don't go after any of Mr. Winston's old friends without first talking to him, he might be persuaded. You could handle the majority of the caseload, and I'd pick up the slack. That would free me up to still do my work for this firm. We could use donor funds for education, an advertising campaign, and other ancillary expenses."

"I like it. I'm interested in the merger, at the very least," Greg agreed. "Then you'd be serving just one master. You could get you love life back on track."

Alex snorted. "Yeah, my love life! Everyone seems to be very interested in my love life all of a sudden. First my father, now you. The only one not interested is a female participant. And with Conner and Mary creating cases for me, I don't have time to do much more than work." Alex didn't want to get side tracked with talk about Charley. He had a full day ahead of him, and his attention needed to be focused on the job. "So, do you want to try to form a coalition of our groups?"

"I do. I think it's a good idea, and since you're so busy, I'll contact the groups and set up a joint meeting. You can draw up the documents to codify the rules, and all members can vote on them at the meeting if they agree to merge."

"Sounds good. I appreciate your help on this," Alex said. "Say, I'm planning to go out to Turtle Island this weekend to check on my house. Would you like to come along for a little beach relaxation on Saturday?"

"I would, but my fiancée is coming back into town on Friday. She's been away on a business trip."

"She's welcome too. Bring her along. I have plenty of room."

"Okay. Let me check with Lisa, and I'll let you know what we decide," Greg replied. "And thanks."

After Greg left his office, Alex turned his attention to his duties for the law firm. The Thompson merger was about to wrap up, barring any last-minute hitch. The negotiations were done, the financing had been worked out, and all that was left was for both parties to sign the final contract. A lot of work went into finalizing an acquisition, and he had been absent for some of it. He made a mental not to get a thank-you gift for his intern and paralegal. They had stepped up while he was on assignment at the beach.

Assignment? Alex thought with a grimace. That word made his stomach queasy. Charley had a right to be angry about the invasion of her life—but not angry at him. If anyone had ever failed an assignment, it was him. He had not learned one thing that Mrs. Maitland didn't already know about Charley. She had even tricked him into bringing Charley to her house so she could get the DNA sample. He prided himself on staying one step ahead of Mrs. Maitland, but she had outfoxed him on the DNA issue. Maybe he had been distracted by a pretty face, as

Mr. Winston had accused.

Alex's return to work meant he was back to being a full-time lawyer. He needed to make up the income he had refused to accept while "on assignment." He had just taken on a new client: a large commercial bakery that wanted to branch out and purchase a small local bakery and cupcake shop, and to expand in airports and other venues across the southeastern United States. They were in preliminary talks on the acquisition at the moment.

According to Alex's father, Mrs. Maitland was making noise again, too. She wanted Alex back as her attorney, since Charley was finished with the stem cell donation. Mr. Gilbert was a very qualified partner in the firm, but he was a quiet, reserved man. He didn't argue with Mrs. Maitland like Alex did when she tried to walk all over him or push him to support every harebrained scheme she came up with. Alex didn't take any of Mrs. Maitland's bullying. Alex had her figured out. She didn't respect anyone she could intimidate and push around. When he gave her advice or flatly refused some of her ideas, Mrs. Maitland would quickly give in. She enjoyed their arguments, but trusted his judgement and counsel. Mrs. Maitland's arguments were mostly for her personal entertainment.

Alex reviewed some of the information on his new client. It was boring reading. He yawned. His two back-to-back late nights were catching up with him. He got up from his desk and made another trip to the coffee pot. He looked at the clock. It was 8:30 a.m. His father should be arriving at the office soon. Alex needed his father's input on the idea he had discussed with Greg. Once he got his father's assessment of the plan to have the firm represent the coalition of different environmental groups, Alex would present it to Mr. Winston.

Fifteen minutes later, Alex paused outside his father's office and knocked on the doorframe. His father was on the phone but beckoned him in. Alex heard the name 'Maitland' as he walked to the window and watched the morning traffic move along the street below. It looked like it would be another sunny day—perfect for a run on the beach. Too bad he wasn't there.

"That was your favorite client," his father said as he hung up the phone. "She wants you back as her attorney. And I think Gilbert is ready to give her to anyone who'll take her."

"That's fine with me. She's already acquired almost everything locally that deals with international shipping, so unless she starts unloading her holdings or branches out, she should be pretty quiet," Alex replied. "I think she's tied up with Dorsey's treatment right now. By the way, how is Dorsey doing? Did Mrs. Maitland say?"

"Dorsey's going into the hospital on Friday to be prepped for the stem cell infusion on Monday. I think some people come home right away afterward, but Mrs. Maitland wants Dorsey to stay in the hospital for a few days as an extra precaution. She's gone to great lengths to get this far. She's taking no chances."

"I can understand that."

Alex was thinking of a way to pitch his new proposal when his father interrupted his thoughts with, "How's Charley? Is she back on the island?"

"Lance said they were planning to go back today. Charley's alright. So far as I know, she only has a sore hip from the procedure."

"Is she still mad at you?" Alex's father shuffled some papers around on his desk and unsuccessfully tried to hide his curiosity. "Your mother and I both hope you'll soon be back on speaking terms."

"I'm not sure when or if that will happen," Alex replied. "Charley's mad at me. I'm mad at her. But some of the steam has evaporated from my anger. I plan on talking with her as soon as I get a chance and can get her to listen."

"Good," Mr. Morgan replied. "Letting small misunderstand-ings fester just creates bigger ones."

"I wouldn't call what Mrs. Maitland did a 'small misunder-standing,' but I need to tell Charley that I had almost nothing to do with the scheme." Alex looked accusingly at his father. "I should never have let myself get talked into it."

"Maybe so, but then you wouldn't have met Charley," his father replied calmly. He straightened in his seat, then leaned forward with his arms on his desk. He looked at Alex. "The time you spent at the beach, working on the 'scheme,' as you call it, created the opportunity for you to get to know Charley. You can't deny that was a good thing."

Alex remained silent. He stared back at his father, refusing to validate his claim.

But his father, once started, wouldn't drop the subject. "How do you plan to get her to talk to you?"

"What's with all the questions, Dr. Phil?" Alex asked, then shrugged. "I don't know. Maybe send Rex over with a note? He seems to get along with her better than I do."

"When your mother and I have a disagreement, I always try to make a grand gesture in apology—even if I think I'm right. I don't just send one dozen red roses. I send two or three dozen, maybe more. It all depends on how bad our disagreement was."

"So that's why there was always a constant stream of floral deliveries at our house," Alex said, unable to hide his smile. As a child, he never saw his parents argue. Maybe they argued in private, but they always presented a united front to Alex and his brother. He once thought he'd have that kind of marriage with Rebecca. He had been naïve in thinking all marriages were like his parents', but a marriage between him and Rebecca would not have been the 'happily ever after' that his parents had found.

"I don't think roses are the solution to my and Charley's sit-uation. But I'll come up with some way to get her to talk to me.

Right now, I need to talk to you."

Alex laid out the plans he and Greg Bennett had discussed earlier. "This law firm needs to do more pro bono work," he told his father. "It's good publicity and shows a commitment to the community. I'd like to have the name and support of the firm when filing environmental cases. That would give our group higher visibility and more clout."

"Hmmm. Interesting. We do need to be more engaged with the community." Alex could see the wheels turning in his father's mind. "What about your work for the firm?"

"If Mr. Winston doesn't want to provide financial support for these cases, I'll get funding some other way. I just need time during the day. Of course, I won't let my regular work for the firm slip in the process. Clay, my intern, is sharp, and he's eager to learn, so he can take on a larger role if it comes to that. He did a good job while I was at the beach."

"Let me see if Winston is in, and we can ask him." Mr. Morgan picked up his phone and spoke with Mr. Winston's secretary for a few minutes. "He's in and said we can come by now."

Alex and his father walked to Mr. Winston office.

"What's up?" Mr. Winston asked as the pair sat down.

Alex got right to the point and explained his plans to set up a new organization—a coalition of environmental groups—and have the firm support their cases on a pro bono basis. Mr. Winston leaned back in his chair and steepled his hands in front of him. He didn't say anything for several seconds.

"Bob, have you mentioned to Alex that Mrs. Maitland wants him back as her attorney?" Mr. Winston finally asked.

Alex started to reply, but a slight shake of his father's head made him stop. His father said innocently, "She does? I don't know, Herb. As you know, what she did is hard to ignore. I'm ashamed that I went along with her scheme. She's the reason why Alex has lost any chance of a friendship or anything more with Ms. Mathews. She's vowed to never forgive Alex. She won't even talk to him now. I don't know if Alex can forgive Mrs. Maitland for that, let alone work with her again."

Mr. Winston looked over their heads and out the window at the bright, sunny sky. He appeared to be deep in thought. "Alex, I'm very sorry about you and Ms. Mathews. It was my fault, too, for letting Mrs. Maitland bamboozle me into her plan. But how about this: if you take Mrs. Maitland back as a client and get her off my back and out of Gilbert's hair, I'll put all the weight of this firm behind you and your organization."

"Go on," Alex replied. He couldn't believe what he was hearing.

"You're an excellent attorney," Mr. Winston continued. "I want to keep you. Even with your short stint at the beach, I've noticed that you're trying to do too many things at once. You can't keep that up indefinitely, or you'll burn out. This Greg Bennett you mentioned—can we count on him helping out when your regular caseload gets too heavy? We could put him on retainer on a case-by-case basis to help with the environmental group's cases. Your position as a senior member of the firm won't change, of course. You'll still be doing mergers and acquisitions."

"That sounds like it might be a sensible trade-off," Mr. Morgan replied before Alex could respond. His forehead wrinkled as he considered Mr. Winston's offer. "What do you think, Alex? Do you think you could forgive Mrs. Maitland for the craziness she cooked up and take her back as a client? I know it's a lot to ask, since she destroyed your chances with Charley."

"Yes, sir. I'm willing to do that. And thank you, Mr. Winston, for doing this." Putting Greg on retainer was more than Alex had hoped for.

"Well, Mrs. Finckney carries as much weight around Charleston as Mrs. Maitland. And if Bennett is a friend of hers and we serve her environmental interests well, maybe she'll move her considerable business over to us." Mr. Winston always looked for the business angle, even in his charitable works.

Alex rose from his chair and shook Mr. Winston's hand. He and his father started toward the door.

"Bob," Mr. Winston called out. Alex and his father stopped and turned back toward Mr. Winston. "You haven't changed since we were in law school together. You're always working an angle, aren't you? I'm not fooled, though. And you're not as sly as you think you are. I work my own angles, and I'm on to your BS. By the way, Mrs. Maitland called me this morning, too—after she talked to you." Mr. Winston chuckled as his old friend and partner grinned and nodded.

"And that's why we make such good partners. We both have a devious streak—but devious for all the right reasons." Mr. Morgan laughed, then closed the door behind them. "That's how you play the game." He grinned broadly at Alex. "When you want something badly, don't show all your cards at once."

"Sometimes telling the truth works, too," countered Alex.

"Knowing when to use which method is key." His father slapped Alex on the back. "Herb is not above using the same tricks on me."

Alex thought about his father's advice as he finished up his day at the firm. Grand gestures, card games. His father was the most honest man he knew, but he wouldn't hesitate to use manipulation if he thought it would further a good cause. His father had advised a grand gesture to get things back on track with Charley. She was very mad at him and it would take more than flowers to change their situation.

Alex was just pulling into his driveway at home when Greg Bennett called. He had contacted all the environmental groups and had scheduled a meeting in the banquet room at a restaurant on the Isle of Palms for the next evening. That was their next hurdle: getting a diverse group of environmentalists to work together. It would be a challenge, since each group thought their cause was more important than all others. Alex had already drawn up a list of rules and bylaws for the group's participants to vote on. Including all segments of their coalition and not making one issue seem more important than the others would be key to convincing them to combine their forces and expertise.

As Alex opened the door to his house, Rex bounded toward him. Alex stooped down to pet him. Charley had only been in his home for only one night, but he felt her lingering presence.

Rex nudged him. "Ah, Rex, old buddy, does the house seem emptier than usual to you?" Rex whined. Alex hugged him. "Yep! To me, too."

The environmentalists were gathered at the restaurant when Alex arrived for the meeting the next evening. The vote to form a coalition was passed quickly once Alex and Greg explained what the meeting was about and how much more power they'd wield if they banded together.

The attendees asked a few questions about the bylaws Alex presented, but soon voted to accept them with only a few minor changes. They next voted to form a leadership committee of three, that would serve as a central point of contact to sort out and prioritize problems. Each faction's leader could ask the committee for volunteers if they needed extra hands during an environmental crisis. Alex and Greg would only get involved if a suspected illegal action was discovered.

The Coalition to Save our Islands for the Future, or CSIF, was now official. Once the meeting adjourned and the participants left, Alex and Greg remained behind to further discuss the legal aspects of the coalition and how they would divide up any cases requiring legal action.

"I asked Lisa about this weekend, and she said she'd love to come out to the beach on Saturday," Greg said as he and Alex prepared to say goodbye in the restaurant parking lot.

"That's great!" Alex gave Greg the address. "I plan to get there late Friday evening and air out the house, so come as early as you like on Saturday. We can either grill or go to The Tides for dinner."

Alex's mood perked up as he started his truck and drove out of the parking lot. Going to the beach always lifted his spirits, but this time, he hoped he'd see Charley, too.

CHAPTER EIGHTEEN

Aunt Beth and Uncle Lance returned to New Jersey early on Saturday morning. Charley waved goodbye to them as they backed out of the driveway, then she returned to the house. As she reached the top of the steps leading to the porch, Charley heard the sound of a vehicle. She looked toward Alex's house just as his pickup pulled into the driveway. He didn't look her way as he got out of the truck and began carrying what looked like bags of groceries up the steps to the house. Rex came out onto the porch to meet him when he opened the door. When had he arrived? This was the first time he'd come back since he stormed away two weeks ago. It seemed much longer than two weeks. She couldn't deny, she had missed him.

He hadn't looked her way as he unloaded his pickup. Did that mean he still didn't want to talk to her? Did she want to talk to him?

Yes, she did want to talk to him., but she was torn between wanting to hear his explanation for collecting her private information and the fear she would be pulled back into a web of lies. She didn't fully trust her ability to listen to her head instead of her heart.

The silence of the house weighed heavily on Charley as she straightened up the bedroom where Aunt Beth and Uncle Lance had stayed. She missed her aunt and uncle, and they likely hadn't even left the state yet. She turned on some music just to fill the house with sound as she worked. It didn't take her long to get the small house in order.

Picking up her camera, Charley went to the back deck and sat down in the shade of the oak tree. At least on the deck, the sounds of the ocean waves and the seagulls would disrupt the silence. Charley began reviewing the pictures she had recently taken during Aunt Beth and Uncle Lance visit. She had quickly healed from the bone marrow donation and had led them on a walking tour through Charleston, taking many more photos along the way.

As she reviewed the pictures, Charley's thoughts turned to Dorsey. She had checked into the hospital yesterday afternoon. She, Aunt Beth, and Uncle Lance had a long visit with Dorsey and her mother at the Maitland estate on Thursday. Charley had worried aloud about what lay ahead for Dorsey, but her sister was upbeat about the upcoming stem cell infusion and its outcome. Mrs. Maitland was insistent that she stay in the hospital for a few days after the stem cell transfer as precaution against infection.

"Don't worry, sis," Dorsey told her. "I've been through worse. This will be easy."

"I know you'll be okay," Charley replied. "I'll just be relieved when it's done and you're on the mend."

Before they left Oak Lane Plantation, Charley asked Mrs. Maitland the question that had been buzzing around in her head like a honey bee trapped in a glass jar for some time now: "Did you know Annabelle Travis?"

"Actually, I did know her, though not very well," Mrs. Maitland admitted. "I once visited her at her home in Charleston. Our search for you had crossed paths. I wanted to know what she had found, but she didn't share much. At the time, she was planning a trip to New York. She wouldn't tell me why she was going, but I suspect it concerned you in some way. She became ill soon after she returned, so I never learned anything about the trip. Did she find you in New York?"

"No. Sadly, she didn't." So her great aunt had been wanting to meet her and that's why she and Alex had been at her gallery exhibit. Charley's anonymity had kept her from meeting Great-Aunt Annabelle and such a meeting would have meant a lot to them both. "I wish she had, though. She sounds like a wonderful lady."

"From all reports, she was. She had great standing in the Charleston community."

Charley thought about asking this new, relaxed Mrs. Maitland for details on the search to find her—specifically, about Alex's role in the search. She quickly decided against it. The timing was wrong since Dorsey was facing a critical, medical procedures and that was where the attention should be focused. Charley was becoming more convinced each day that Mrs. Maitland was the driving force behind the spying. She wanted a full explanation, but she'd rather hear it directly from Alex.

Charley left the Maitland estate with another tidbit of information that fleshed out the picture in her mind of Annabelle Travis. Everyone Charley had met who knew Annabelle spoke highly of her.

As Charley sat on the deck and scrolled through and assessed the quality of her photographs, her thoughts mulled over Dorsey's upcoming procedure. Charley was proud of her little sister. Thus far, Dorsey had shown only strength and courage in the face of a life-threatening disease. Charley wouldn't even contemplate that Dorsey wouldn't survive the cancer. They had just found each other and they needed each other.

"Hi," a voice said from the edge of the deck.

Charley jumped. Why did everyone around here keep sneaking up on her? She looked toward the steps that led to the yard below.

A blonde head was sticking up over the edge of the deck. The head was soon followed by a petite body that climbed up the steps. "You must be Charley. I'm Lisa," the blonde woman said. At Charley's questioning look, she added, "Alex's friend. I'm staying at his house."

"You're a friend of Alex's?" Charley's stomach clenched then relaxed. Of course Alex had other friends—other women friends.

"Well, I just met him this morning, but I like him. I think we're friends," Lisa replied.

"This morning? You're staying at his house?" Charley asked. She was struggling to hold a coherent conversation while processing Lisa's comment. Alex had met this woman this morning, and she was already staying at his beach house? He worked fast.

Lisa peered closely at Charley, confused. Then, suddenly, her eyes cleared, and she nodded. "Oh, I see. Of course. You don't know who I am. I'm here with my fiancé, Greg. Alex invited us to come out for the weekend. We just arrived a short time ago. I was going for a walk when I noticed you sitting up here. I decided to come up for a chat. I apologize if I'm bothering you. I can leave." Lisa turned toward the steps.

"No, don't go," Charley said quickly. "I'm the one who should apologize. I was engrossed in my photos, and it took me a minute to switch back to reality. I'm sorry. I sounded like an idiot. Sit down and visit. Please. Can I get you something to drink?"

"No, we just finished a late breakfast. Any more liquid, and I'll start sloshing. Would you like to come with me while I finish my walk on the beach?" Lisa invited.

"Sure. That sounds great. Come inside while I put my camera away. We can leave through the front door."

Charley led the way into the house. Lisa looked around as she followed Charley inside. "These beach houses are so pretty. And the island is nice, too. I've lived in Charleston all my life, and I barely knew Turtle Island was here, much less that it's such a lovely place."

"I'm a newbie in the area, but I think it gets overshadowed by the larger islands and those that are more populated. Alex says it's a constant fight to keep it from becoming just another building site, like some of the other islands."

"Alex and Greg are kindred souls," Lisa said, smiling, "fighters of polluters and development like superheroes. They can get wound up once they get on the subject."

Charley grabbed her sunglasses from the counter, then led the way out the front door. They crossed the road, cut through the dunes in front of Charley's beach house, and walked toward the beach. By the time they had walked to the pier, turned around, and walked back to Charley's house, they were chatting like old friends. Lisa was friendly and very talkative, so there was never a lull in the conversation. They paused at the bottom of the stairs to Charley's house before saying goodbye.

"We're going to The Tides for dinner tonight. Why don't you join us?" Lisa asked.

"No, I couldn't. I'd better not," Charley replied haltingly. She hated the thought of the lonely evening that stretched out before her, but she'd feel strange tagging along without Alex inviting her. If he ignored her or was cold to her she'd be humiliated. That type of behavior didn't sound like Alex, because he was always courteous and a perfect gentleman to anyone he met. And he'd been friendly—his teasing comments notwithstanding—on Wednesday when she stayed at his house. She was just looking for an excuse—a weak excuse—to avoid a potentially awkward situation. She was unsure of what to expect from him since their blowup.

"Please come. Alex suggested that I invite you if I saw you on my walk. I know he wants you to come. And I need someone to talk to when the guys start talking shop."

"I… I don't know." Charley was weakening. "Are you sure Alex wants me to join you?"

"Yes. He does," Lisa assured her. "I know you and Alex are having a spat right now—Greg told me—but just think of it as friends having a casual dinner together."

Spending the evening with Alex, even if he was mad at her, would be better than sitting alone in the beach house, staring at the walls, with only the sound of the ocean to keep her company. And she'd like to get to know Lisa better. "Okay. But I'll meet you there. That way, if I become uncomfortable, I can leave."

"Great!" Lisa said. "We'll see you there around 6:30 p.m." Lisa turned and jogged toward Alex's house and up the steps. She waved to Charley when she reached the porch and then disappeared inside the house.

Charley drove to The Tides feeling nervous about seeing Alex again. Would he be warm and relaxed as he'd been when they bantered back and forth on Wednesday at this house? Or would he be as cold and hostile as he'd been during the meeting at the Maitland estate? She was about to find out. Charley parked her car, then made her way to the front door of the restaurant.

Alex was standing just inside, watching the door and chatting with the hostess when Charley stepped inside. He excused himself and approached Charley. He didn't speak at first, but paused in front of her and just looked into her eyes. Charley tilted her chin and steadily returned his gaze, as she tried to hide the nervous tightening in her stomach. After a few moments, Alex turned and offered her his arm. "Shall we join the others?" he asked.

Charley took his arm, and he placed a warm hand over hers. He guided her toward the table where Greg and Lisa were sitting. Other diners looked up as they made their way through the crowded restaurant. They nodded and called out friendly greetings to both of them, "Hi, Alex. Hi, Charley." Charley was now welcomed just like Alex, and viewed as a permanent Turtle Islander.

Alex introduced Charley to Greg as they sat down and opened their menus. Alex gave his recommendation on the variety of dishes.

"Alex," Manny called as he approached their table. "Welcome to all of you." He included Greg and Lisa in his greeting. Then, he turned to Charley. "Charley, good to see you back again. And with Alex. I was worried when you two were no-shows recently." He laughed and clapped Alex on the shoulder. "Don't screw this up, Alex."

Charley started to deny Manny's implication that they were together, but Alex interrupted. "It hasn't been that long since we were here, but I'm not stupid, Manny." He put his arm around Charley's shoulders and pulled her closer. "No screw-ups. I promise."

Manny gave him a thumbs-up, then walked on to greet other diners.

Charley eased away from Alex's arm and looked across the table at Greg and Lisa. They were both following the by-play between her and Alex. As Charley searched for something to say, the waiter arrived and began pouring their wine. Happy to have the interruption, Charley went back to looking over the menu.

They placed their orders, and Lisa started the conversation. "Alex tells me that you're a travel photographer. I imagine you've been all over the world. Do you work for a specific publication?"

"I used to be a staff photographer and content writer for
one magazine, but went freelance a couple years ago, though
I'm still with the same travel and adventure magazine. I thought
there'd be less travel as a freelancer. There was, but I found
myself unable to turn down most jobs. The lure of the road, I
guess," Charley replied.

This was Charley's usual canned response to anyone who
asked about her job. She always avoided explaining why she decided to go freelance. But this time, her statement to Lisa about
not turning down jobs, made her realize that her effort to save
her marriage to Daniel had been only a halfhearted attempt.
Their love had died when he cheated on her the first time. The
broken trust was something she couldn't get past, and even
adjusting her travel schedule hadn't helped with that.

"That sounds exciting, but so much traveling must be very
grueling," Lisa noted.

"It is, but I've taken this summer off. I'm still doing a few
stock photos and putting together a book of photos about the
Lowcountry, but I'm not traveling."

"What's your favorite subject to photograph?" Lisa asked.

"I particularly like landscapes, historical landmarks,
wildlife, and candid photos of people. Wildlife is my favorite, though, because they're more challenging. You can't pose
wildlife. But there's an abundance of great subjects of all kinds
in this area," Charley replied. "What about you? What gets you
up in the morning?"

"I'm a child psychiatrist, and my passion is helping kids who
struggle with life's problems—problems they didn't create," Lisa
replied.

"I could have used you when I was a kid," Charley said without thinking.

Lisa, Alex, and Greg all looked at her. Alex reached out and touched her hand under the table.

"I… uh… I mean when my father died unexpectedly."

Aunt Beth had tried to coax Charley into attending therapy sessions over the years, but Charley's loyalty to her mother kept her from divulging her mother's behavior to anyone. Aunt Beth conducted her own therapy sessions. She explained to Charley that Debra was sick and didn't realize she was neglecting Charley. As Charley grew older, she accepted that her mother's life had died along with her husband.

"That must be a very gratifying career," Charley said to Lisa.

"The death of a parent is a traumatic event for a child. And yes, I find child psychiatry very gratifying," Lisa replied. "I work mostly with children who have learning difficulties and behavioral issues. My patients struggle to fit in. Their brains are wired differently from those of other children, and they don't always know why they act the way they do. I try to give them the skills to navigate and manage their differences in a world where they often feel like outcasts among their peers."

"That sounds amazing. What you do makes my career choice seem silly," Charley said.

"I disagree," Lisa replied. "Your photography brings beauty to the world, and nothing brings attention to a problem like a photo of endangered species, melting glaciers, or people under pressure to survive the circumstances they find themselves in, like poverty."

"You should see her in action," Alex said. He gave them an embellished account of the day they crouched in the marsh, awaiting the egrets' first flight. "I tried to leave, but she threatened to break my leg if I moved. I thought the birds were never going to leave the nest. But she was right, and the photo was worth the wait."

"He's exaggerating," Charley said as she poked Alex in the ribs with her elbow. "If you've taken a few thousand similar photos, you develop a feel for the right moment." She looked at Alex and added, "You just need to remember that much-needed lesson in patience."

"I remember everything that happened that day," Alex replied as he looked steadily at her. "Everything."

Charley looked away, unable to keep the warmth from her cheeks.

"Ahem." Greg cleared his throat and changed the conversation to the newly formed coalition of environmentalists. He and Alex shared the details with Charley and Lisa of how the central committee would work together to handle divergent environmental interests and problems.

"There's power in numbers," Greg said.

"It also provides an orderly way to marshal the troops in case of an emergency," Alex added. "Hurricane season will be here soon, and there could be any number of problems that will require the group's attention."

They finished their dinners, gave compliments to Manny for the great food, and walked out into the parking lot.

"Let's go back to my place and open a bottle of wine," Alex suggested. He included Charley in the invitation. "We can sit on the front porch and watch a spectacular Carolina moon rise over the water."

"I..." Charley hesitated. This was starting to look like two couples, rather than one engaged couple and two others going solo. She wasn't as mad at Alex as she once had been, but she didn't want to get sucked back into trusting him completely—at least, not yet. Not until he explained his part in the collection of data on her.

"Please come," Lisa encouraged. "I want to hear more about your travels. You're just next door. You can leave at any time."

"Alright," Charley agreed. "I'll come over for a little while."

Charley climbed into her car and drove back to the beach

house. As she pulled into the driveway, a figure rose from the bottom step and walked toward her. Alex and his guests had reached the beach house before Charley, but he had walked over to her house and was waiting for her.

"You don't have to escort me," Charley said. "I don't think I'll get lost crossing the lawn to your house."

"I don't know about that." Alex laughed as he held the car door so she could slide out. "You got lost the day you drove out to Oak Lane Plantation."

"This is slightly different. But what makes you think I got lost?"

"I was behind you. I saw you take the wrong road at the crossroads. Another clue was how long it took you after that to get to Mrs. Maitland's."

"Aren't you the detective? Why didn't you stop me if you knew I was taking the wrong road?" Charley asked.

"And have you run me into a ditch?" Alex joked. "Not a chance."

"Maybe I was looking for scenic shots for my photo book."

"Whatever you say." Alex smiled. "Since I'm your escort, let's go." He put his arm around Charley's back and started guiding her toward his house. They had taken only a few steps when he stopped and turned toward her. "I've been wanting to do this all evening." He bent his head and kissed her lightly on the lips.

"What are we doing, Alex?" Charley whispered when the kiss ended. The sweetness of his light kiss made her want more, but under the circumstances, that wasn't a good idea.

"I'm kissing you," Alex replied. He reached out and brushed her cheek with his fingers. He slowly pulled back from her. "You're right of course. And our guests are waiting for us. We need to figure this out—and soon."

"I know," Charley agreed. They turned and walked toward Alex's house and joined Lisa and Greg on the porch. The evening passed quickly as they talked about a wide range of topics. Rex found a place at Charley's feet and refused to move.

As Alex had promised, a spectacular Carolina moon rose over the water and streaked the ocean in liquid silver as a soft breeze blew inland. The sweet smell of the ocean wafted across the porch where they sat and created a perfect setting for a pleasant evening. When the party broke up after midnight, Alex escorted Charley to her door. He placed another brief parting kiss on her lips. Then, with a soft, "Goodnight," he moved toward the porch steps.

Charley closed the door, walked to the front window, and stood in the darkened living room and watched Alex cross the yard and climb the steps to his house. He was soon hidden in the shadows of the porch as he entered the house. Where had her anger and outrage gone? A brief, friendly kiss was all that was needed to make her forget everything that had happened between them. She was once again caught in Alex Morgan's web—a dramatic thought, but one that described her confused state.

That's exactly where you want to be: entangled and ensnared in Alex's web! Her inner voice had been rather quiet over the last few days, but now, it woke up and pointed out the obvious. *Face it, Charley Mathews, your feelings for Alex are anything but anger.*

As Charley made her way to her bedroom, she couldn't deny that her anger at Alex had mostly dissipated. But 'caught in Alex Morgan's web'? This was the beach, so a more appropriate response to her head chatter came to mind. She whispered it quietly: "I'm swimming with the tide while praying I don't get swept out to sea and left stranded."

CHAPTER NINETEEN

Charley slept late the next morning. She showered and dressed, then had a leisurely breakfast and finished her photo review, that Lisa had interrupted yesterday. She made a sandwich and decided to take it and her camera to the beach in the afternoon. Alex's truck and Greg's car were both gone. Maybe they were still organizing their new coalition or meeting with the various groups involved.

Charley had hoped to photograph the porpoises that played in the water just off the beach. They usually appeared around this time of day, but none had showed by the time she had walked to the pier and back. Her photos today were mostly routine beach scenes—pelicans and seagulls and some interesting cloud formations. The porpoises would have been a nice addition to her book, but not every shoot turned out successfully. She gave up and walked back through the dunes toward her house.

The late afternoon sun had moved lower in the sky by the time she arrived home. Alex still wasn't back. He hadn't shared his plans for today, but why should he? Neighbors didn't share everything they did. He had to work at the law firm tomorrow, so going back to the mainland today would be the smart and convenient thing to do. Charley was still reliving last night. In the light of day, Alex's quick kiss could hardly be described as passionate, and was more likely due to the beautiful and enjoyable evening they were sharing. So why could she not get it out of her mind? The memory was pleasant. That's why.

The next morning, Charley drove into Charleston to see Dorsey. She parked in the cancer center parking lot and took the elevator up to the floor where the infusion patients were located. Mrs. Maitland and one of her assistants were sitting in the waiting room when Charley walked in.

"How is she?" Charley asked as she sat down beside Mrs. Maitland.

"She's tired and weak from the chemo, but positive about the procedure. She's ready. The doctors are inserting the tunneled catheter now. Once she's awake from that, she'll be taken to the transplant unit for the infusion. For now, we just wait," replied Mrs. Maitland.

"When will we be permitted to see her?" Charley asked.

"I've asked for her to be put in special isolation for at least the first twenty-four hours. She can't have any visitors during that period. After that, we can visit so long as we take extra safety precautions," Mrs. Maitland replied. "I know everyone thinks I'm an old fool and being overly cautious, but, Charley…" Mrs. Maitland's voice broke, before she quickly steadied it. "I can't lose her. I'll do everything—everything I can—to protect her." Mrs. Maitland nervously twisted her hands together. She showed, what was for her was, an unusual vulnerability. With Dorsey's disease, Mrs. Maitland had met something she couldn't shape and mold to her liking.

Charley reached over and squeezed her hand. "I understand, and you're not a fool at all. Take no chances. It's the right thing to do until she's stronger."

Someone stopped in front of them. Charley looked up to find Alex looking down at Mrs. Maitland. He nodded to Charley.

"How is Dorsey?" he asked, addressing Mrs. Maitland. "I have a meeting nearby in a few minutes, but I wanted to stop by and check on her—and you. How are you both doing?"

"She's fatigued, but the doctors are prepping her for the transfusion as we speak. She seems ready to get it done. Thank you for stopping by."

Alex waved away Mrs. Maitland's thanks. "Well, of course I'd stop by to check on you," Alex said before turning to Charley. She rose from her chair with the intention of walking him to the door when he left, but Alex surprised her by pulling her closer and briefly kissing her on the temple, then he released her. "I have to go, but keep me updated, okay?" He touched her arm. She nodded, and with a wave, Alex turned and quickly exited the waiting room. Charley's eyes followed him until he disappeared down the hallway and turned toward the bank of elevators.

"Alex is a good man," Mrs. Maitland said, bringing Charley's attention back to her. "I trust him with all of my business decisions, even though I like to give him a hard time over most of them. But he knows it's a game with me." Mrs. Maitland paused, then added, "Hmmm. I wonder why he didn't kiss me before he left." She looked at Charley, with a mischievous quirk of her eyebrow.

Charley waved away Mrs. Maitland's speculative gaze. "It wasn't a real kiss," she protested. "Just a friendly air-kiss—a combo hello and goodbye. He just forgot to kiss or hug you."

"Now that, I believe." Mrs. Maitland laughed, and her mouth thinned into a skeptical smile. "Believe it or not, this old lady fell in love once upon a time. I can recognize the signs.

That young man has someone on his mind, and it's not me."

"Well… I…" Charley stammered. "He's very busy so he has lots of different things on his mind."

Charley sat with Mrs. Maitland until Dr. Baker came and informed them that everything had gone well with the stem cell infusion and that Dorsey had been moved back to her room in the isolation ward. "The room has a window," Dr. Baker said, "so if you'd like to see Dorsey, you can."

Mrs. Maitland dismissed her assistant, and she and Charley walked toward Dorsey's room. They stopped in front of a room with three large windows that gave them a good view inside. Dorsey lay on her back in the hospital bed with her eyes closed. The attending nurse said something, and Dorsey opened her eyes slightly and offered a weak smile when she saw them standing outside the window. She gave a brief thumbs-up. Charley's heart squeezed as she looked at Dorsey, her brave sister. She had only recently found her, and like Mrs. Maitland, she desperately wanted the infusion to work.

Charley and Mrs. Maitland stood by the window just long enough to see Dorsey and let her know they were there. Charley left soon after that. Dorsey didn't need to feel like a fish in a bowl with an audience peering in at her. Charley had a couple appointments scheduled in Charleston, but she would return to the hospital later in the day before going back to Turtle Island.

Since moving to Turtle Island, Charley had put off any decisions about her future, preferring to take a breather before tackling the issue. But recently, she had returned to the problem and had begun to seriously consider what she wanted to do. Her editor had given her until the end of the summer to decide, but Charley had come up with a couple ideas that were worth exploring now. If her appointments went as she hoped—and since selling the beach house was off the list of things to do— her decisions about her future would be made.

Charley's first appointment was with Mrs. Sanders at Charleston's Convention and Visitors Board, commonly called CVB. Last week, she had submitted her resume online for a position in their Destination Marketing Office, or DMO. She had an interview today.

Mrs. Sanders, a friendly, middle-aged woman, welcomed Charley into her office and offered her a seat in front of her desk. "I've looked over your resume and online portfolio," Mrs. Sanders said. "I must say, your past experience is impressive. You've visited and photographed places all over the world. Why do you want to move to Charleston at this juncture in your career? Can we expect you to remain with us long-term if we hire you?"

Charley explained what brought her to Turtle Island. "I'll admit that, at first, I wondered why I was even here, in a place so different from my home in the New York and New Jersey area. But it didn't take me long to fall in love with everything about the region. It's a photographer's dream. But mostly, it's been meeting the people—from the proud Gullah Geechee people who still honor their African roots, to the distinguished families that have kept family names and traditions alive through the centuries—that has caused me to want to stay in the area."

"You've met some of our Gullah Geechee citizens?" Mrs. Sanders asked in surprise.

"Yes, on Pawleys Island. I met a wonderful family there," Charley replied. "But I also love the historical nature of Charleston and the surrounding area." Charley realized she was gushing, but what she said was true. In a very short time, she had fallen in love with South Carolina. "As for whether you can count on me staying here," Charley continued, "yes, you can. I've done all the traveling I want to do in my job. I'm ready to stay in one place, and what place is more perfect for a photographer than this region?"

"We like passion in our employees," Mrs. Sanders replied with a laugh then repeated the phrase Charley frequently heard. "I'd say you have been bitten by the Lowcountry bug." She looked down at a printed copy of Charley's resume on her desk. "Another thing in your favor is that you were also a content writer at your last job. Mr. Carson, who is retiring at the end of the summer, is a wonderful photographer, but the written word is beyond his abilities. He was hired before we had an online presence, so we've had to hire a freelance writer to write the stories that go with his photos. We would expect you to do both jobs."

"I actually prefer to do my own writing. I'm at the sites of the photos, so I pick up the flavor of the setting and a feel for the subjects. I like for readers to experience places through both my eyes and my words. I believe my personal perspective helps enhance my photographs."

As the interview ended, Mrs. Sanders advised Charley that she'd have to speak with the director of the board, but Charley was a strong contender for the job. She also assured Charley that her outside work under her pseudonym would not be a problem.

Charley left the CVB office and walked along King Street. The job in the Destination Marketing Office would pay less than her job at the New York magazine, but with no rent to pay and with income from her outside work, she could live comfortably. Plus, she should be receiving her half of the money from the sale of the New York townhouse any day now. If everything worked out as Charley expected, she might be able to buy a small house on the mainland where she could spend the winters or stay during icy weather that closed the bridges. A house on the mainland would make working in the city easier and safer when the hurricanes came ashore.

Charley soon arrived at her second appointment of the day. She opened the door of the Lower King Street Art Gallery and entered. The gallery owner met her at the door.

"You look familiar," Leana Barry said as Charley introduced herself.

"I bought a painting here not long ago. Gena Middleton's painting," Charley replied.

"Oh, yes, I remember now! But I didn't know you were Ce Ce Kane. I had one of your photos here not long ago. I purchased it at an art show in New York—the gentoo penguins. I donated it for a charity fundraiser."

Charley nodded, but didn't mention that Alex had paid thirty thousand dollars for it at the auction. "My real name is Charley Rainier-Mathews. I made our appointment today as Ce Ce Kane, the professional name I use for my exhibited photos and books. The first gallery owner I worked with thought that a little mystery surrounding the photographer would help sell my work, since I was new on the scene."

"I see. Well, mystery does sell."

"I asked to meet you today," Charley said, "because I wanted to pitch an idea. Would you be interested in exhibiting some of my photography in your gallery?"

"I like your work, that's for sure," Leana replied. "I have room for a couple right now, maybe more as space opens up. I could take them on consignment. And Charleston has several art festivals each year, so we could include your photography in our exhibits at those. It would be good exposure for you and would also elevate our exhibits to another level. People come from all over for our art festivals."

"That sounds perfect," Charley said. "Just let me know what you need on my end. I've brought a thumb drive of prints that are currently available to show."

Charley and Leana looked over the prints, and Leana selected two. One was of the Morris Island Lighthouse situated next to algae-covered boulders, with the rising sun reflecting off the lighthouse beacon. Beach grasses swayed in the breeze. The second photo was of a rustic building sheltered by several large oak trees that Charley had photographed at the Firefly Distillery on Wadmalaw Island.

Charley left the gallery and walked toward Broad Street. Leana had given her directions to a photo lab located there that reproduced and mounted high-end professional photographs. As Charley neared the photo lab, she noticed that the Winston, Morgan, and Gilbert Law Firm was located in an office building close by.

Charley gave the thumb drive to the young man in charge of the photo lab, along with instructions for printing and mounting the large, gallery-sized displays.

"It'll take approximately forty-five minutes to an hour before they'll be ready," the lab tech told her.

Rather than wait, Charley decided to go next door and say hello to Alex.

As she stepped off the elevator on the fourth floor and headed toward the reception area, she noticed several black-and-white photographs displayed on the wall. She stopped to take a look. The photos were mostly scenes from Charleston's early days when it was still a sleepy coastal town and most streets were paved with cobblestones. There were several photos of the historic homes located along on the Battery seawall and a few of plantation houses located outside the city limits.

"There you are," a voice said from behind her. A hand reached out and braced itself against the wall near her head, practically pinning her between the wall and the hand's owner. "I was wondering when you'd come looking for me."

Charley looked around. Eric Winston stood close, almost touching her with his body.

"Um… I was looking for Alex," Charley replied as she ducked and tried to slip under his arm.

He dropped his arm lower, further trapping her.

"You need to step back," Charley said calmly. Fire sparked in her eyes as she stared into Eric's smug face.

"Eric," barked a voice from a short distance away. "Your client is waiting for you at reception."

Eric dropped his arm and slowly turned toward the reception area, but not before running his hand down Charley's arm.

Charley tried not to shiver. She now understood why Eric Winston so easily pushed Alex's buttons. Alex had kept her photo out of Eric's hands at the cost of an enormous sum of money, and for that, she was grateful. She turned to see Alex's father, Bob Morgan, standing in the doorway down the hallway. He scowled at Eric's retreating back, then beckoned Charley to come into his office.

"Alex isn't here right now," Mr. Morgan said as he closed the door behind her. "He's at a property that one of his clients wants to purchase. I'm sorry you were greeted like that. Eric's behavior is not the norm around here, thank goodness. His father keeps hoping he'll change, but it doesn't seem to be working."

"I had business next door, so I thought I'd pop in for a short visit while I waited and give an update on Dorsey."

"Alex will be sorry he missed you. He said he saw you this morning—at the hospital?"

"He did. I was there until Dorsey's procedure was done and she was moved to isolation."

Charley gave Mr. Morgan a more recent update that Mrs. Maitland had texted her a short time ago. Dorsey was more awake and the infusion has gone as expected. No problems to report.

"I plan to go see her again after I leave here and before I go back to the island."

Charley visited with Mr. Morgan for almost an hour before she excused herself to return to the photo lab. Mr. Morgan walked her to the elevator. Charley was relieved because she didn't want to encounter Eric Winston again.

"I'll tell Alex that you were here." Mr. Morgan looked thoughtful for a moment, then added, "He'll be mad at me for saying this, but that's what parents are for: to meddle and irritate their grown children. Alex is a good person. And he works too much. But I think he works too much because he doesn't have a reason not to." Mr. Morgan looked expectantly at Charley. His candor surprised her.

"I know," she said with equal candor. "We plan to talk soon to try to resolve our disagreements." Everyone seemed to be championing Alex today. Since her anger at him had fizzled to an ember, she didn't need much convincing to recognize that he was a good man. But he needed to explain his part in the file he had on her.

"Good. That's good." Mr. Morgan nodded, visibly relieved. "Oh, and come by the house. Karen would love to see you again."

"I will. I'd like to see her again, too," Charley replied. With a wave, she entered the elevator.

The photos were ready when Charley returned to the photo lab next door. The technician had done an excellent job. She made arrangements to have them delivered to the Lower King Street Art Gallery.

Charley walked back to her parked car, then drove to North Charleston and the cancer center. Dorsey was sitting up in her bed when Charley arrived. She looked much stronger than she had that morning. Mrs. Maitland was not there, but Charley was sure she was in the vicinity or on her way to the hospital. Dorsey was in good spirits and laughed as she and Charley communicated using a combination of miming, sign language, and loudly spoken words through the window. They shared a laugh when Charley finally deciphered one of Dorsey's more complex messages: "Help me! My mother is holding me hostage!"

Charley left the hospital encouraged that Dorsey was going to be alright. She texted Alex with an update on Dorsey's condition. Only a moment passed before he texted back: "Great news! Will stop and see her again shortly."

Charley visited Dorsey daily over the next four days. On Friday, Dr. Baker gave them permission to go into her room and visit.

"Our team thinks she can be released to go home tomorrow," he informed Mrs. Maitland after he had checked Dorsey's vitals. "Her red blood cell count is increasing as expected. It will do her good to be home, around familiar surroundings, and out of this room." He smiled at Dorsey, who nodded emphatically. "But," he continued, "I expect you to come in for weekly blood draws so we can follow your blood cell count. If your count drops, we'll need to do a blood transfusion. But with the progress you're making right now, I don't expect that to happen."

"I was thinking that we'd have a nurse come to the house and do the blood draws," Mrs. Maitland said.

"Mother!" Dorsey protested. "I can't stay cooped up all the time. I'll need to get out of the house. I promise to be careful at all times."

"Going home will be good for her," Dr. Baker advised, "and coming back for the blood draws won't endanger her, so long as she's careful. She knows what to do. Rest assured, you can return to the hospital if Dorsey's condition changes or anything major happens." He turned and headed out of the room. "Call me at the slightest sign of a cold or fever or if you just need to talk or ask questions."

Charley promised Dorsey that she would come see her once

she had settled in at home.

On the drive back to the island from the hospital, Charley received a phone call from Mrs. Sanders at the Destination Marketing Office. The director of the CVB wanted Charley to come in the following week to meet with him and talk salary. If they could agree on a salary, Mrs. Sanders told her, the job would be Charley's.

Things were falling into place for her, career-wise. It looked like she was going to be a permanent resident of Turtle Island.

CHAPTER TWENTY

Charley arrived at Oak Lane Plantation on Saturday afterncon just after midday. She joined Dorsey in the solarium, a sunny room lit by two skylights and wide windows framed by pink azaleas mixed with dwarf honeysuckle in the backyard. Charley, her face covered by a mask, sat down across from Dorsey, leaving a wide space between them. Charley was taking no chances on spreading germs that might be harmful to her sister.

After they had discussed a wide range of trivia ranging from movies to music, Dorsey turned to the topic Charley had been dreading. "Tell me about your mother," Dorsey said. "What is she like?"

Charley pulled up her legs, tucked them underneath her, and leaned her head back against the cushion of the chair. "How does one explain Debra Mathews to someone who has never met her?" she asked out loud. She lifted her head from the back of her chair and looked at Dorsey. "My mother is nothing like your mother."

She would give Dorsey the abbreviated version now. Maybe

later, she would give a more in-depth description. Dorsey didn't need to hear about all the sadness that surrounded her and her mother's life once her father had died.

"My mother was unable to take care of me after my father was killed in car crash. She went from being a loving mother to an emotionally absent mother. She was so distraught at first that she couldn't even take care of herself. That's why I went to live with Aunt Beth and Uncle Lance and they raised me. My mother, to her credit, realized she wasn't giving me the care I needed."

Dorsey nodded. "Tell me about your father. Do you remember him?"

"My father was a wonderful, fun-loving man. My mother and I were the center of his world. He could make anything we did together fun—even chores. We would sometimes wash the car together in our driveway. He could have taken it to a professional detail shop, but we enjoyed doing it together. Our clothes would be soaked by the time we finished." Charley smiled as she recalled the times when the hose would get away from her and the house windows would end up as wet as the car. She shared with Dorsey the fun things they did together as a family and how happy they were. It felt a bit odd describing her parents to Dorsey—her sister. They were technically Dorsey's parents, too, but then again, they weren't. "My parents had a wonderful marriage, and our home was filled with love, but all that ended with his death."

"I lost my father ten years ago," Dorsey said. "He was very quiet and reserved, but deep down, I knew he loved me. You can just feel it, you know? He treated me like I was his biological daughter."

"I do know. A DNA connection is nice," Charley replied, "but that's not all there is to parenting. I'm glad that you found a good home, sis. And I'm ecstatic that I found you."

Charley and Dorsey soon turned to more pleasant topics. Dorsey wanted to know all about Charley's travels and the countries she had visited and photographed. Charley shared brief details of her marriage to Daniel, their subsequent divorce, and how she came to be living on Turtle Island through her inheritance from Aunt Annabelle.

"But tell me about you," Charley said. "What career path have you chosen?"

"I want to be a teacher. I will be one, once I recover and complete my degree at the University of South Carolina. I'm almost done. Math is what I love and I want to teach high school kids."

"A teacher? And a math teacher at that? And you can endure teenagers all day?" Charley laughed. "I'm very impressed!"

"My mother wanted me to go into the family shipping business in some capacity, but running a large company doesn't interest me the way it does her."

"Teaching is a noble profession," Charley said. "Filling young minds with knowledge is very important. I think it might be even more challenging than running an international corporation."

"It can be challenging, but also very rewarding," Dorsey agreed. "I like shaping young minds. You can see tangible results—kinda like with your photography."

Charley soon noticed that Dorsey was getting tired, so she said goodbye and headed home. On the drive back to the island, Charley acknowledged that, regardless of the invasion into her private life in the search to find her, she was grateful that she and Dorsey had been brought together. She had found another piece of her life.

Charley arrived home shortly after six p.m. Her heart leaped when she saw Alex's truck parked in his driveway. Maybe she would get to see him this weekend.

Charley had received a text from Leana Barry, letting her know that she had space for another photograph, so Charley settled down on the back deck with a glass of sweet tea to look through her collection to select a photo. She again came across the one she had taken of Alex on Pawleys Island. She wished again she could see his eyes that were hidden behind his dark sunglasses. Did he have the teasing twinkle in his eye that he often had when he looked at her? Or was his mind on something other than her? She sighed and reluctantly moved on to the next photo.

A few minutes later, Charley's phone pinged with a text message from the photo's subject: Alex. "Please meet me on the beach in front of the dunes in fifteen minutes," it read.

Charley wanted to ask why, but just replied, "Alright." She'd find out when she got there.

She left the deck and went inside to change clothes and freshen up. She left the house, then angled toward the tall dunes located between their beach houses.

As Charley walked through the opening in the dunes, she saw Alex seated not far away on a blanket. The blanket was held down by a picnic basket, as a strong ocean breeze tugged against it. He silently watched her as she approached and sat down on the blanket across from him.

"Are you ready for our talk?" Alex asked. At Charley's nod he opened the picnic basket and took out two glasses, a bottle of lime-flavored water, and a container of mini fried catfish rolls from The Tides.

"I hope you haven't eaten." Alex opened the flavored water, poured a glass, and handed it to Charley.

"No, and I'm starved," Charley replied. She raised her eyebrow as she accepted the glass. "Lime-flavored water?"

Alex nodded toward the 'No Alcohol on the Beach' sign behind them. He filled his own glass, then held it out toward her. "Not wine, but I hope it will suffice for a toast for our long-awaited discussion. A toast to clearing the air and making a fresh start."

"I can drink to that," Charley said as she touched her glass to his. "May the sea breezes of Turtle Island blow away all mis-understandings." She took a sip of her water, then asked, "Who goes first?"

"I will," Alex replied. He passed the catfish rolls to Charley, then took one for himself. He chewed slowly, as if he arranged his thoughts. "Okay, I'm discarding the pretty speech I had prepared. I'm just going to lay it all out for you and give you the truth."

"Good idea. The truth always works best."

"I wasn't the one who did the investigation into your back-ground. Mrs. Maitland hired a private investigator, and he com-piled the information on you. I never even opened the folder, so I didn't know what was in it."

"But you had it at your house. Why, if you had nothing to do with it?"

"I'm getting to that," Alex replied. "What I did do was accept the folder—reluctantly, I might add—just to keep it out of the hands of anyone else. It was a boneheaded decision and I'm not proud I agreed to it in exchange for a summer at the beach. That sounds very selfish and immature, I know. But my reasons weren't all about a summer at the beach." Alex went on to tell Charley in detail about the scheme cooked up by his bosses for him to get close to her and to find out if she was who Mrs. Maitland was looking for; how Mrs. Maitland was afraid to ask her directly. "She wanted an intermediary to break the news to her if you turned out to be someone else. This all sounds crazy, even to me, but I took the folder, stuck it in the desk drawer, and forgot all about it."

"So, you *were* spying on me?" Charley asserted. She wasn't

going to let him off easy.

"No. I told my father that I wouldn't do that, but I agreed that if you let something slip, I would let them know… if I thought it was relevant. Of course, since I didn't know what was going on, I'm not sure how I would have recognized what was and wasn't relevant. After I met you, the plan to get close to you wasn't a hard sell."

"You admit it, then. You were spying on me."

"No," Alex repeated, his voice rising in frustration. "Did I ever pump you for information? No, I didn't. What I meant was, once I met you, I was interested in getting to know you for reasons that had nothing to do with the plot cooked up by the crazy gang at my office. Plus, they threatened to give the job to Eric Winston if I didn't go along. I couldn't let that happen to you—or *any* female."

Charley shivered at the thought of having Eric Winston chasing after her. That was reason enough to accept that Alex had chosen the best course.

"At first, I didn't know why Mrs. Maitland was looking for you. If I had known about Dorsey's illness, it might have made the whole scheme more palatable—but just barely."

"Well, I'm glad you didn't give the job to Eric. What a creep!" Charley did an exaggerated shiver. "I was horrified, and hurt. I trusted you. Spying on me didn't fit the picture I had formed of you. I wondered if I had let myself be duped into seeing you the way I *wanted* to see you. And you did have the folder."

"I understand," Alex said as he reached over, picked up his phone, selected some music, and then laid the phone down on the blanket.

"I've trusted other people before, and have been deceived. 'Once bitten, twice shy'" Charley took another catfish roll and passed them back to Alex. "I now understand why you did what you did. And finding Dorsey has been the best thing that's happened to me in a long time. It's taken a lot of the sting out of being spied upon. Is that *everything* you've been hiding from me?"

"I skipped school once when I was a sophomore in high school," Alex replied with a deadpan expression. "My parents still don't know, so keep my secret, will you?"

"Let me guess. It was because of a girl," Charley laughed, "and those raging teenage hormones."

"Partly. I took Kym Wainwright to see *The Lord of the Rings*. Her father wouldn't let her go out with boys after dark. But mostly, I just wanted to see the movie." Alex shook his head. "Another plot that sounds foolish now because I couldn't even enjoy the movie. I kept looking around, expecting my father to grab me from behind." He laughed, then sobered. "Now, it's your turn. What's with all the names? And why the secrecy?"

"It's a lengthy tale. Want more water?" Charley asked. "You'll need it." Alex held out his glass, and Charley topped it off, then filled her own glass. She decided to share the whole sordid tale, not the abbreviated version she had shared for most of her life. She wanted to clear the air, as promised. She had never told anyone except Aunt Beth—not even Daniel—the full story of what had happened after her father was killed.

Charley began her story by repeating what she usually shared with those closest to her: how her father was killed when she was eight; how she tried to feed herself and her mother after Debra took to her bed; how she managed to hide her condition from her neighbors and teachers. "My mother fell apart when we lost my father. She took both of our lives down with her." Charley said as she described her mother's depression, and how she became dependent on alcohol. "I think she hoped that she'd die, too. She was totally wrapped up in her grief and didn't think of anyone else—not even me." Charley paused and swallowed.

Alex moved from his side of the blanket and tried to pull her into his arms.

"No," Charley said as she shrugged off his arm. "Don't distract me. Let me get this out." She picked up a handful of sand and let it drift slowly through her fingers. She raised her head, and her eyes fixed on a far-off point somewhere out in the ocean as she remembered those frightful days.

"As an eight-year-old child, I didn't know that the authorities would likely take me away from my mother if my secret life was discovered. So, my secrecy was driven by my humiliation. I didn't want anyone to know what was going on in my house. I lied to our neighbors, my teachers and stopped visiting my best friend. I was ashamed of my mother and her condition. I didn't understand then, that she couldn't help it. Aunt Beth called frequently, but I lied to her, too and told her that my mother didn't want to talk to her. I was keeping a secret, but I was also pretending that the awfulness of my life wasn't real."

Charley took a sip of water and looked at Alex. He sat quietly, concern wrinkling his brow. "I was scared all the time in the quiet, lonely house. One day, someone rang the doorbell. It was probably a solicitor, but I hid in a closet for three hours, shaking and crying, afraid that someone had come to harm me. I saw shadows in my room at night, and my dreams were filled with faces peering in my window. I worried that we would starve when our food supply ran out." Charley took a drink of water, then recounted the scariest part when she couldn't wake her mother that day and had called Aunt Beth. "I didn't understand death, so I was afraid my mother was dying that day". Charley could still remember the wave of relief that washed over her when Aunt Beth walked through the door.

"Somehow, Aunt Beth convinced my mother to go to a rehabilitation center. Once that was done, she took me to live with her in New Jersey.

"My name was changed from Mathews to Rainier because I was taunted and bullied at school and called an orphan. Aunt Beth and Uncle Lance gave me the protection of their name for as long as I wanted to keep it. Even as a child, I learned that it's sometimes *who* you are, not *what* you are, that counts. The taunting stopped immediately. Uncle Lance was their hero, so the bullies were impressed that I knew him and shared his name."

"You kept the name?" Alex asked. "Even after you were grown?"

"Yes. I thought about changing it back to Mathews as I got older, but stayed too busy to do it. Then, I married Daniel, and it seemed pointless. When I came to Charleston—where my father grew up—I decided to reclaim my Mathews identity for him. So, I had Mr. Lewis file the paperwork to legally change it back to Mathews."

"I'm so sorry," Alex said. He reached out and picked up Charley's hand. "You never went back to live with your mother?"

"No," Charley replied sadly. "My mother was a broken woman. She wasn't an alcoholic in the traditional sense. She just couldn't deal with my father's death. I was never on her list of priorities. In fairness, she couldn't help herself, and she probably didn't want me around her new lifestyle, either."

"That must have been very hard for a child to understand," Alex said. He turned her hand over and kissed her palm.

"Sometimes I was angry about it, but Aunt Beth was a wonderful surrogate mother, so that helped. Kenneth, my mother's current husband, is the third man she's married since my father died. I think she was always searching for someone who would make her feel the same way my father had."

Charley looked at Alex. "I think her marriage to Kenneth

might last. That's why I got upset when she told me that someone had called her looking for information about me. Digging
up our past could be devastating for her."

"It wasn't me," Alex said. "I let it slip in front of Mrs. Maitland that your mother lived in Miami. I imagine she was the
one who called. She has blinders on when she sets her sights on
something. In this case, Dorsey's health is all that matters to her.
I'm truly sorry about that."

"I can see Mrs. Maitland doing that," Charley said. "She's
as strong-willed as my mother is weak. But there! You have
the whole sordid story of my past. And if you're curious, I am
stronger than my mother—more like Aunt Beth."

"I knew that the day you almost knocked me cold with the
door at Benji's." Alex rubbed the spot above his eye. The red
mark had faded weeks ago, but he was happy to remind her of
the incident whenever possible.

"I don't mean physically," Charley replied laughing.

"I know. There's nothing weak about you. But how did Ce
Ce Kane get into all this? And you did hide that from me." Alex
leaned back and stretched his legs out alongside her. He looked
accusingly at her.

"Oh, that!" Charley replied. "I almost forgot." She looked at
Alex and smiled. "It's not as nefarious as the look on your face
indicates. As a newbie in the art scene, the first gallery owner I
showed with felt I needed some mystery. 'Ce Ce' is from Charlotte Christine, and 'Kane' is my mother's grandmother's name."

"But why did you keep it a secret?" Alex asked. "You had
several chances to tell me."

"I'm sorry I didn't tell you. When you were looking at the
photograph on my wall—the one Aunt Annabelle bought at my
exhibit—I felt awkward piping up and declaring, 'I took that
photo.' I had only just met you. You'd have thought I was making it up, wouldn't you?"

Alex thought for a moment before replying, "Maybe. I don't know. But when I bid on the photograph at the auction, why didn't you tell me then?"

"Truthfully, I was in shock when I saw my work put up for bid hundreds of miles from New York. I meant to tell you on the way home from the ball, but you barely spoke to me."

"I apologize for that, too. It had nothing to do with you. I was mulling over and examining mistakes of my past. You have permission to kick me if I ever ignore you again."

"I'll remember that," Charley said with a laugh. "By the way, I'm sorry you spent so much money on the photograph."

Alex waved his hand, dismissing the comment. "It was for a good cause. And I wasn't about to let Eric Winston outbid me."

"He egged you on, you know," Charley said. "Intentionally."

"I was aware of what he was doing, but it didn't matter. I had planned to donate that amount anyway. Well, twenty-five thousand, actually. But I was also prepared to bid whatever it took to outbid Eric."

"I take it that you and Eric aren't close."

"An understatement. We aren't even friends, but I try not to let it show. I think his dad keeps him around in the hopes that he'll eventually grow up and into the job."

"An awfully big hope from what I've seen," Charley said. She added cautiously, "So, are we good? Is there anything else you want to know?"

"No. I understand," Alex replied. He gazed up at the sky, then leaned over and turned up the music slightly. A country song—a slow ballad—was playing. "Have you ever danced in the sand?" he asked.

Charley shook her head, and Alex rose and pulled her up from the blanket. She kicked off her shoes as he put his arms around her. Charley rested her head beneath his chin and snuggled closer to his chest. They moved slowly together in the soft sand. As the music ended, Alex twirled Charley away from him, then back into his arms. He started to kiss her, but was interrupted when his phone pinged with a text. He bent, picked up his phone, and looked at the screen.

"Do you have some other place you need to be?" Charley asked. Irritated by the interruption, she sat down on the blanket. Work calls that interrupted a private moment had been unusual in the time she'd spent with Alex, but they'd been a normal occurrence with Daniel—and something she never got used to.

"Right here with you is where I need to be." Alex sat down and scooted close to her. "Listen," he said quietly as he draped his arm across her shoulders.

Charley quieted and listened. At first, all she heard was the ocean, but soon the noise of an airplane over took the sound of the waves. A small airplane came into view over the water just off the beach. A large banner trailed behind it.

Alex pointed toward the banner. It read, 'Charley, I'm sorry!'

"What?" Charley exclaimed as she read the banner. "You did this?" She turned to look at Alex, shook her head, and laughed.

"My father said I should make a grand gesture to apologize to you. This is the grandest I could come up with. I was stalling with my 'sand-dancing' because the pilot was running late. My text just now was from his crew, letting me know he was on his way."

"It's the grandest apology I have ever received!" Charley looked from the banner to Alex and back again. "I can't believe this!"

"This is a further apology for my part in Mrs. Maitland's scheme," Alex said, pointing to the banner.

"I should have let you explain," Charley replied. "But I was shocked and angry."

"You were *very* angry with me, but you had a right to be,"

Alex acknowledged as he watched the plane loop back, make one more pass over the ocean, dip its wings, and then fly out of view. He turned toward Charley. "So, now you have to come up with a grand gesture of your own—for hiding your pseudonym. What will it be, Ms. Mathews?"

"This," Charley said as she reached out and placed her hands on either side of his face. "I'll need to repeat it several times to compete with a banner and an airplane, though." Charley kissed him gently.

Alex pulled her closer and deepened the kiss. "I like your grand gesture," he said softly. He ran his fingers down her cheek, then followed the outline of her lips. "And the promise of repeats."

"I love you, Alex," she whispered. She had never trusted anyone enough before to say "I love you" first—not even to Daniel. She always blamed her hesitation on her mother's abandonment and the fear of another rejection. The truth may have been that she had never been as confident in love before as she was with Alex.

"I love you, too, Charley. I love you regardless of what name you use," Alex said as he nibbled gently at her lips. "Rainier, Mathews, Kane—whatever." He whispered the names as his breath played softly across her lips.

"You sure do talk a lot, counselor," Charley whispered. "Stop teasing me and kiss—"

Her words were cut off as Alex followed her instruction and kissed her deeply. Then, he slowly pulled away, stood up, and reached for her hand. "Come on. Let's go home. There's a bottle of wine waiting to be opened to celebrate our new beginnings and honesty with each other."

"Home," Charley repeated as Alex pulled her to her feet.

"Yes." Alex grabbed the blanket and picnic basket and wrapped his free hand around her waist. "Home—or homes, in our case."

Charley hadn't felt completely at home anywhere since that horrible day in Atlanta a lifetime ago. But she now knew where she belonged. Her Mathews ancestors, her father, and a newly discovered sister were all born here, and that rooted her firmly in the Lowcountry soil. The love she shared with Alex further anchored her to this place. Charley had come to Turtle Island on a whim, but she'd found love, and with the right man this time, and in the process found the new path she'd been searching for.

As a bronze Carolina moon began to glow on the distant horizon, the evening tide crashed against the shore then rippled back to sea. Nature's nightly ritual between the changing tides, the moon and the earth went unnoticed as Charley and Alex walked arm in arm toward home and toward their future together.

www.ingramcontent.com/pod-product-compliance
Lightning Source LLC
Chambersburg PA
CBHW022140170626
46807CB00005B/2011